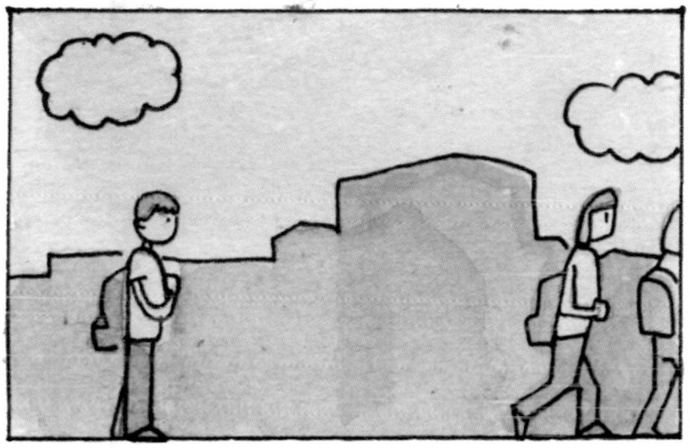

LEVEL UP

GENE LUEN YANG THIEN PHAM

:01
First Second
New York & London

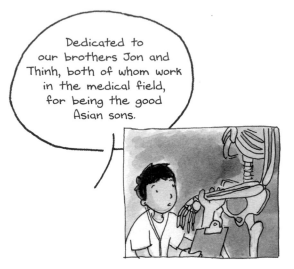

Dedicated to
our brothers Jon and
Thinh, both of whom work
in the medical field,
for being the good
Asian sons.

Text copyright © 2011 by Gene Luen Yang
Illustrations copyright © 2011 by Thien Pham
Compilation copyright © 2011 by Gene Luen Yang and Thien Pham

Published by First Second
First Second is an imprint of Roaring Brook Press,
a division of Holtzbrinck Publishing Holdings Limited Partnership
175 Fifth Avenue, New York, New York 10010
All rights reserved

Distributed in Canada by H. B. Fenn and Company Ltd.
Distributed in the United Kingdom by Macmillan Children's Books, a division of Pan Macmillan.

Cataloging-in-Publication Data is on file with the Library of Congress
Paperback ISBN: 978-1-59643-235-2
Hardcover ISBN: 978-1-59643-714-2

First Second books are available for special promotions and premiums.
For details, contact: Director of Special Markets, Holtzbrinck Publishers.

Book design by Marion Vitus
Printed in China

FIRST
EDITION

First Edition 2011

BY ART
WE LIVE

Paperback: 1 3 5 7 9 8 6 4 2
Hardcover: 1 3 5 7 9 8 6 4 2

http://www.jaderibboncampaign.com/

PRESS START
TO BEGIN

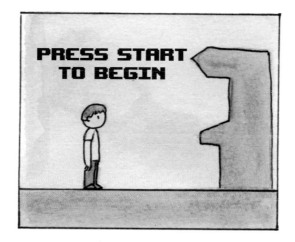

I saw my first arcade video game when I was six

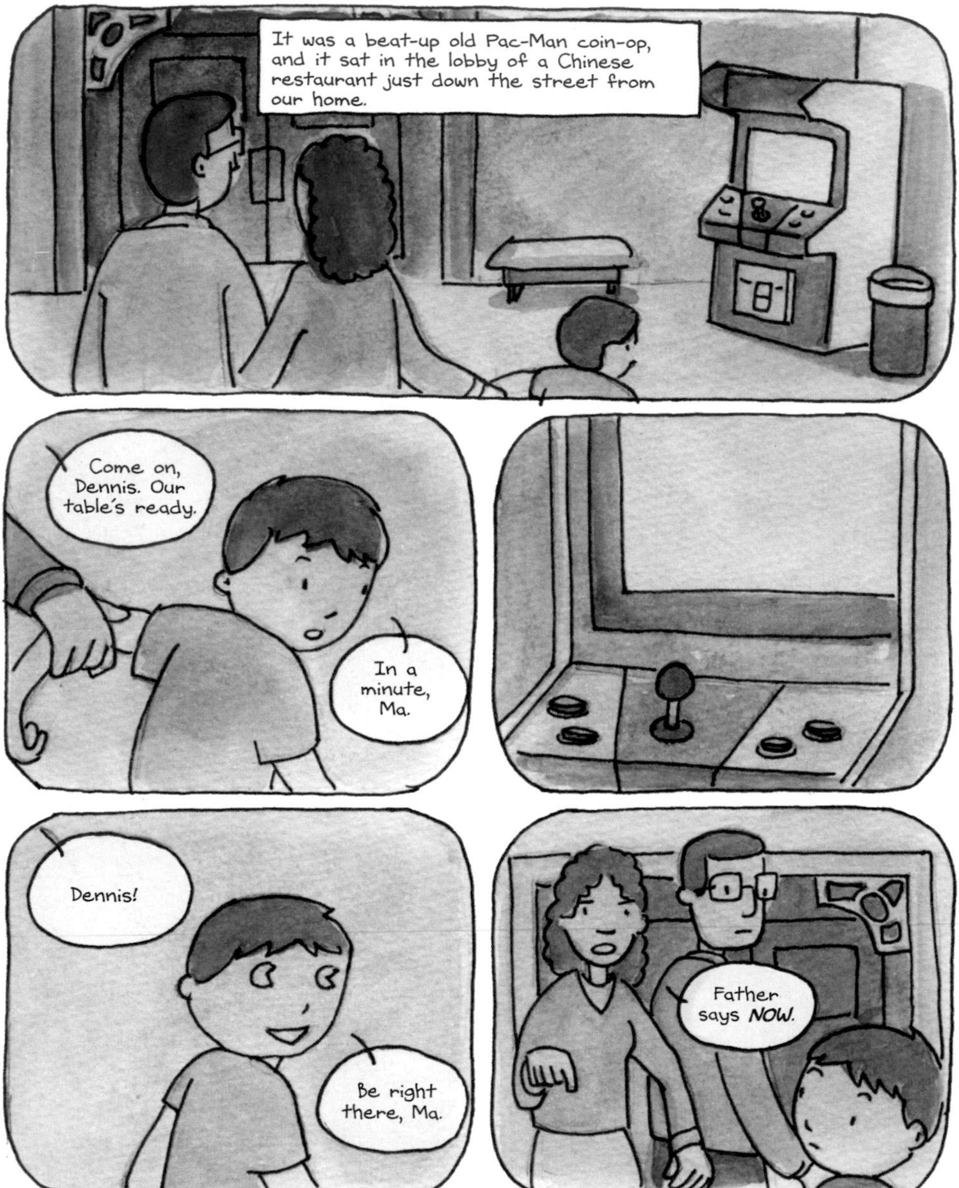
It was a beat-up old Pac-Man coin-op, and it sat in the lobby of a Chinese restaurant just down the street from our home.
Come on, Dennis. Our table's ready.
In a minute, Ma.
Dennis!
Be right there, Ma.
Father says *NOW*.

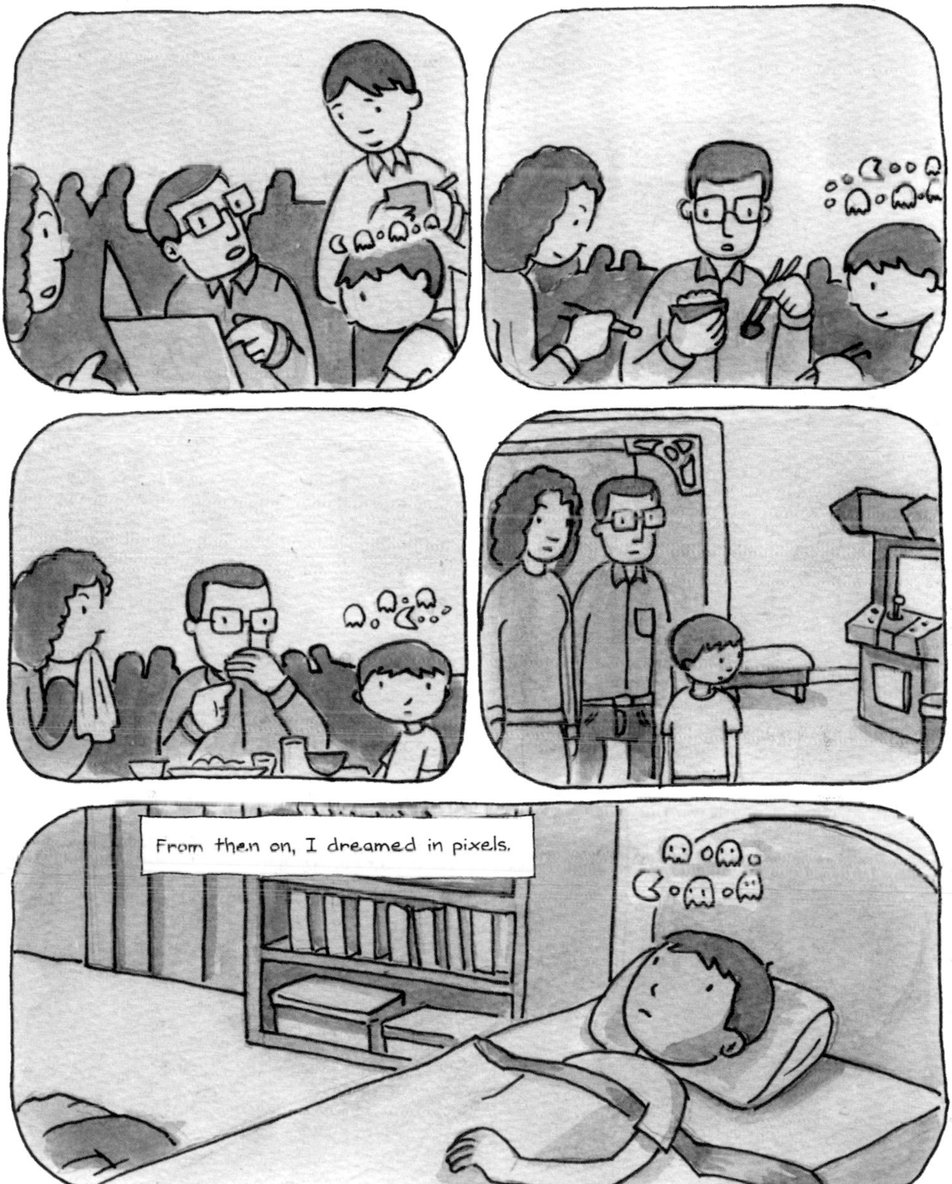
From then on, I dreamed in pixels.

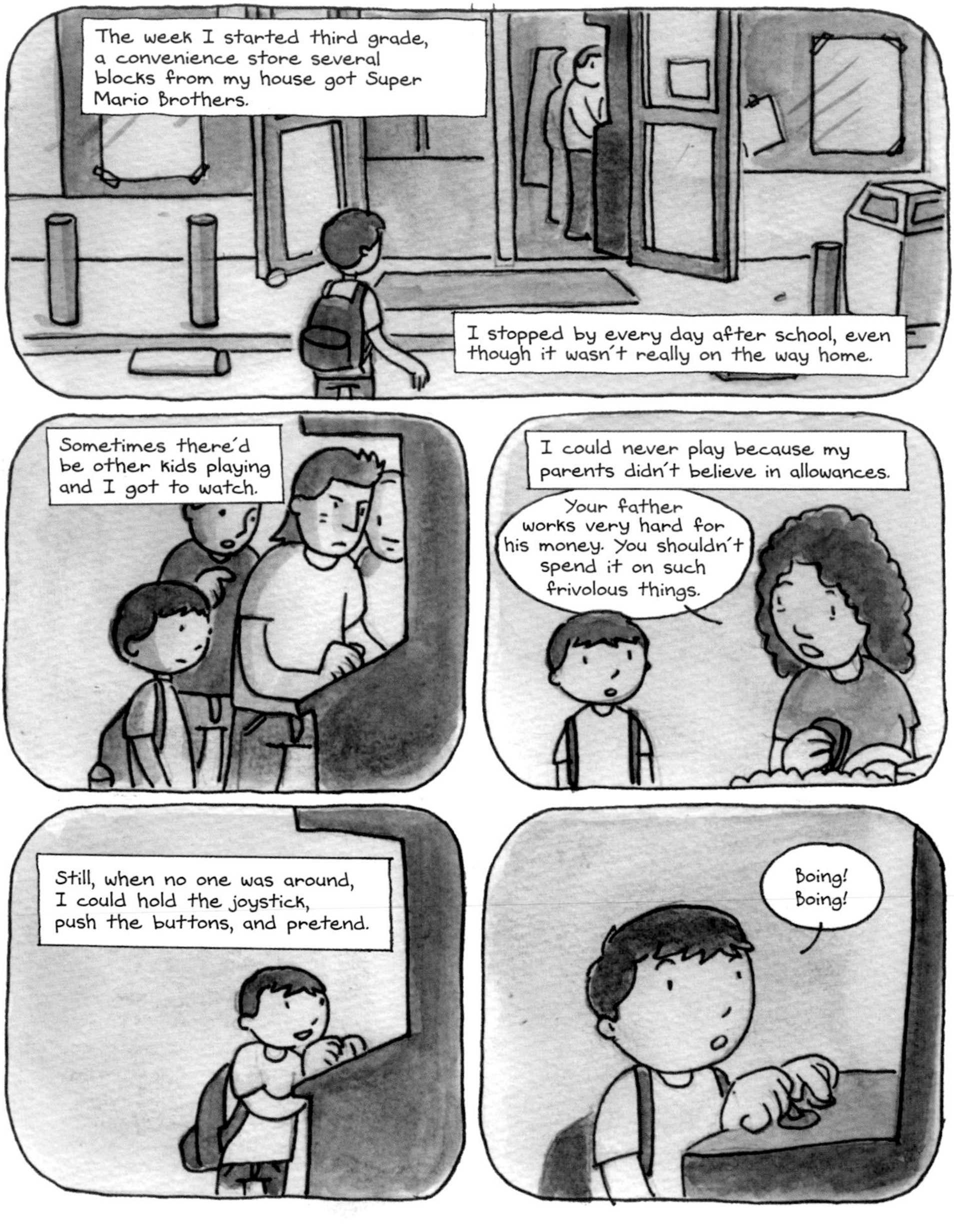
The week I started third grade, a convenience store several blocks from my house got Super Mario Brothers.
I stopped by every day after school, even though it wasn't really on the way home.
Sometimes there'd be other kids playing and I got to watch.
I could never play because my parents didn't believe in allowances.
Your father works very hard for his money. You shouldn't spend it on such frivolous things.
Still, when no one was around, I could hold the joystick, push the buttons, and pretend.
Boing! Boing!

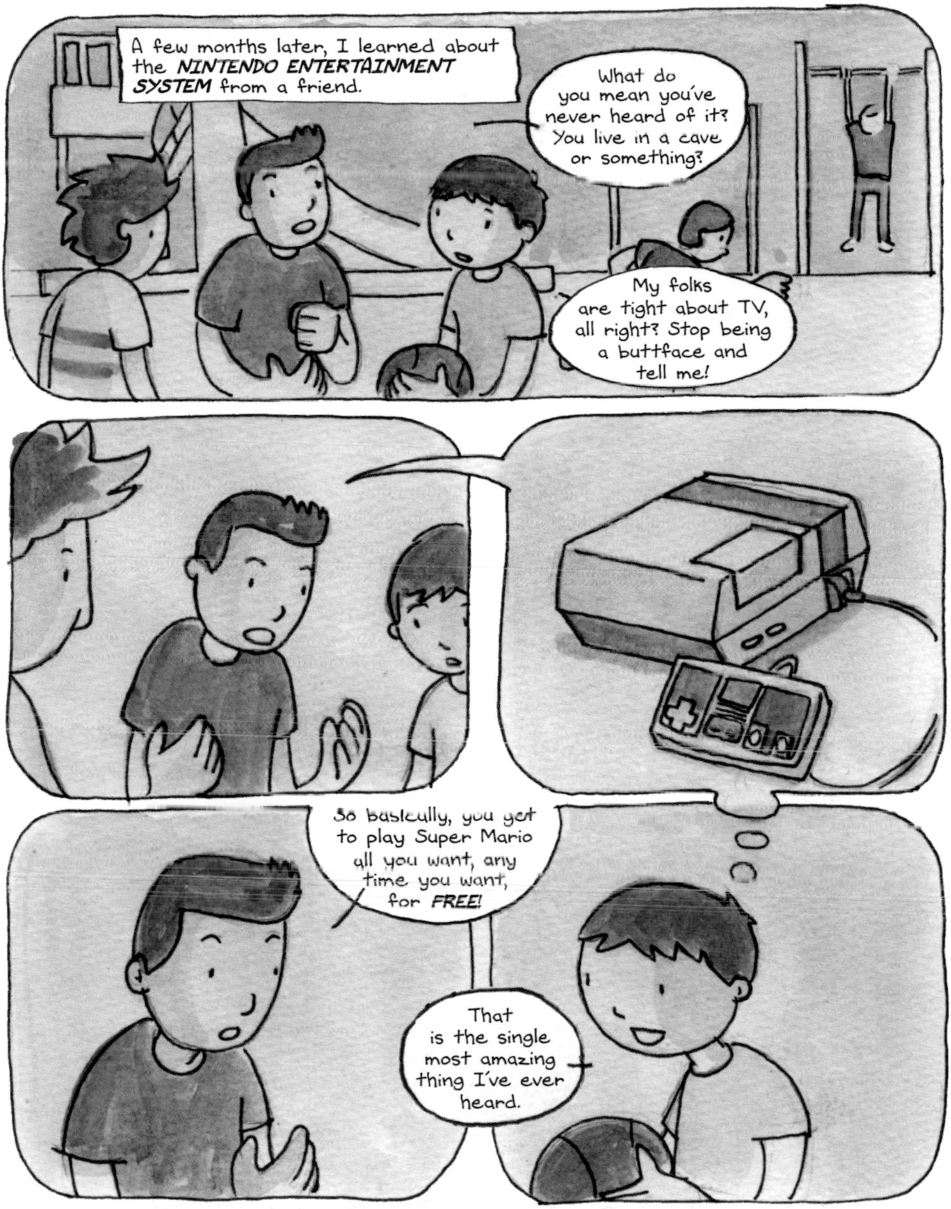
A few months later, I learned about the **NINTENDO ENTERTAINMENT SYSTEM** from a friend.
What do you mean you've never heard of it? You live in a cave or something?
My folks are tight about TV, all right? Stop being a buttface and tell me!
So basically, you get to play Super Mario all you want, any time you want, for **FREE!**
That is the single most amazing thing I've ever heard.

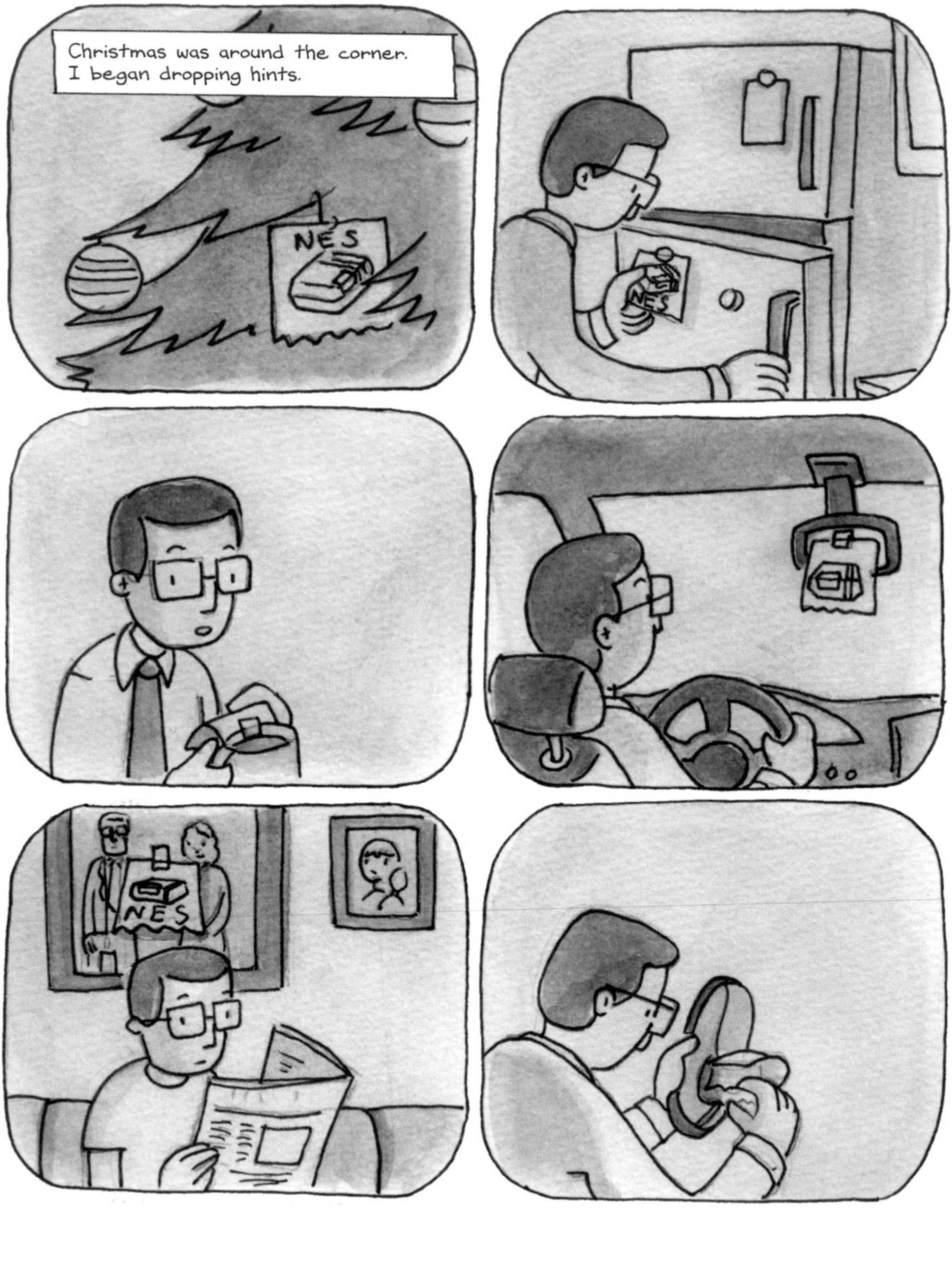
Christmas was around the corner.
I began dropping hints.
NES
NES
NES

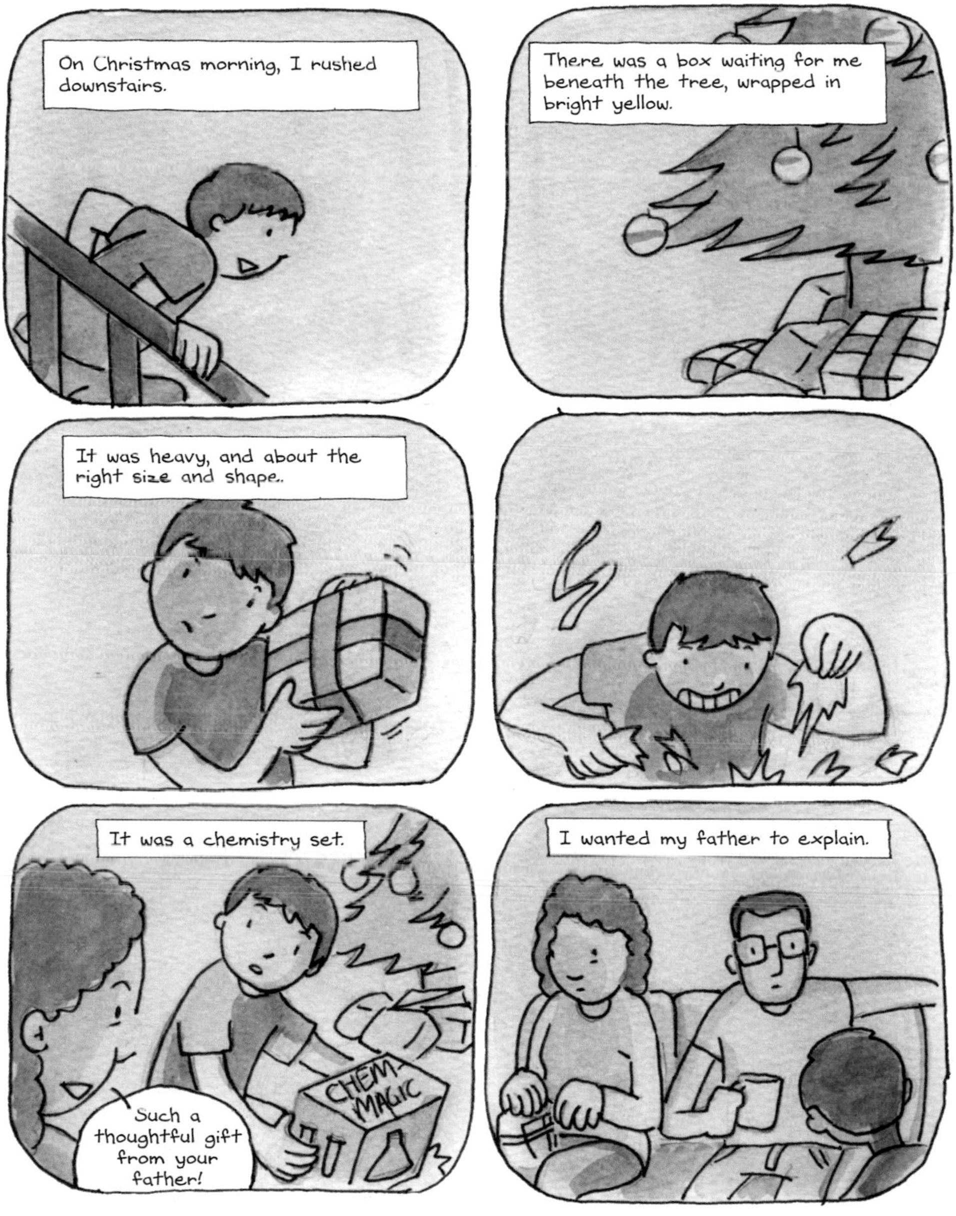
On Christmas morning, I rushed downstairs.
There was a box waiting for me beneath the tree, wrapped in bright yellow.
It was heavy, and about the right size and shape.
It was a chemistry set.
CHEM-MAGIC
Such a thoughtful gift from your father!
I wanted my father to explain.

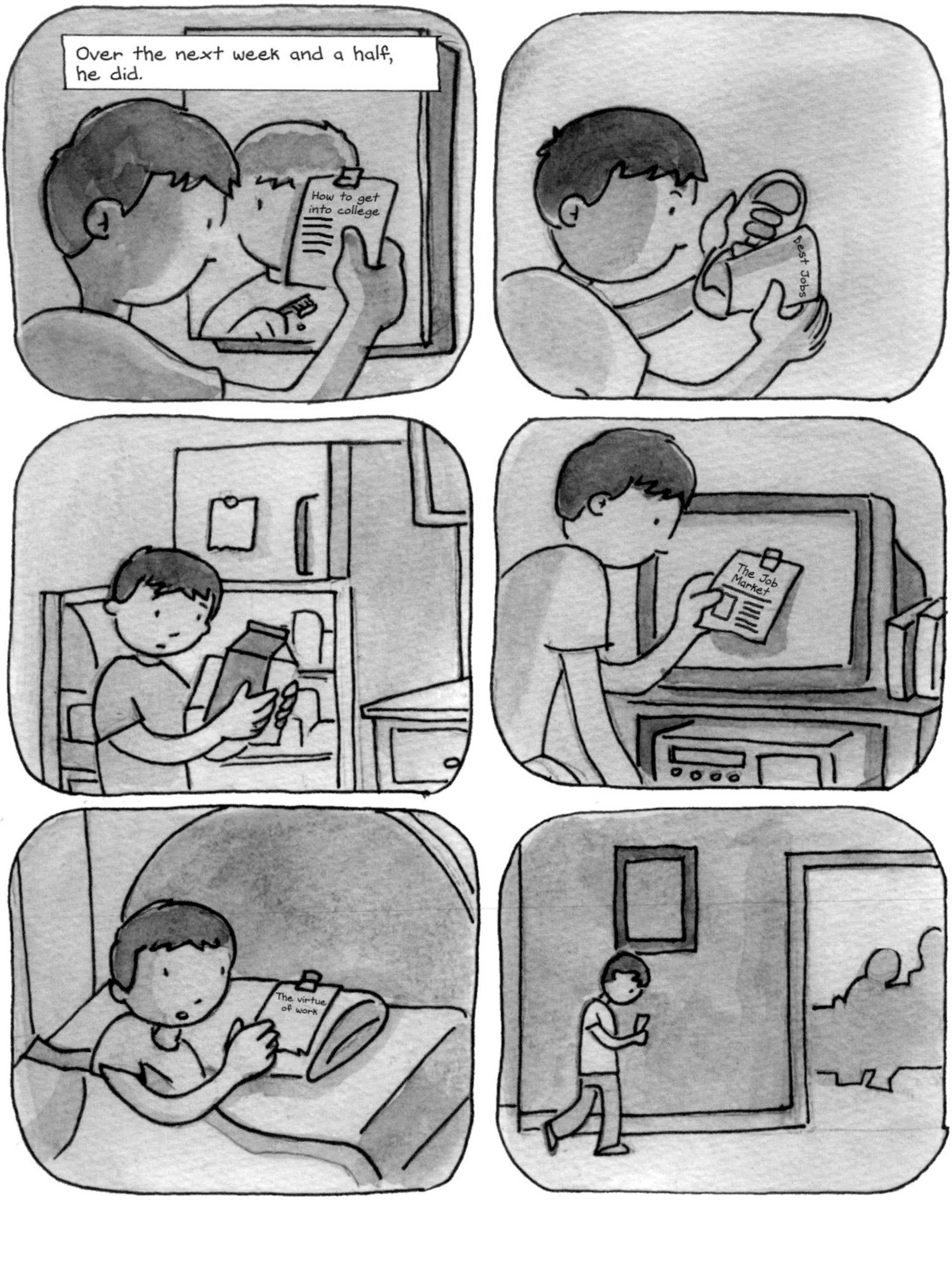
Over the next week and a half, he did.
How to get into college
Best Jobs
The Job Market
The virtue of work

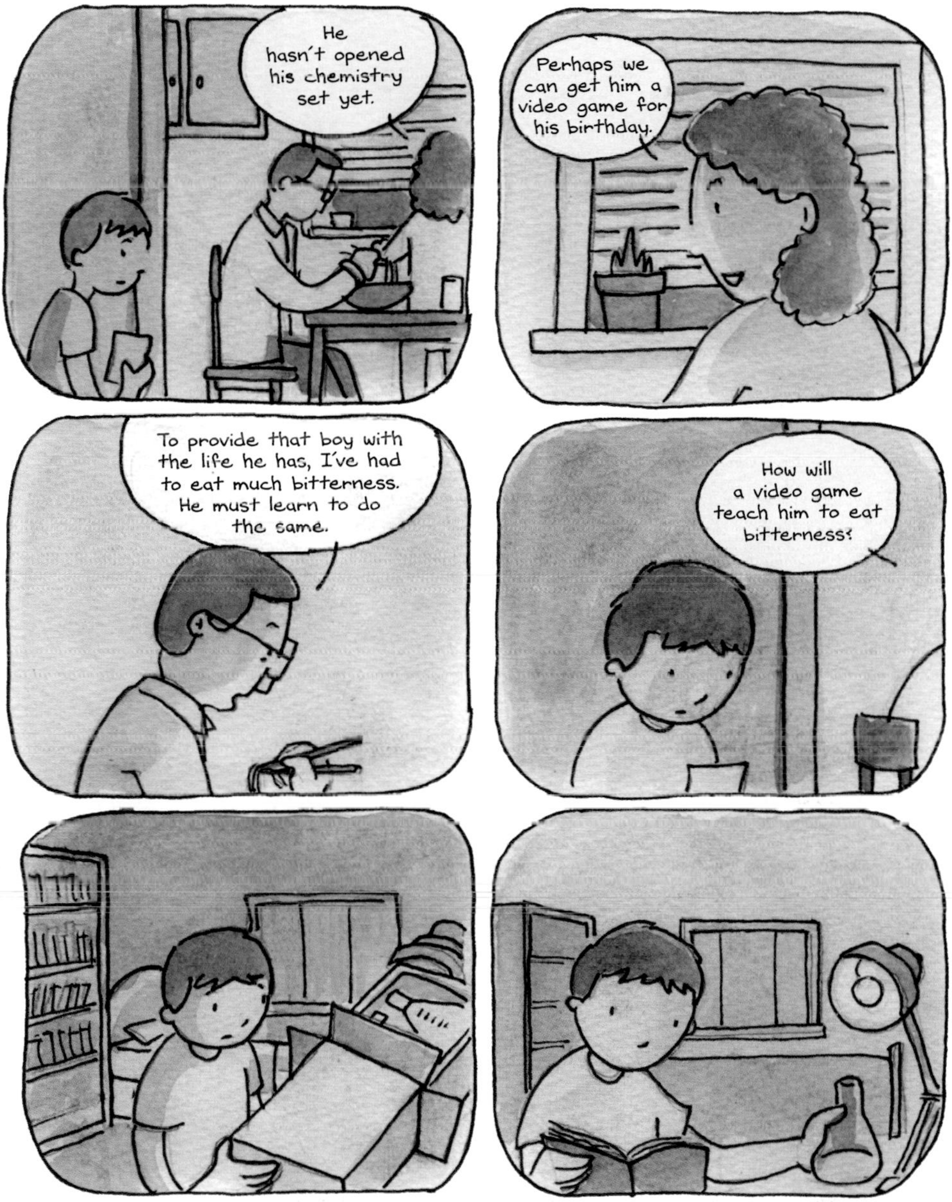
He hasn't opened his chemistry set yet.
Perhaps we can get him a video game for his birthday.
To provide that boy with the life he has, I've had to eat much bitterness. He must learn to do the same.
How will a video game teach him to eat bitterness?

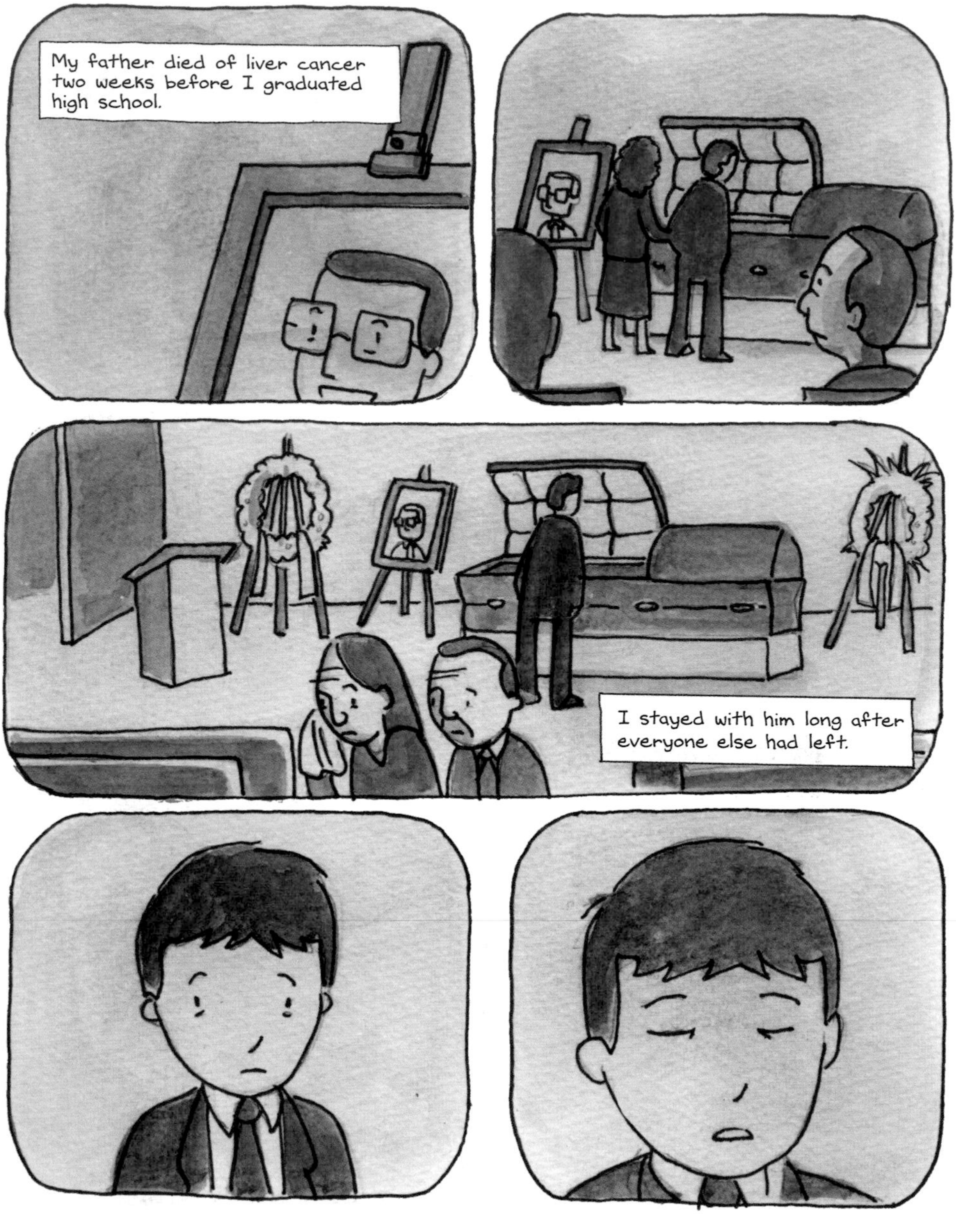
My father died of liver cancer two weeks before I graduated high school.
I stayed with him long after everyone else had left.

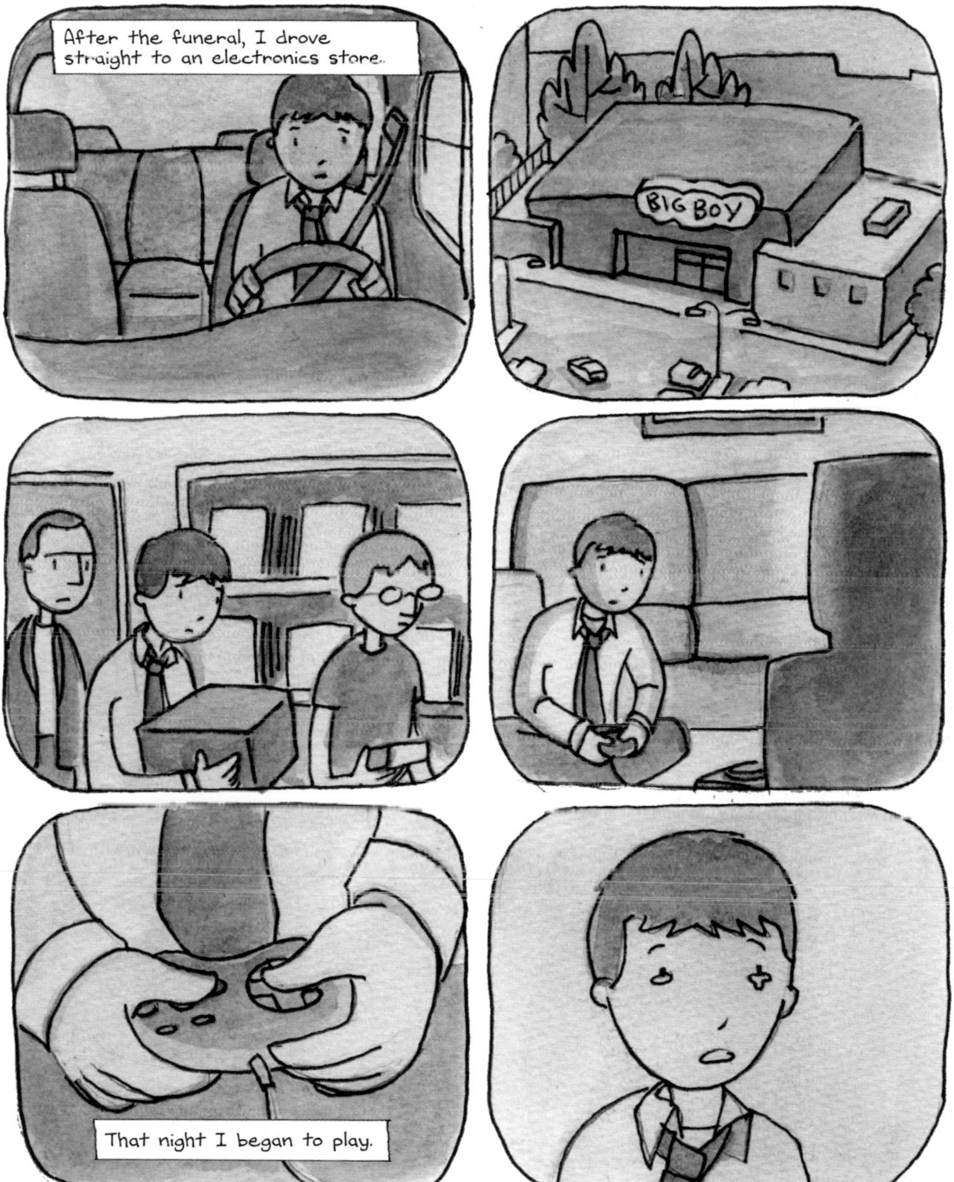
After the funeral, I drove straight to an electronics store.
BIG BOY
That night I began to play.

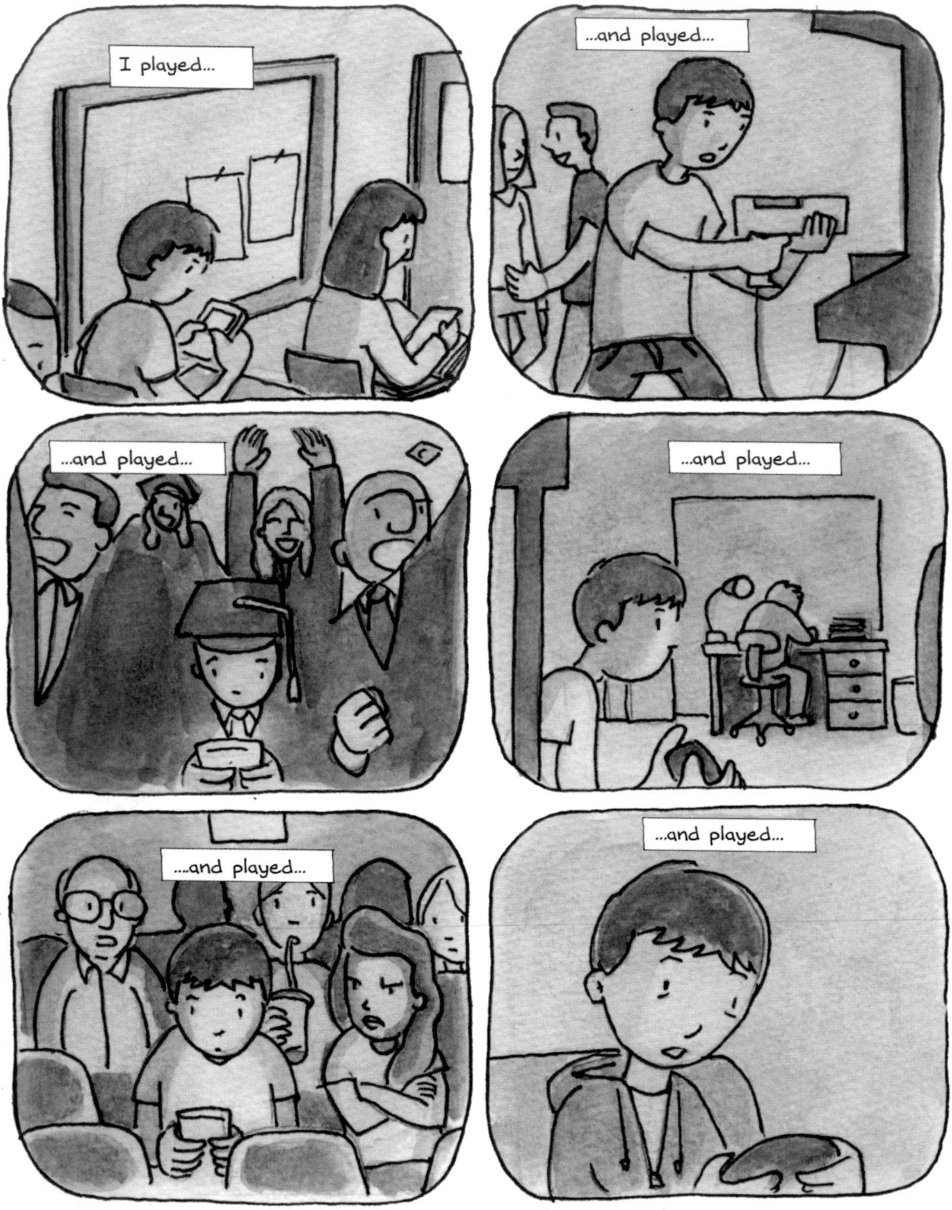
I played...
...and played...
...and played...
...and played...
....and played...
...and played...

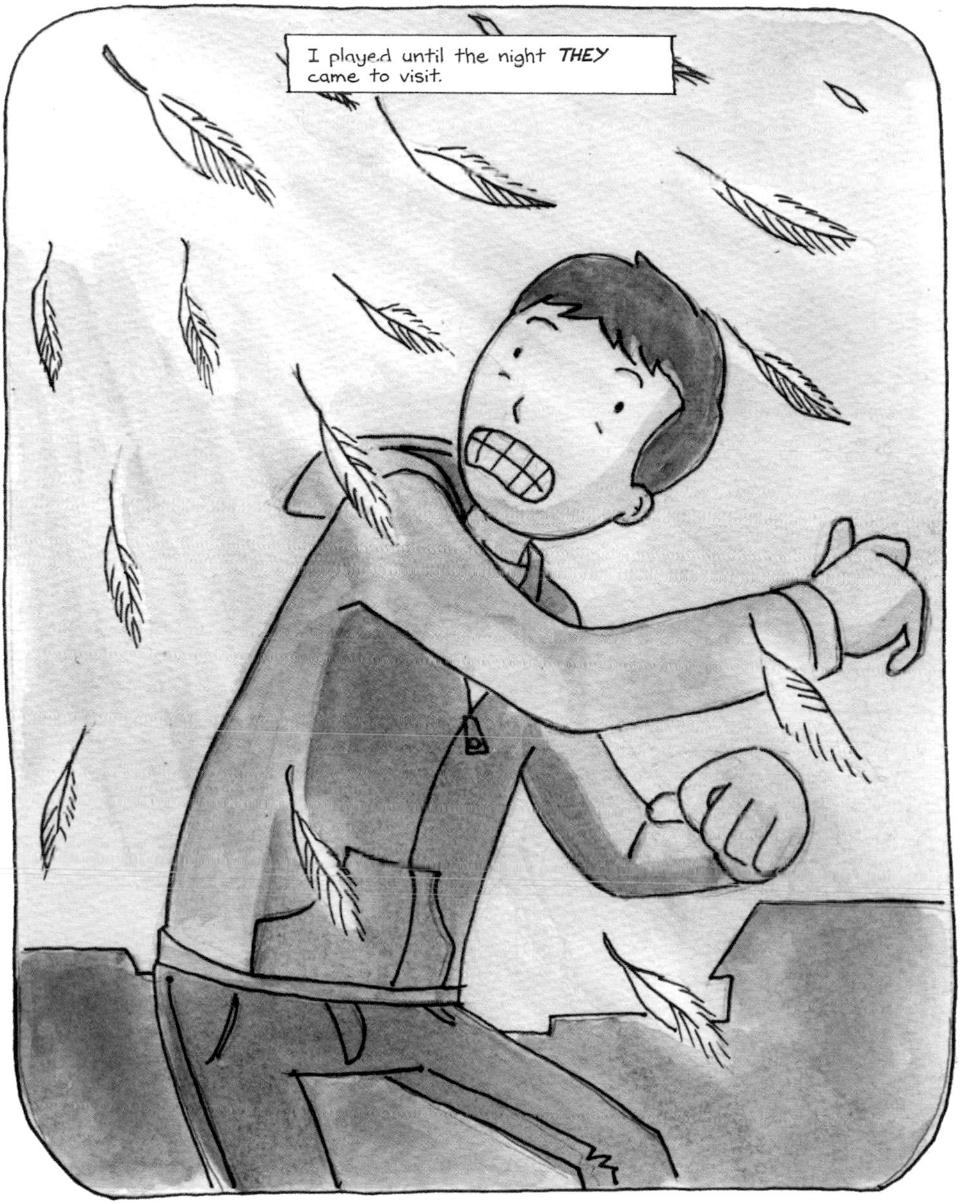
I played until the night THEY came to visit.

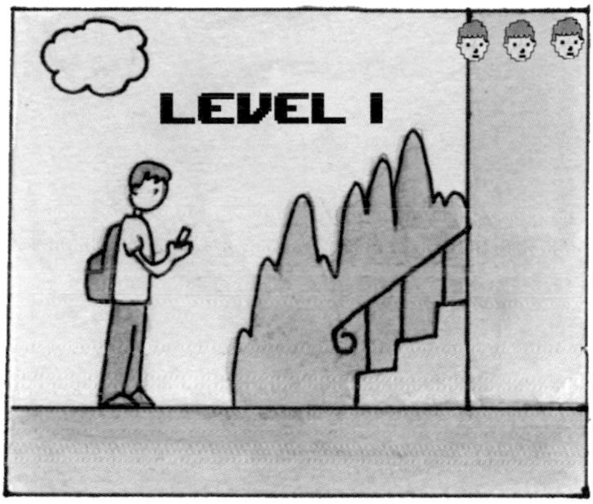
LEVEL 1

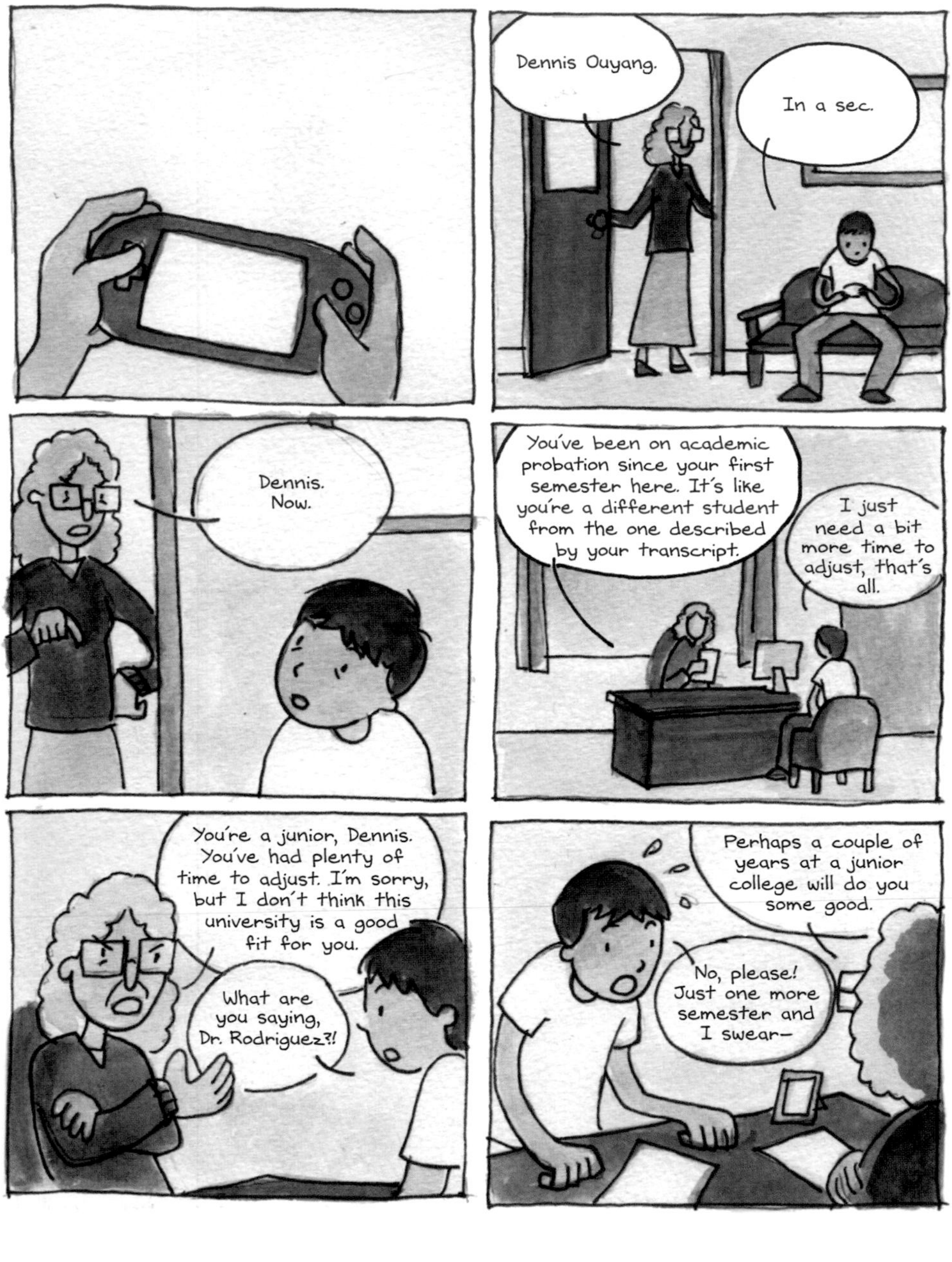
Dennis Ouyang.
In a sec.
Dennis. Now.
You've been on academic probation since your first semester here. It's like you're a different student from the one described by your transcript.
I just need a bit more time to adjust, that's all.
You're a junior, Dennis. You've had plenty of time to adjust. I'm sorry, but I don't think this university is a good fit for you.
What are you saying, Dr. Rodriguez?!
Perhaps a couple of years at a junior college will do you some good.
No, please! Just one more semester and I swear—

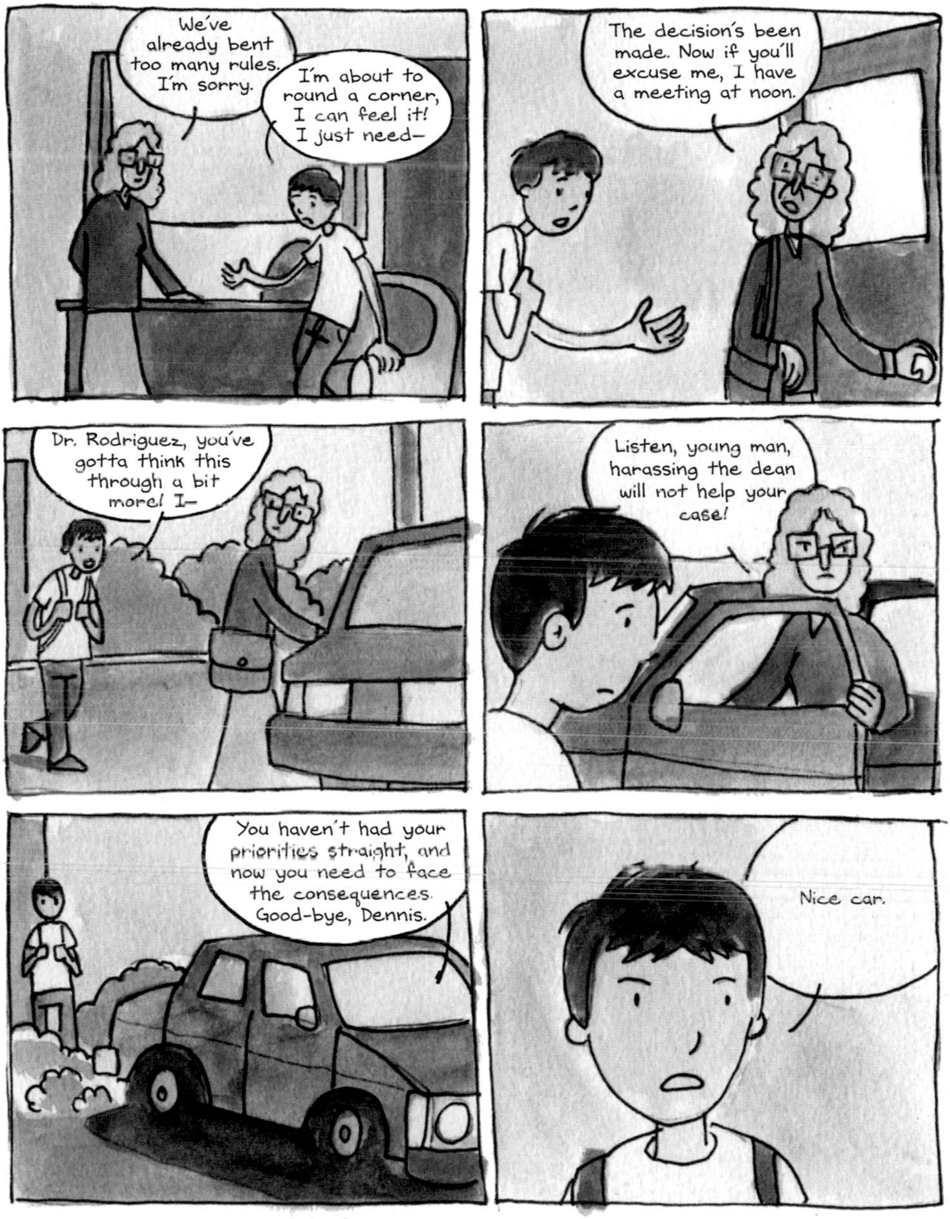
We've already bent too many rules. I'm sorry.
I'm about to round a corner, I can feel it! I just need—
The decision's been made. Now if you'll excuse me, I have a meeting at noon.
Dr. Rodriguez, you've gotta think this through a bit more! I—
Listen, young man, harassing the dean will not help your case!
You haven't had your priorities straight, and now you need to face the consequences. Good-bye, Dennis.
Nice car.

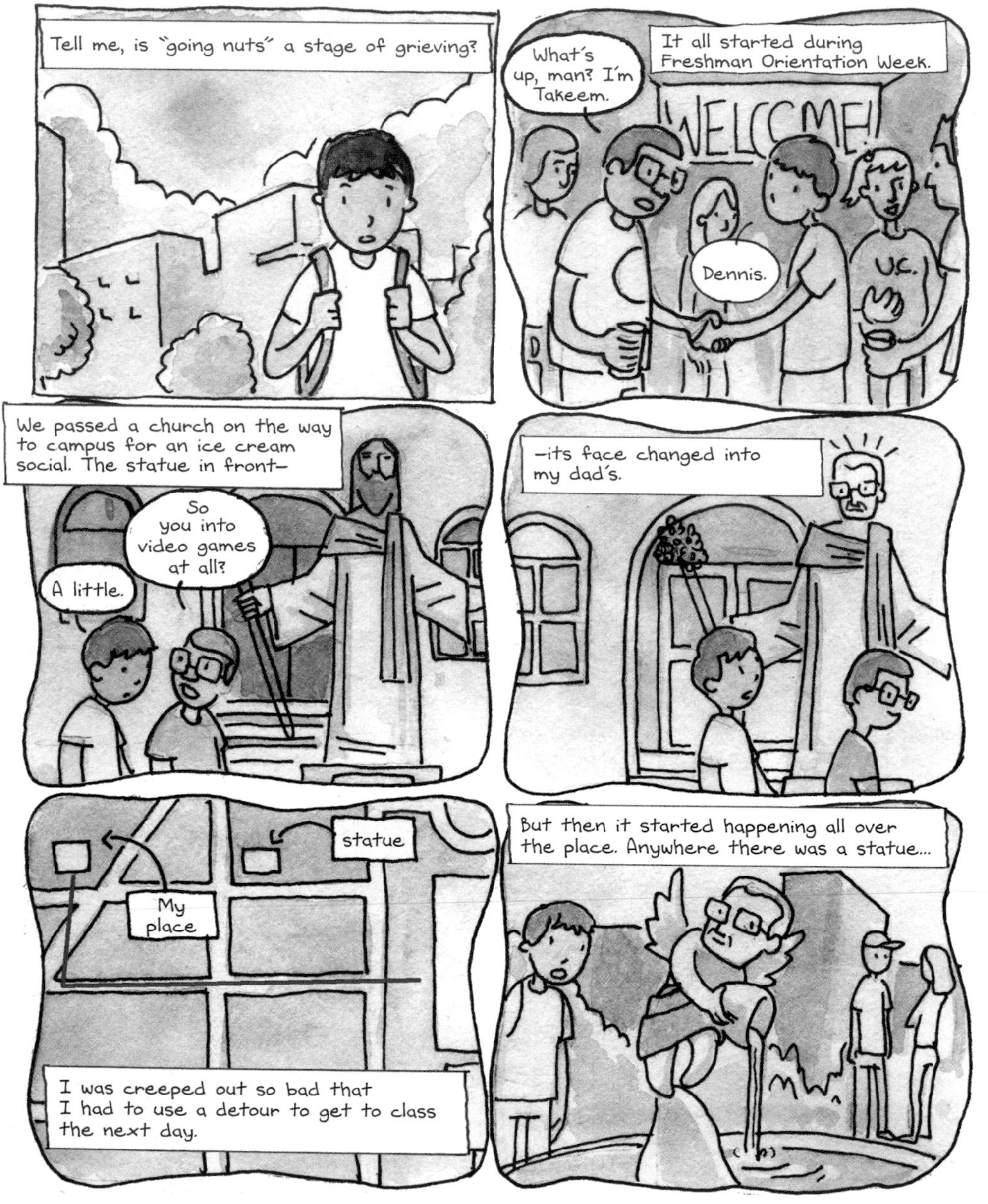
Tell me, is "going nuts" a stage of grieving?
It all started during Freshman Orientation Week.
What's up, man? I'm Takeem.
WELCOME!
Dennis.
U.C.
We passed a church on the way to campus for an ice cream social. The statue in front—
So you into video games at all?
A little.
—its face changed into my dad's.
statue
My place
I was creeped out so bad that I had to use a detour to get to class the next day.
But then it started happening all over the place. Anywhere there was a statue...

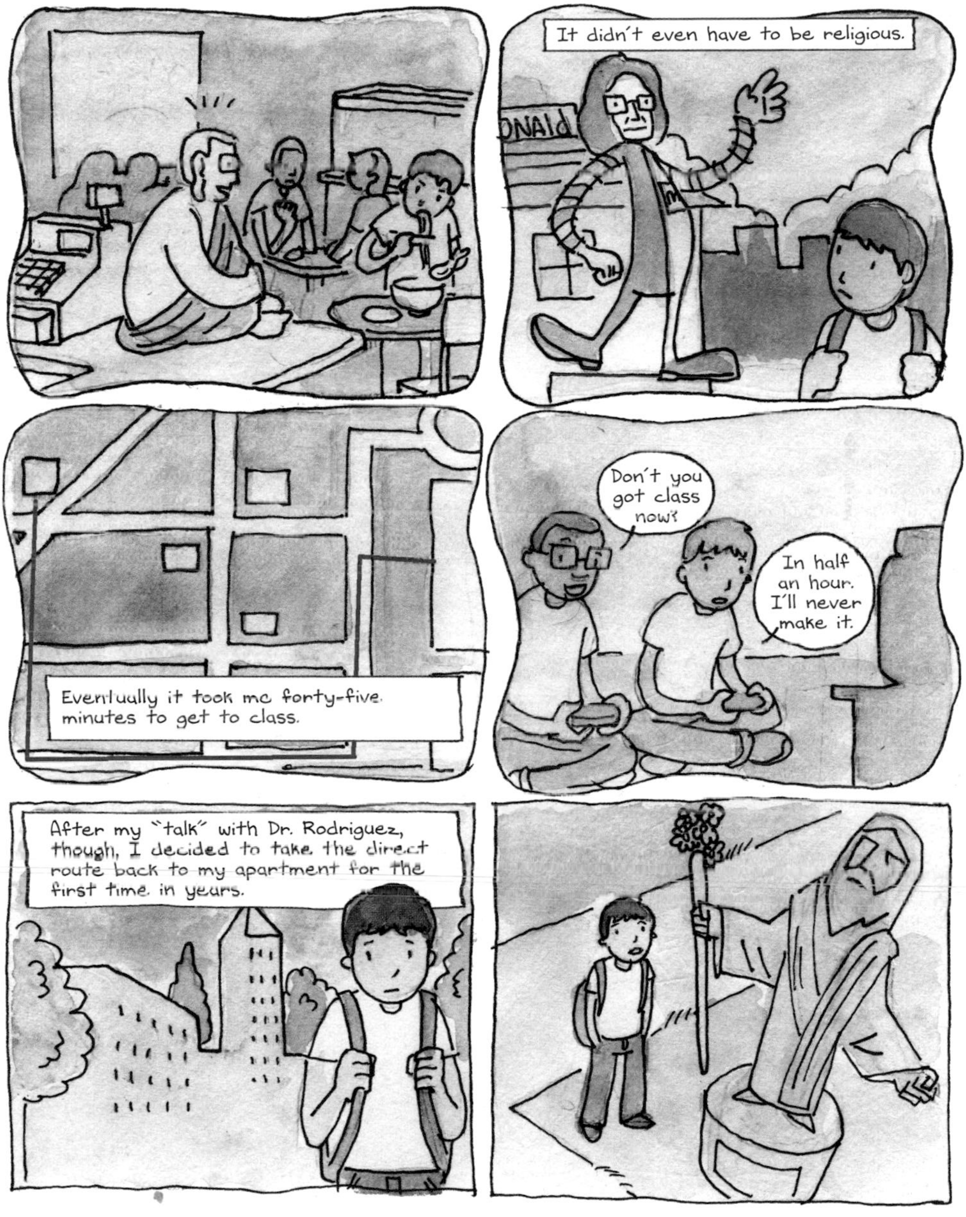
It didn't even have to be religious.
ONAld
Eventually it took me forty-five minutes to get to class.
Don't you got class now?
In half an hour. I'll never make it.
After my "talk" with Dr. Rodriguez, though, I decided to take the direct route back to my apartment for the first time in years.

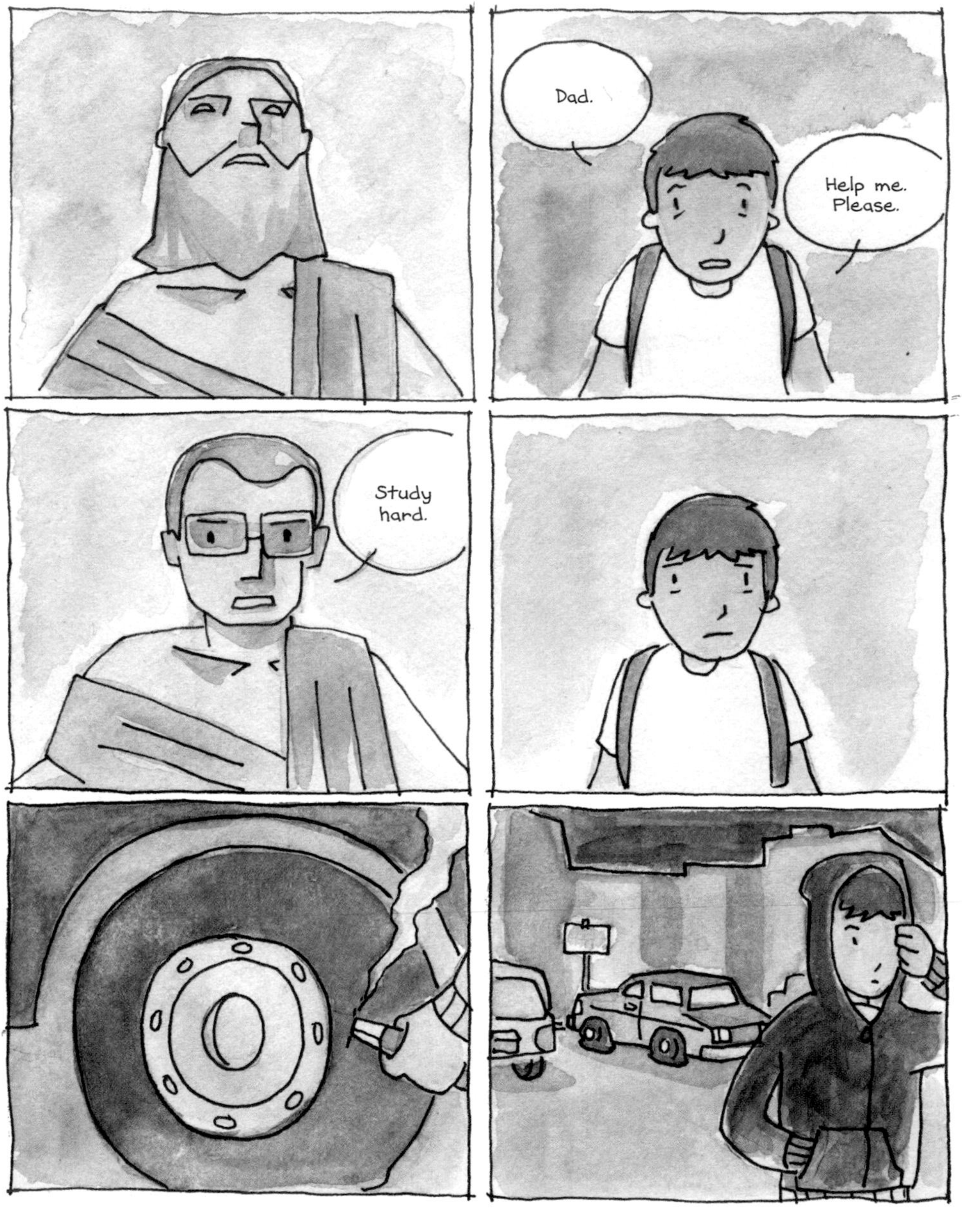

Dad.
Help me. Please.
Study hard.

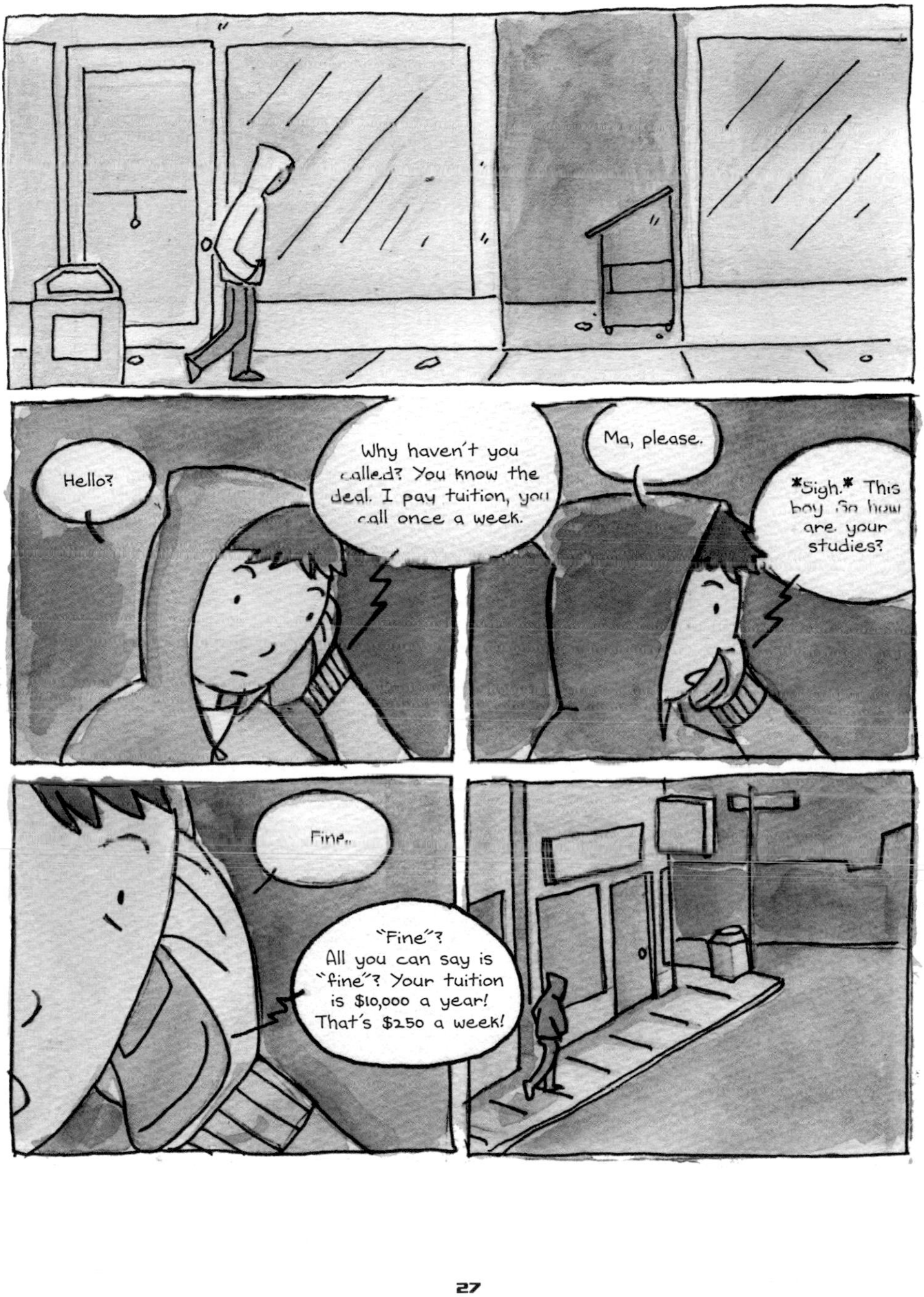
Hello?
Why haven't you called? You know the deal. I pay tuition, you call once a week.
Ma, please.
Sigh. This boy. So how are your studies?
Fine.
"Fine"? All you can say is "fine"? Your tuition is $10,000 a year! That's $250 a week!

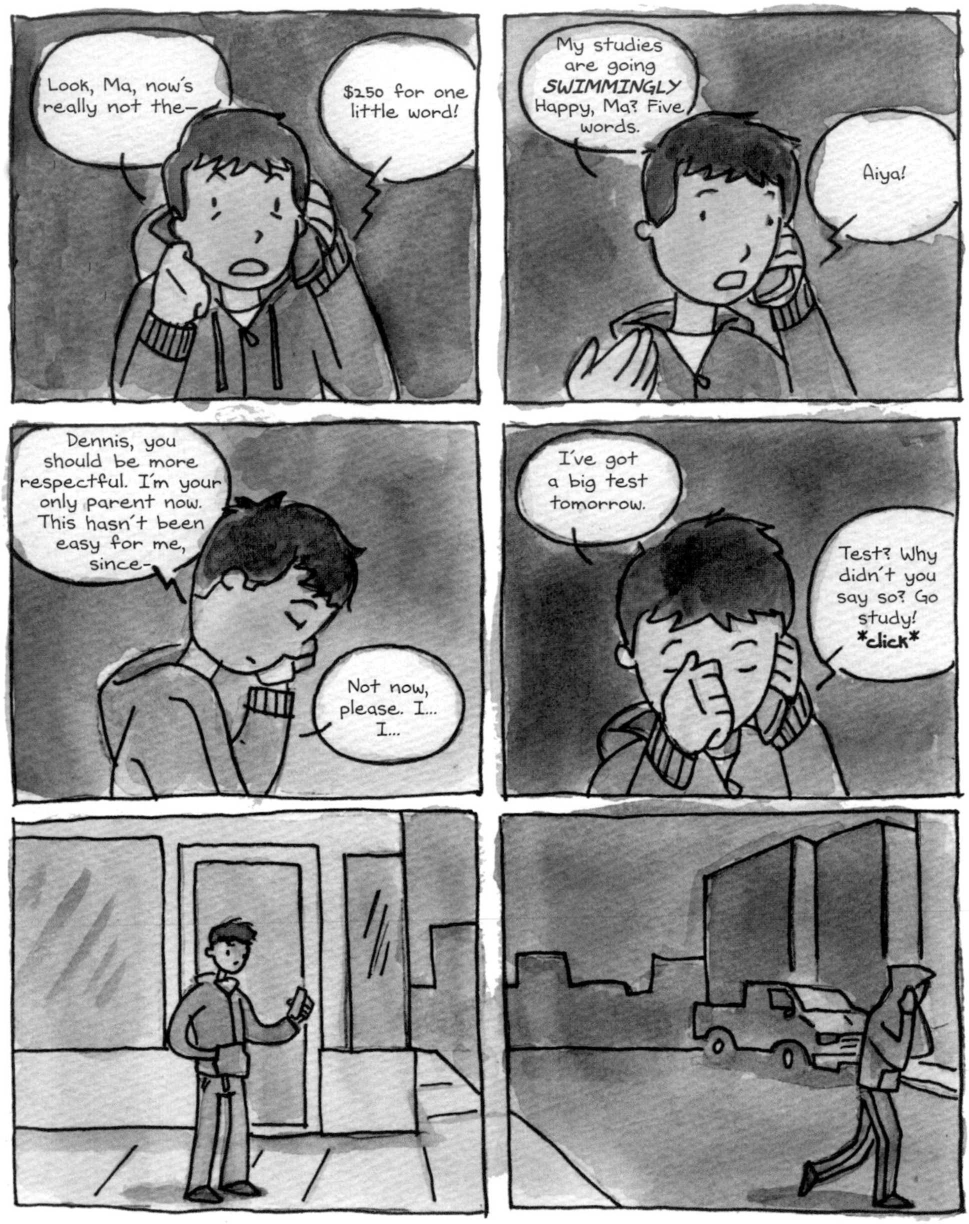
Look, Ma, now's really not the–
$250 for one little word!
My studies are going SWIMMINGLY Happy, Ma? Five words.
Aiya!
Dennis, you should be more respectful. I'm your only parent now. This hasn't been easy for me, since–
Not now, please. I... I...
I've got a big test tomorrow.
Test? Why didn't you say so? Go study! *click*

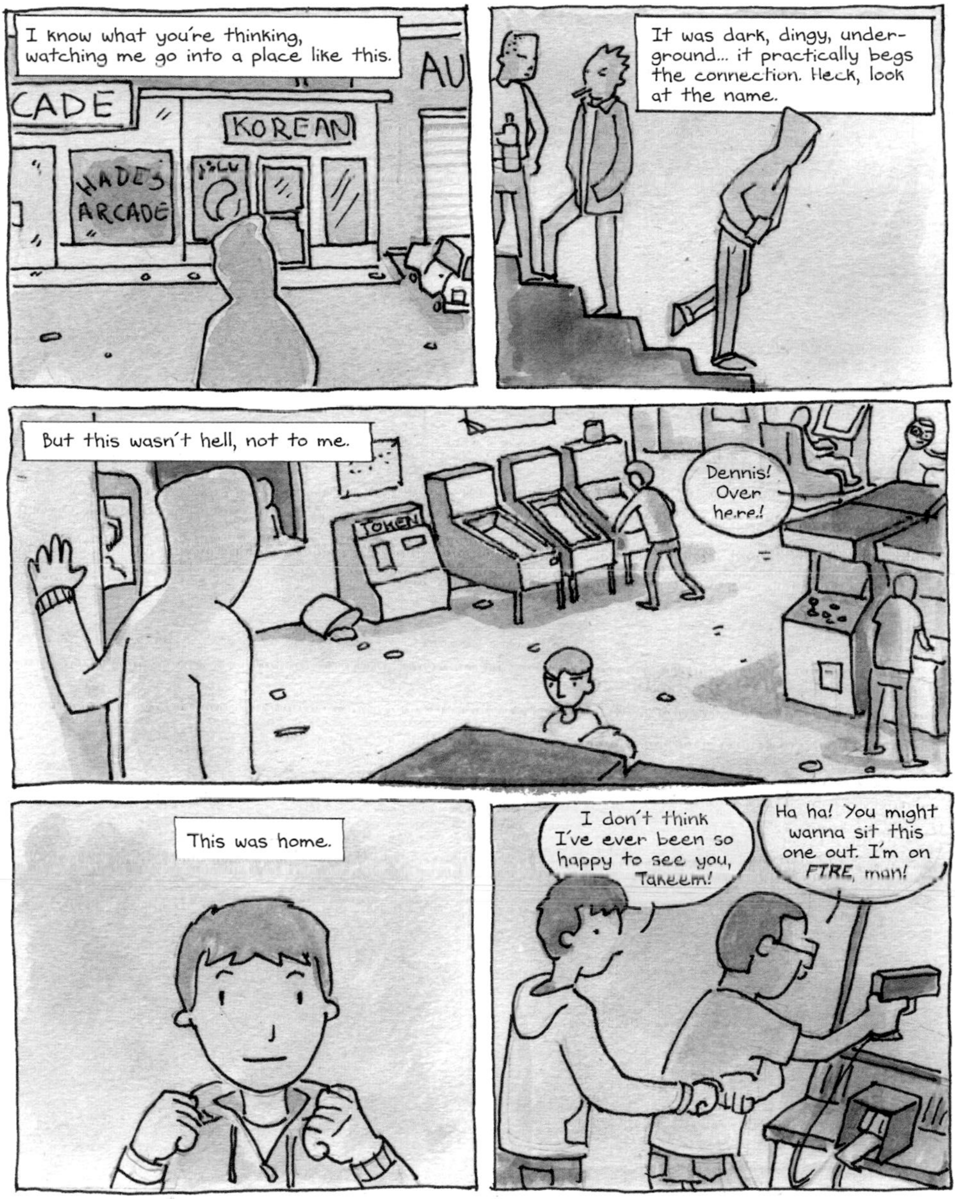
I know what you're thinking, watching me go into a place like this.
CADE
AU
KOREAN
HADES ARCADE
It was dark, dingy, underground... it practically begs the connection. Heck, look at the name.
But this wasn't hell, not to me.
TOKEN
Dennis! Over here!
This was home.
I don't think I've ever been so happy to see you, Takeem!
Ha ha! You might wanna sit this one out. I'm on FIRE, man!

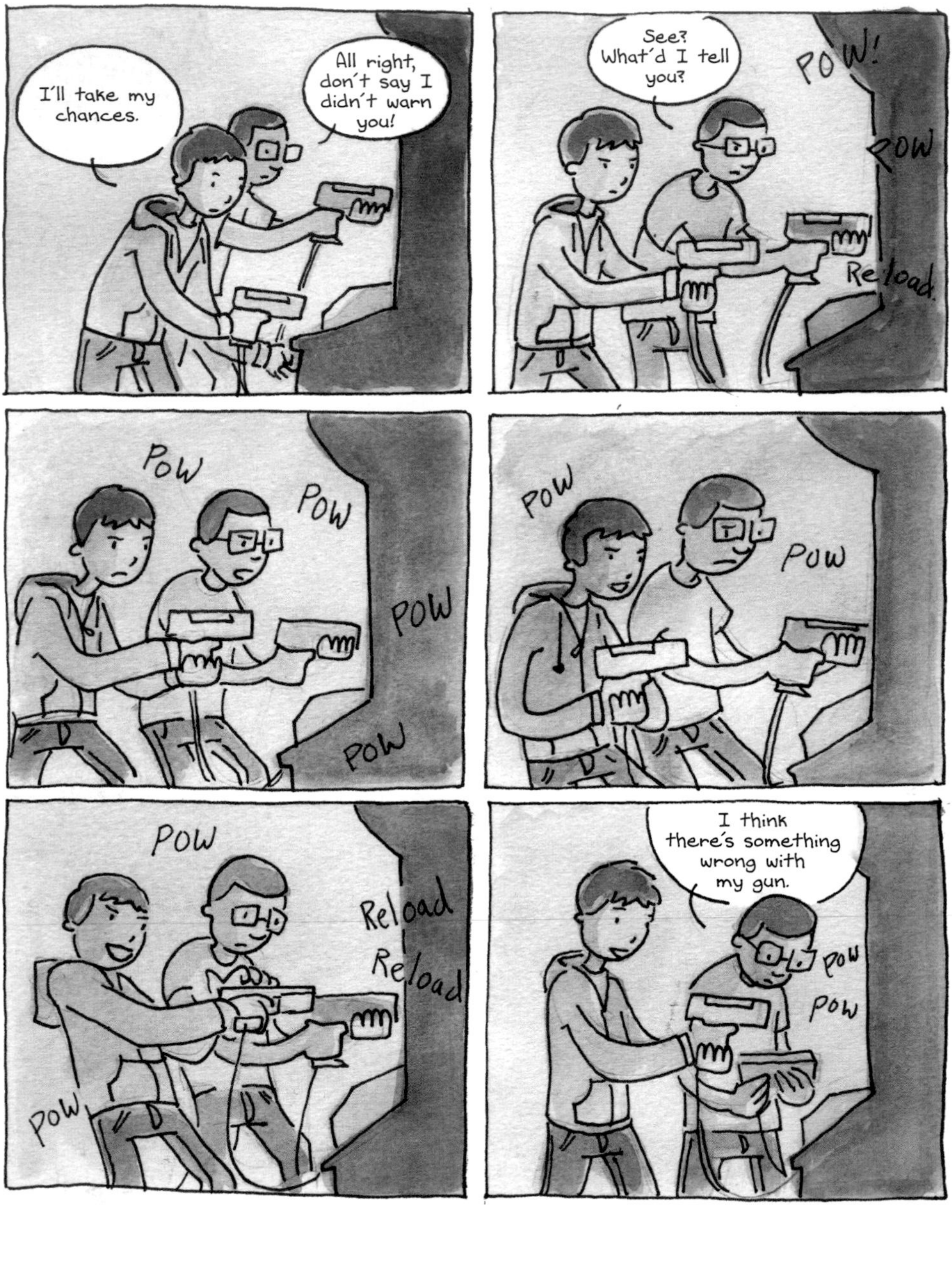

I'll take my chances.
All right, don't say I didn't warn you!
See? What'd I tell you?
POW!
POW
Reload
POW
POW
POW
POW
POW
POW
POW
Reload
Reload
POW
I think there's something wrong with my gun.
POW
POW

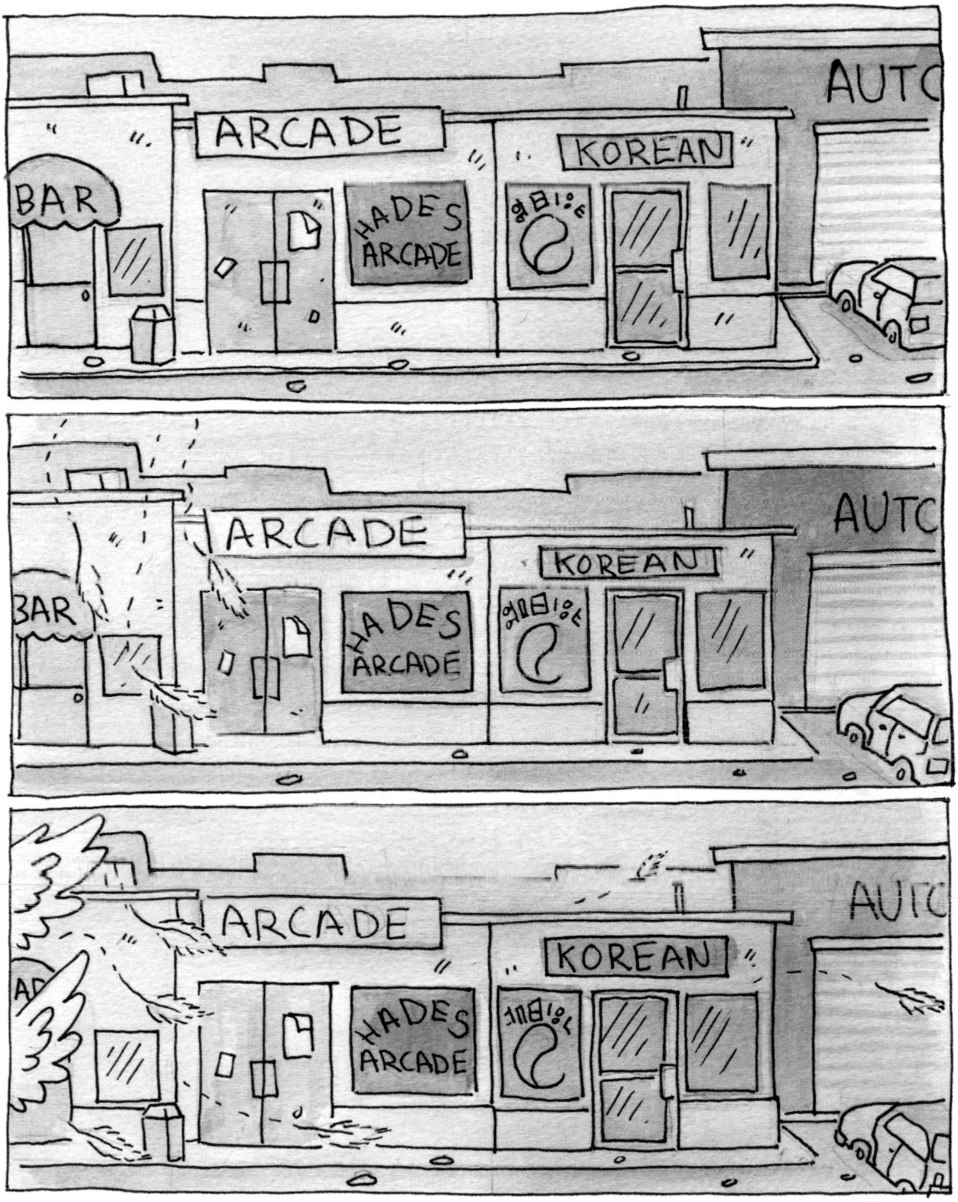
ARCADE
KOREAN
BAR
HADES ARCADE
ARCADE
KOREAN
BAR
HADES ARCADE
ARCADE
KOREAN
HADES ARCADE

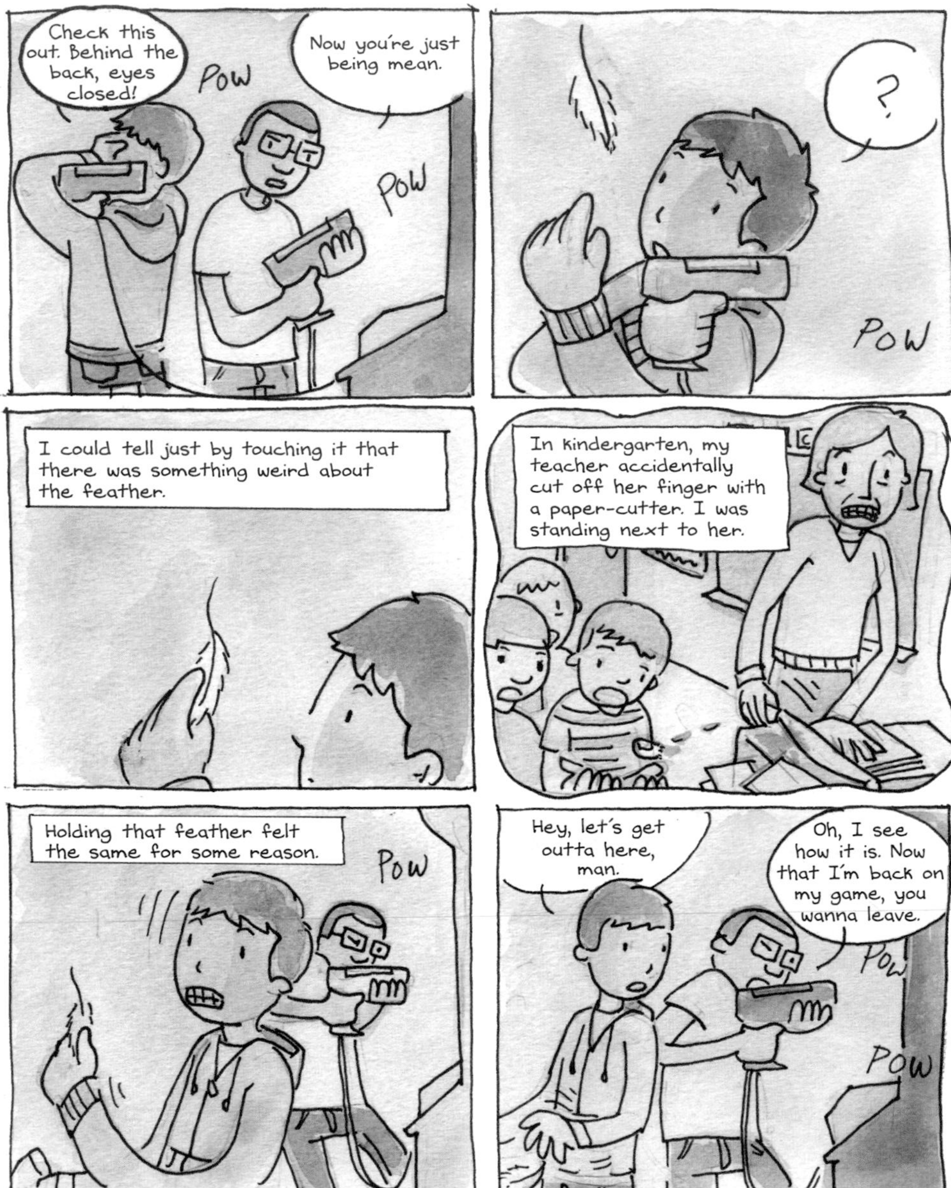
Check this out. Behind the back, eyes closed!
POW
Now you're just being mean.
POW
?
POW
I could tell just by touching it that there was something weird about the feather.
In kindergarten, my teacher accidentally cut off her finger with a paper-cutter. I was standing next to her.
Holding that feather felt the same for some reason.
POW
Hey, let's get outta here, man.
Oh, I see how it is. Now that I'm back on my game, you wanna leave.
POW
POW

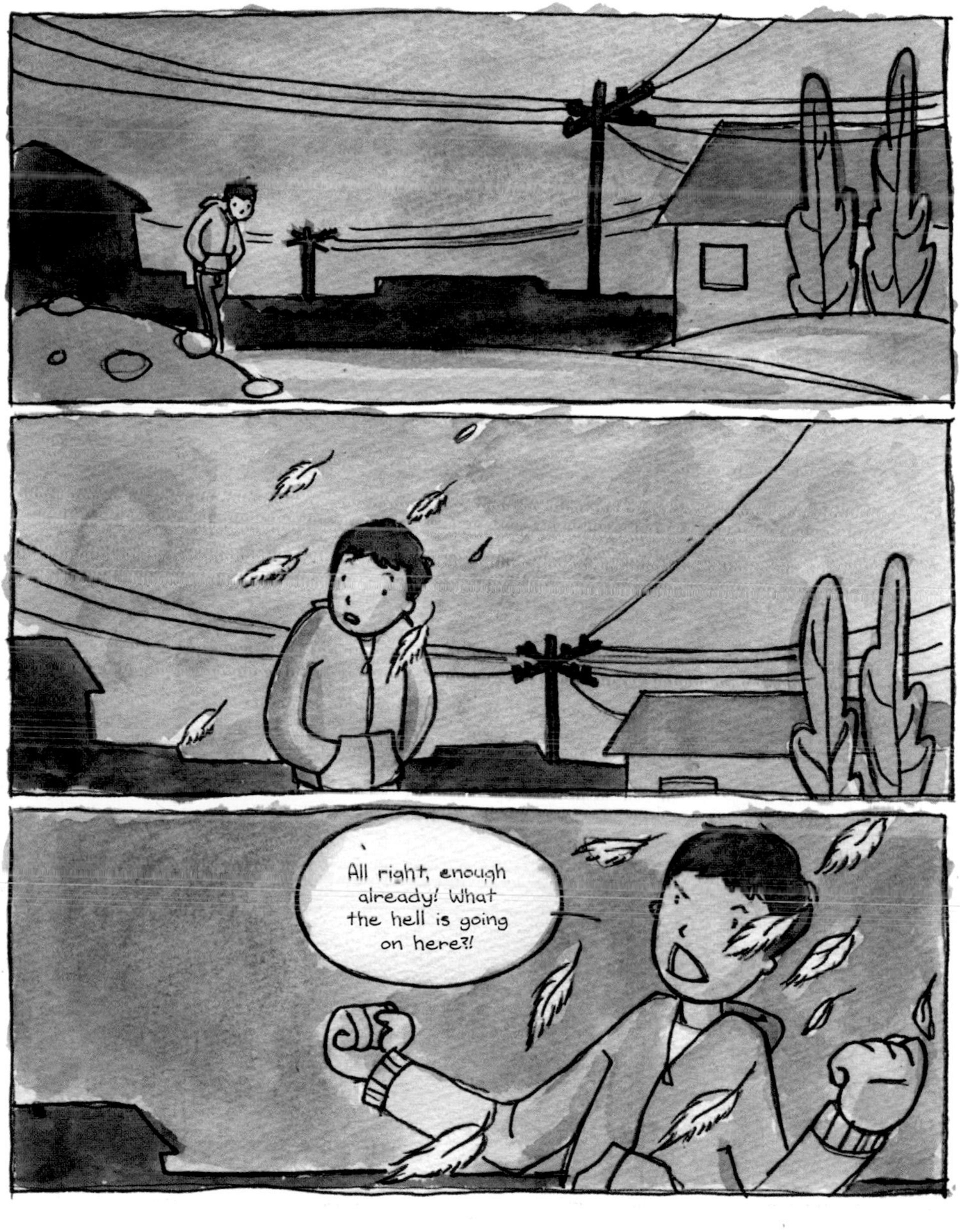
All right, enough already! What the hell is going on here?!

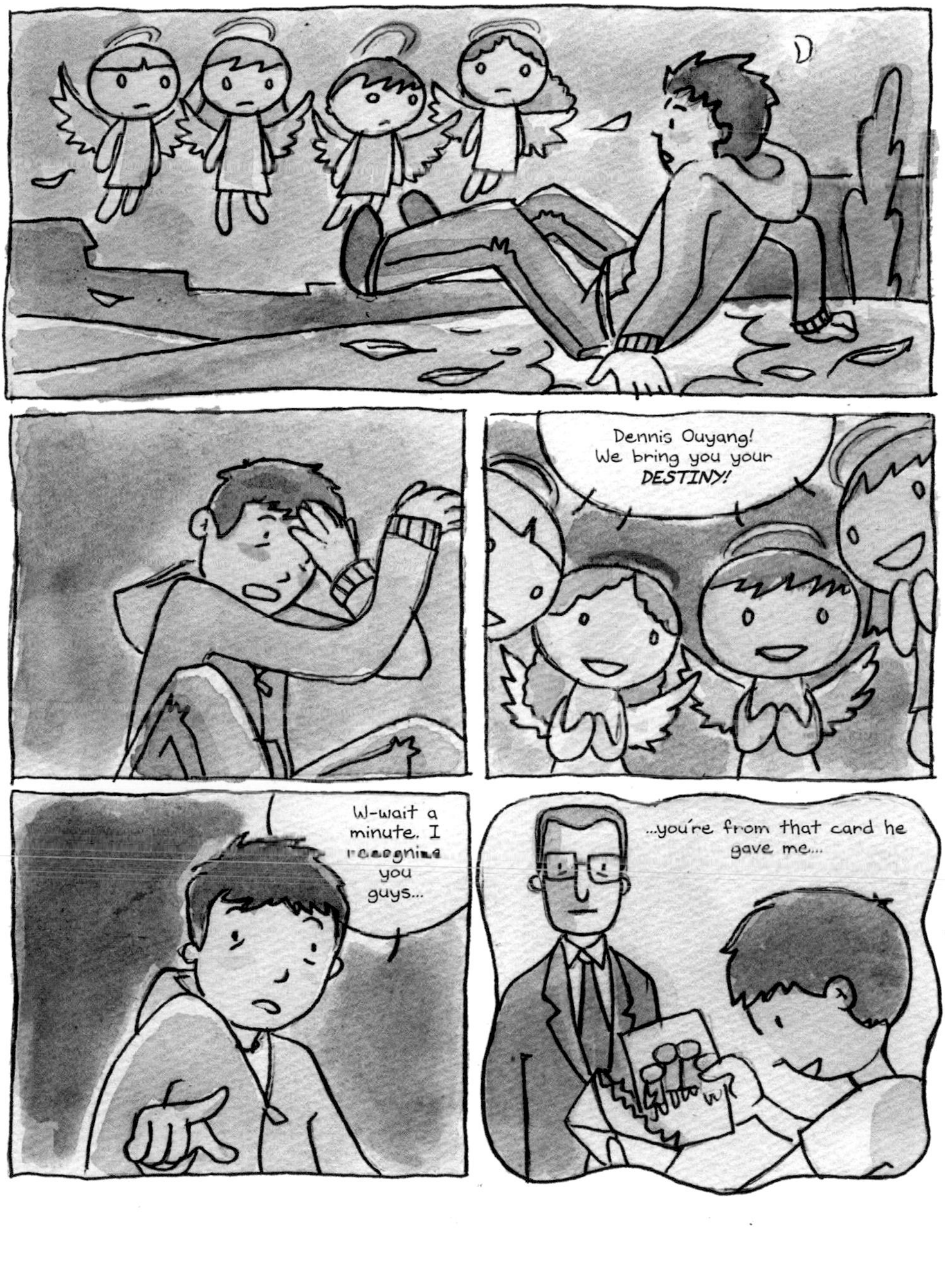
Dennis Ouyang! We bring you your **DESTINY!**
W-wait a minute. I recognize you guys...
...you're from that card he gave me...

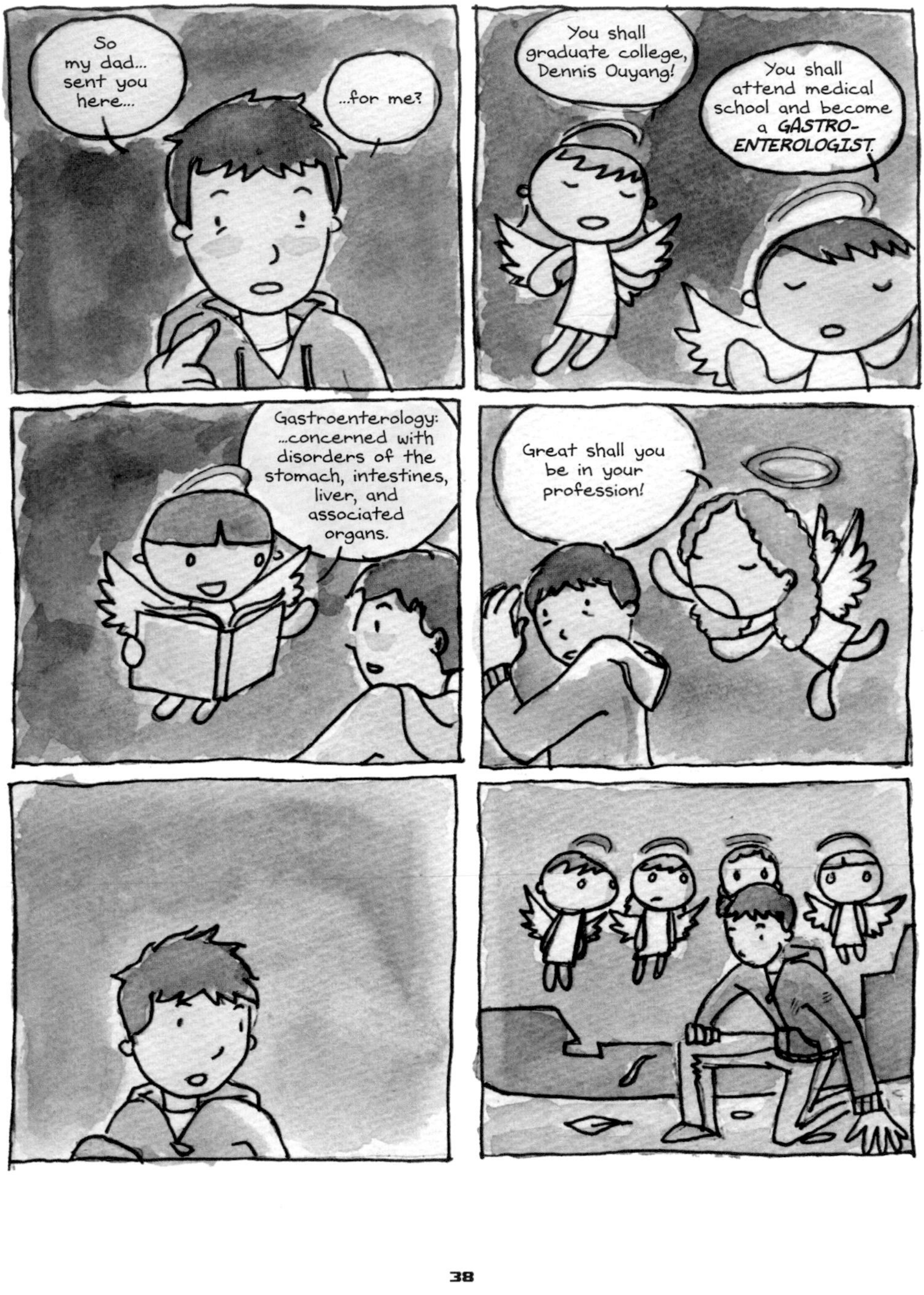
So my dad... sent you here...
...for me?
You shall graduate college, Dennis Ouyang!
You shall attend medical school and become a GASTRO-ENTEROLOGIST.
Gastroenterology: ...concerned with disorders of the stomach, intestines, liver, and associated organs.
Great shall you be in your profession!

44

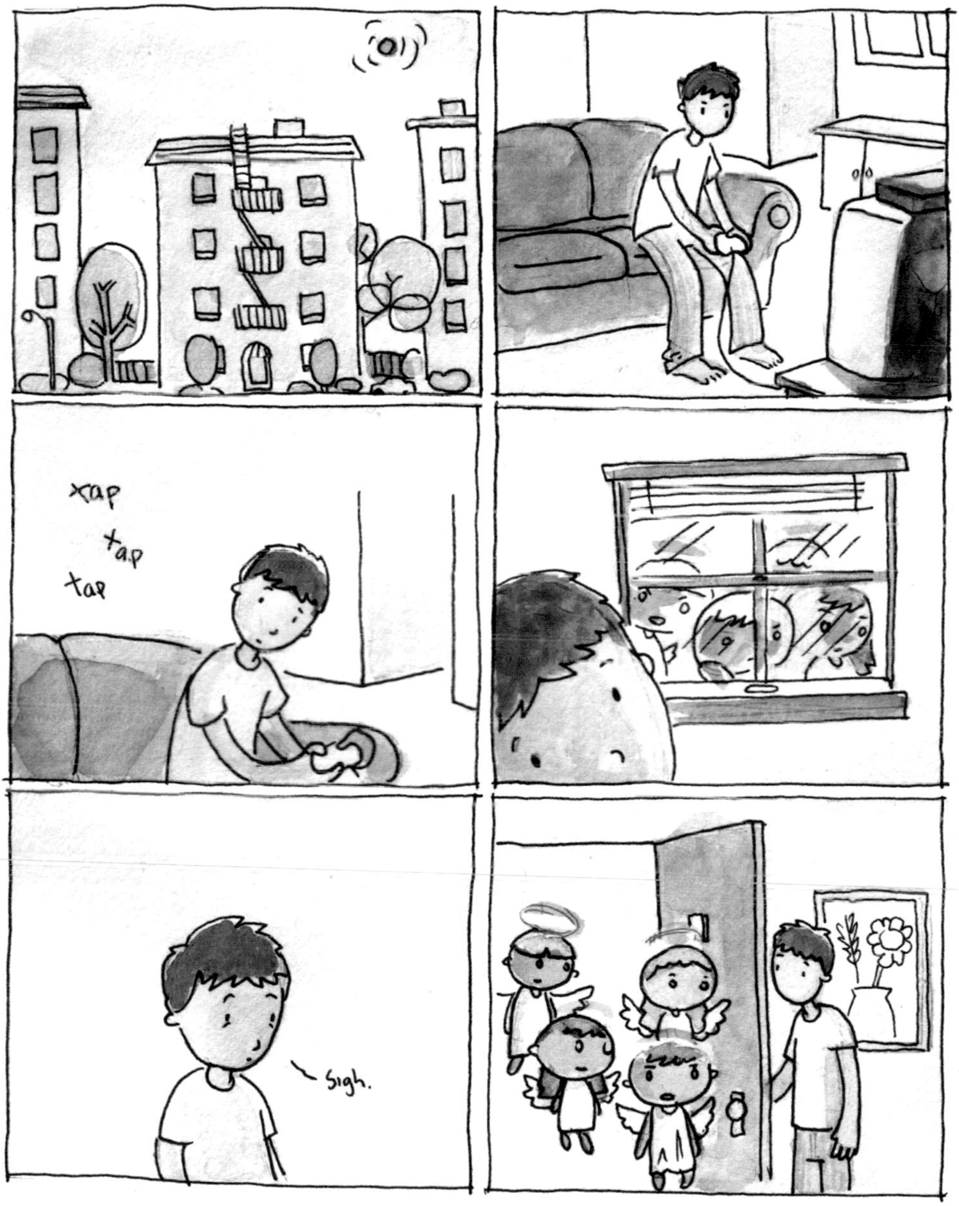
tap
tap
tap
Sigh.

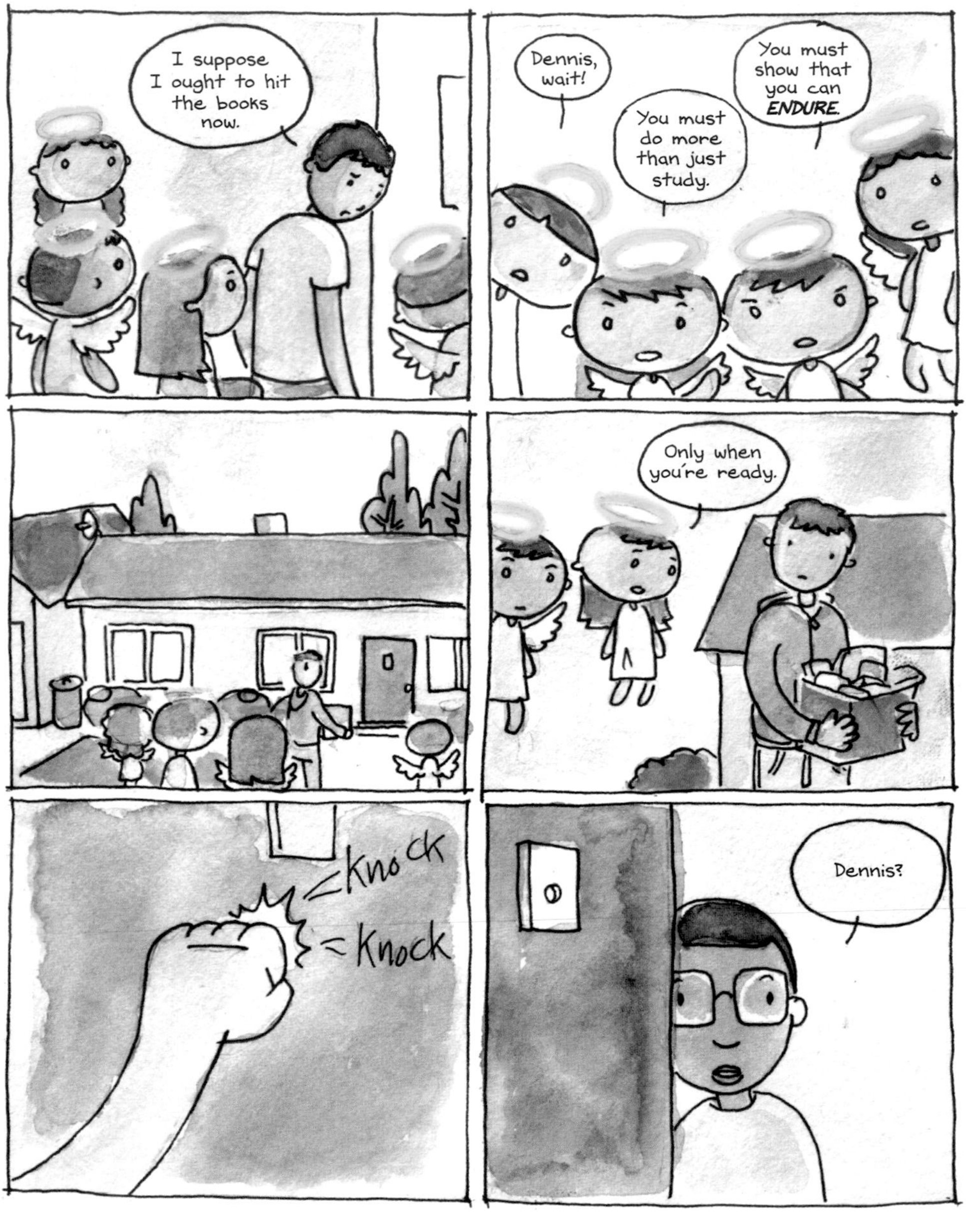

I suppose I ought to hit the books now.
Dennis, wait!
You must do more than just study.
You must show that you can ***ENDURE.***
Only when you're ready.
Knock
Knock
Dennis?

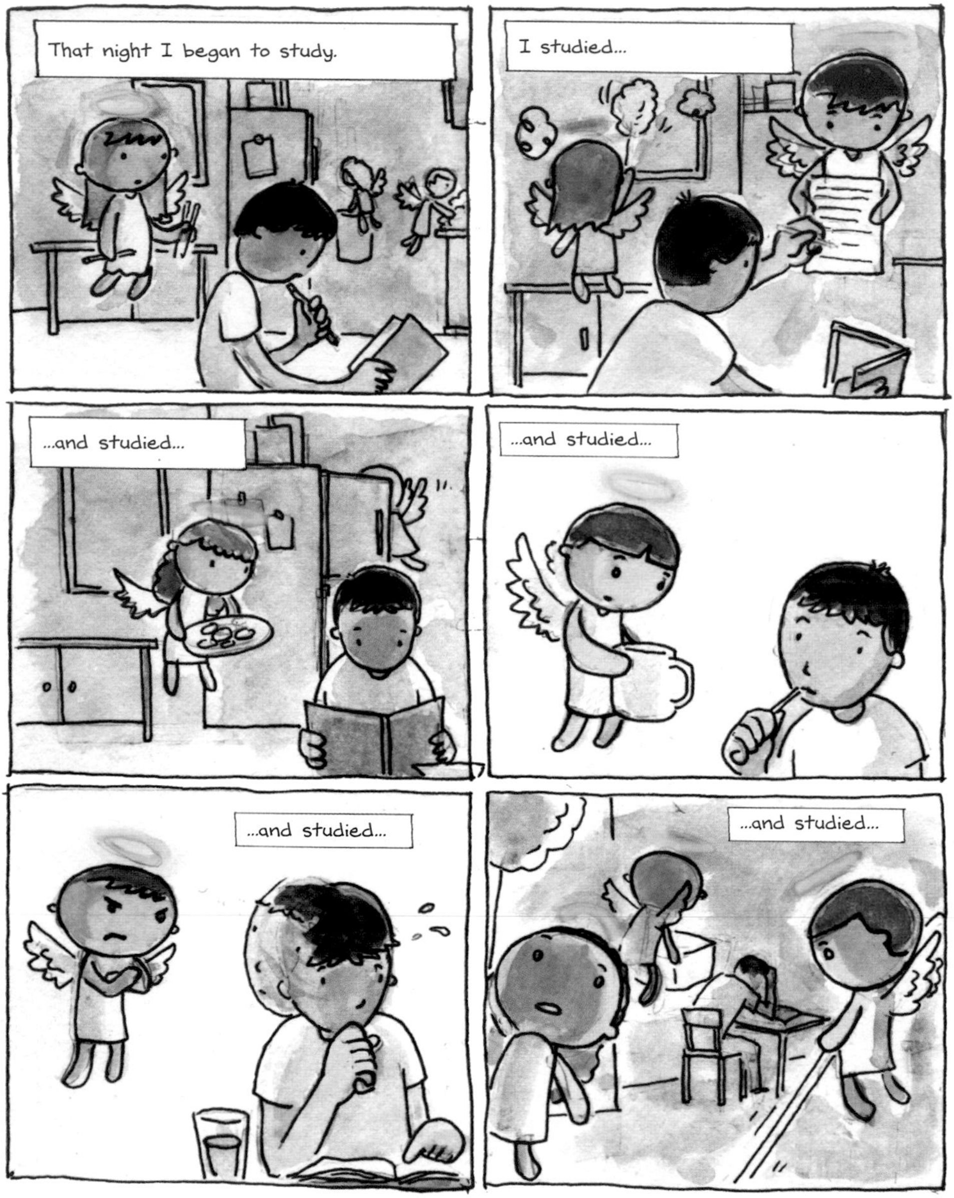
That night I began to study.
I studied...
...and studied...
...and studied...
...and studied...
...and studied...

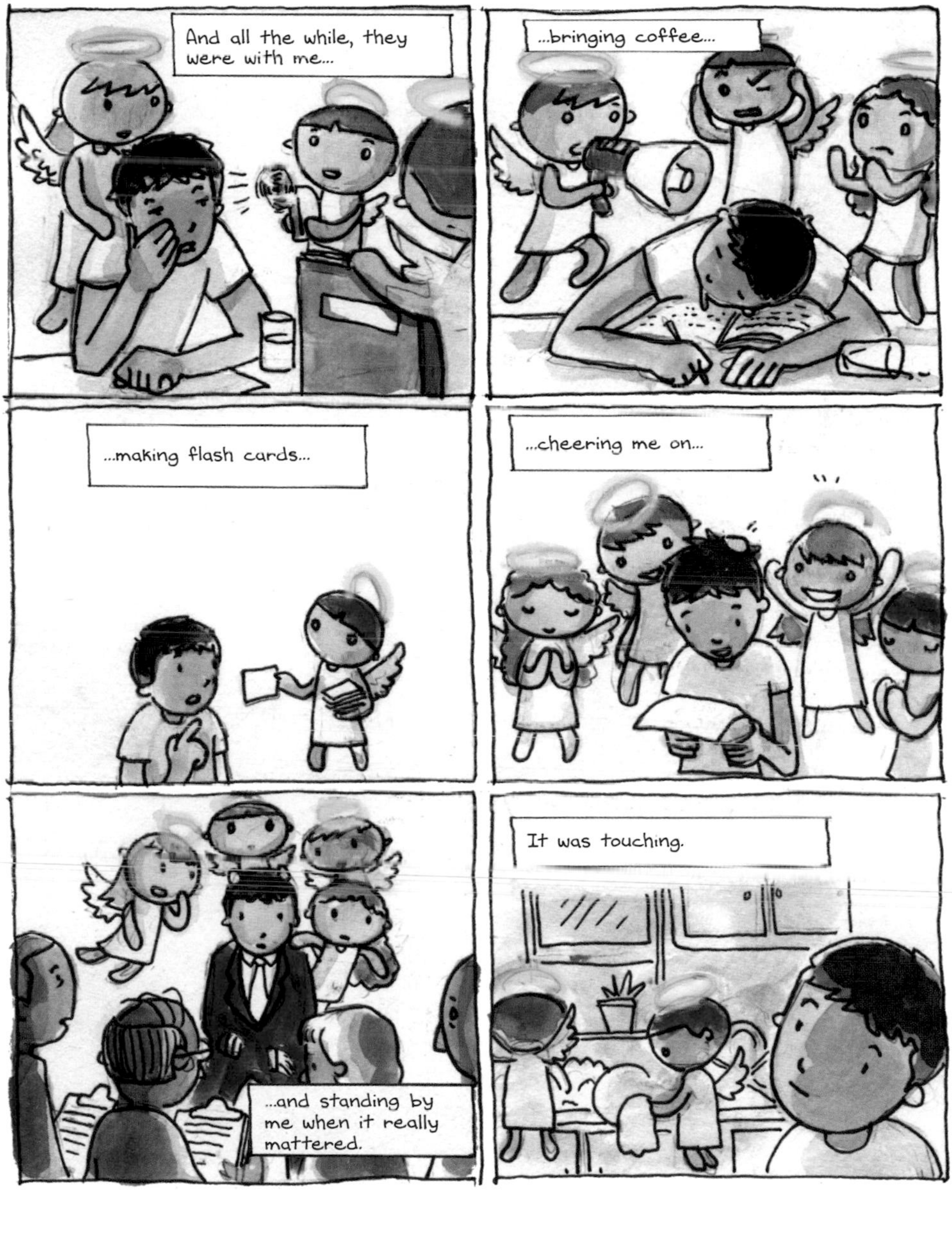

And all the while, they were with me...
...bringing coffee...
...making flash cards...
...cheering me on...
...and standing by me when it really mattered.
It was touching.

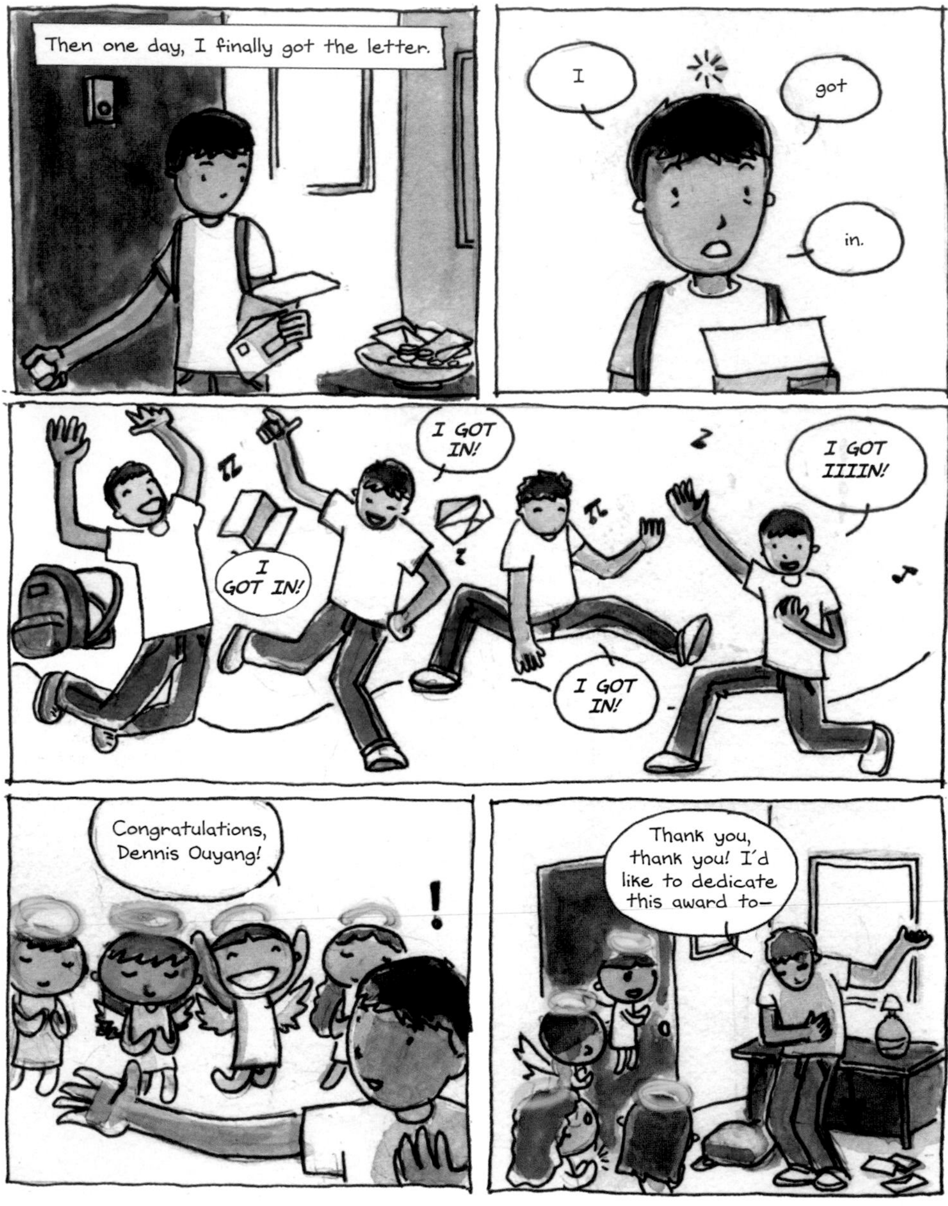
Then one day, I finally got the letter.
I
got
in.
I GOT IN!
I GOT IN!
I GOT IN!
I GOT IIIIN!
Congratulations, Dennis Ouyang!
!
Thank you, thank you! I'd like to dedicate this award to—

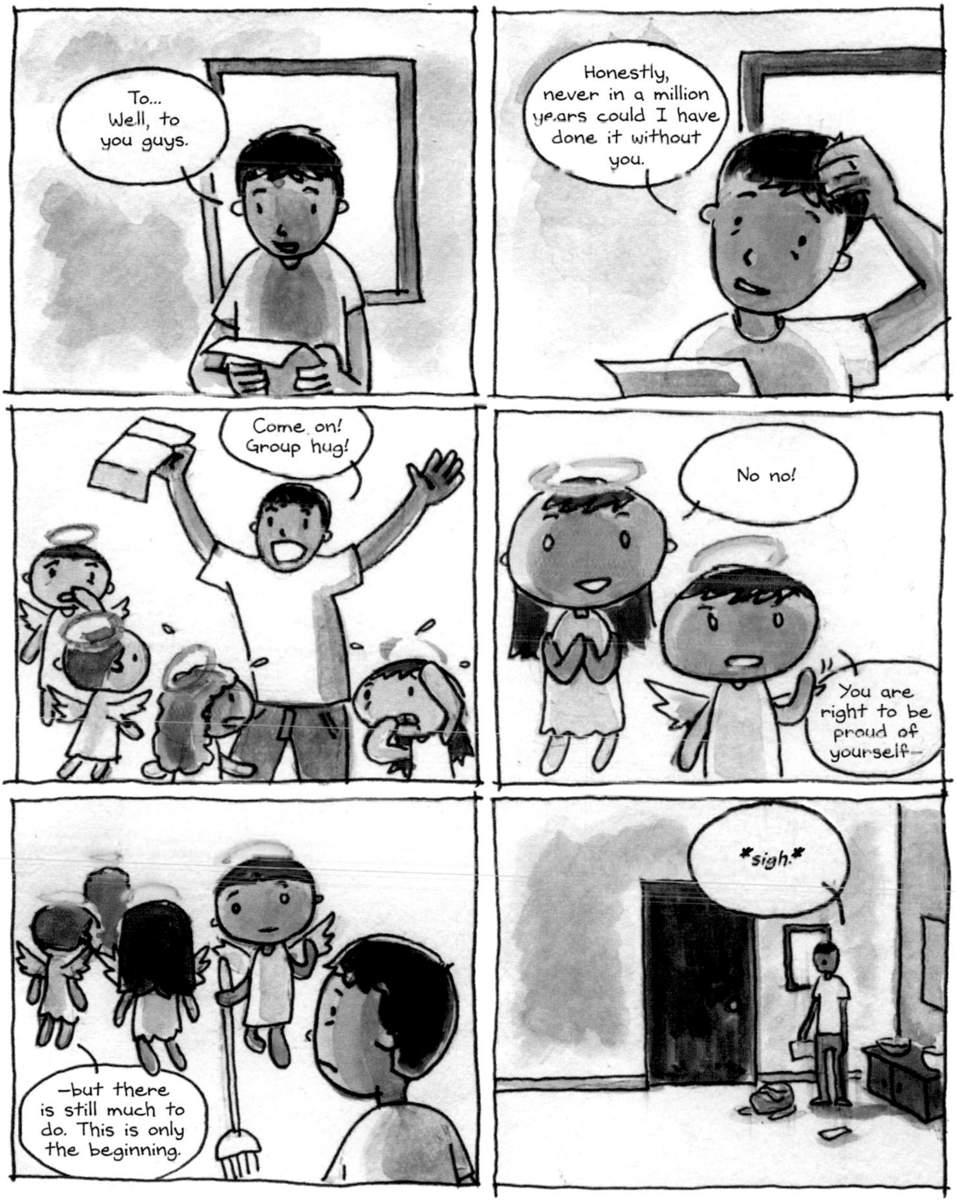
To...
Well, to
you guys.
Honestly,
never in a million
years could I have
done it without
you.
Come on!
Group hug!
No no!
You are
right to be
proud of
yourself—
—but there
is still much to
do. This is only
the beginning.
sigh.

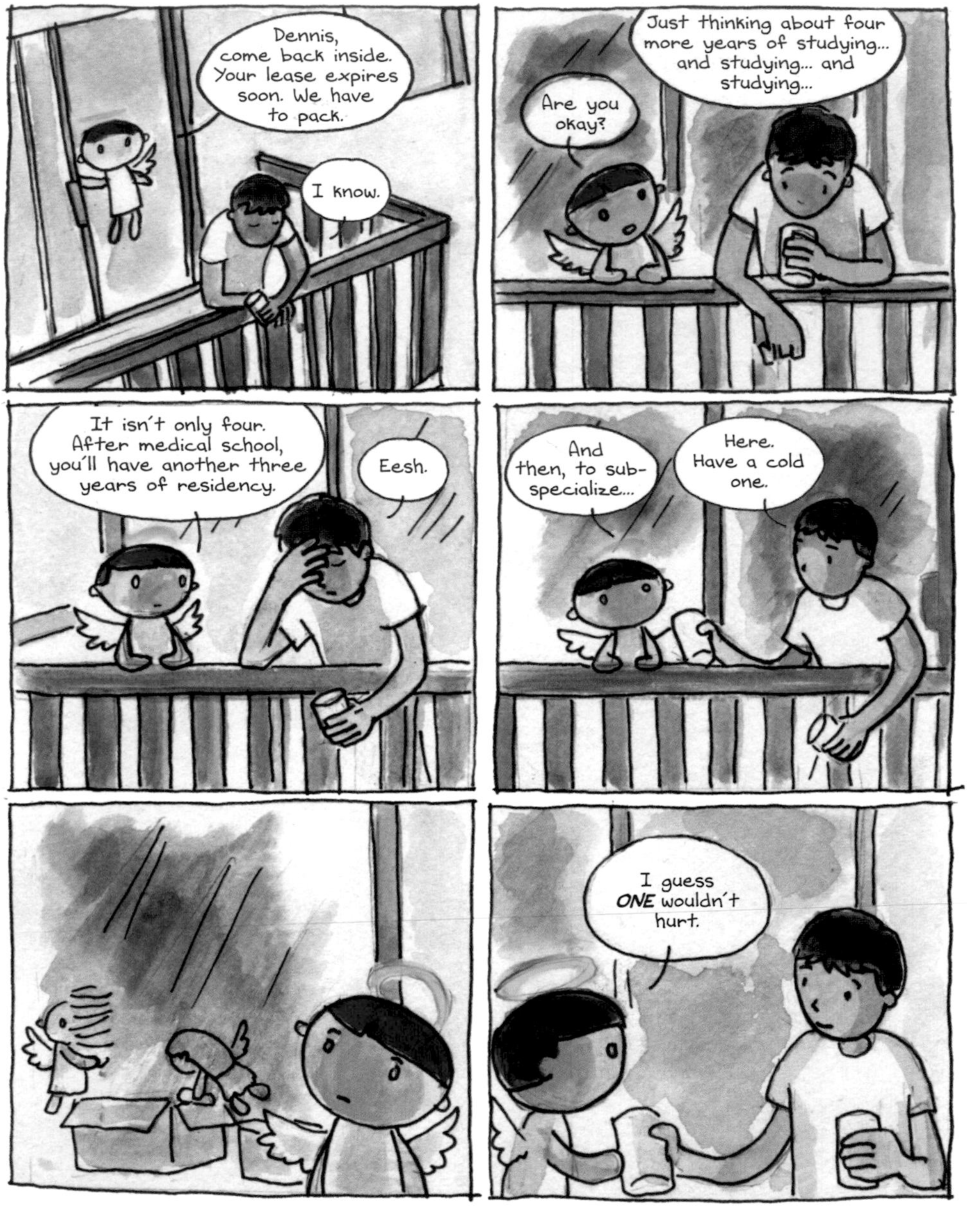
Dennis, come back inside. Your lease expires soon. We have to pack.
I know.
Are you okay?
Just thinking about four more years of studying... and studying... and studying...
It isn't only four. After medical school, you'll have another three years of residency.
Eesh.
And then, to sub-specialize...
Here. Have a cold one.
I guess ONE wouldn't hurt.

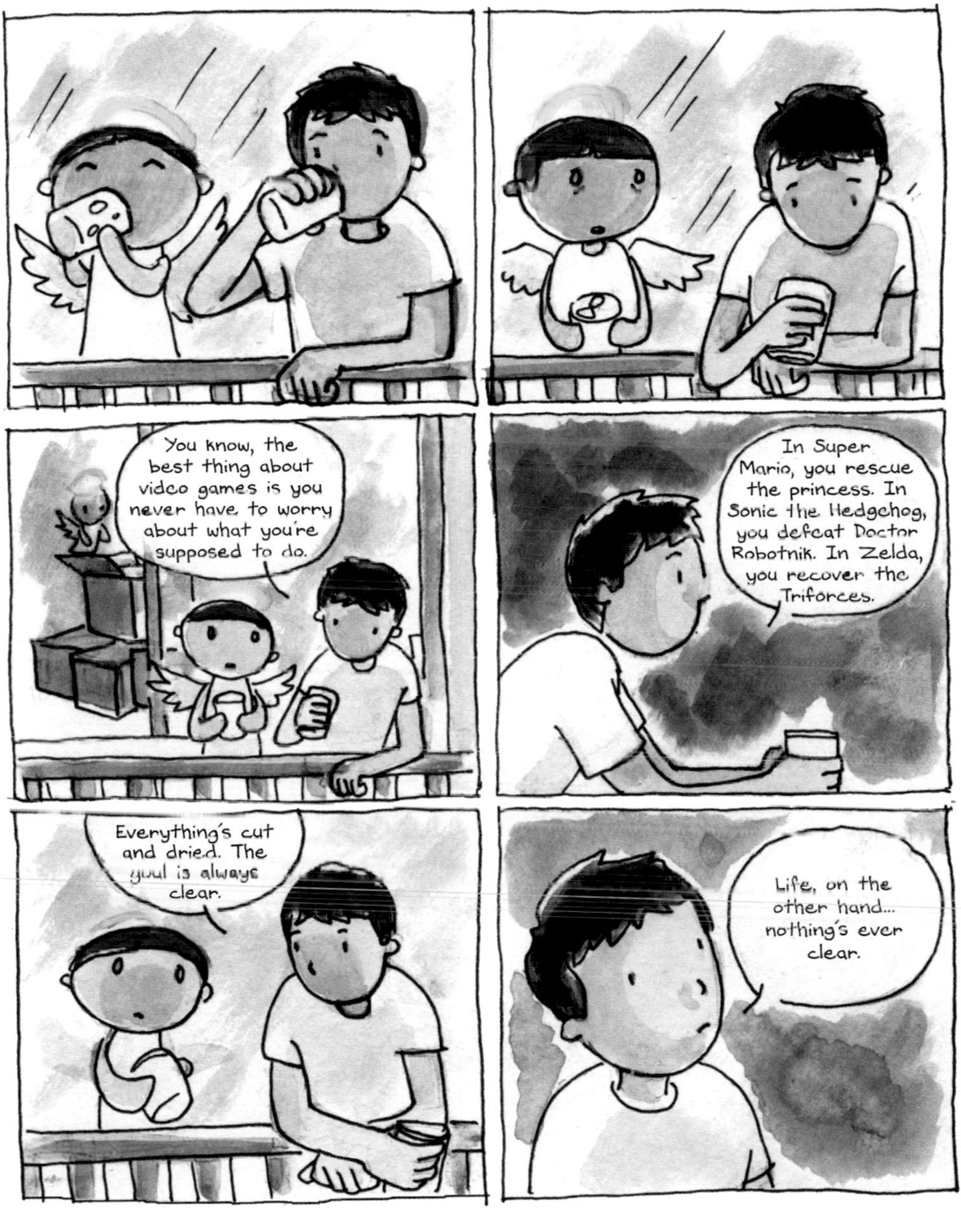
You know, the best thing about video games is you never have to worry about what you're supposed to do.
In Super Mario, you rescue the princess. In Sonic the Hedgehog, you defeat Doctor Robotnik. In Zelda, you recover the Triforces.
Everything's cut and dried. The goal is always clear.
Life, on the other hand... nothing's ever clear.

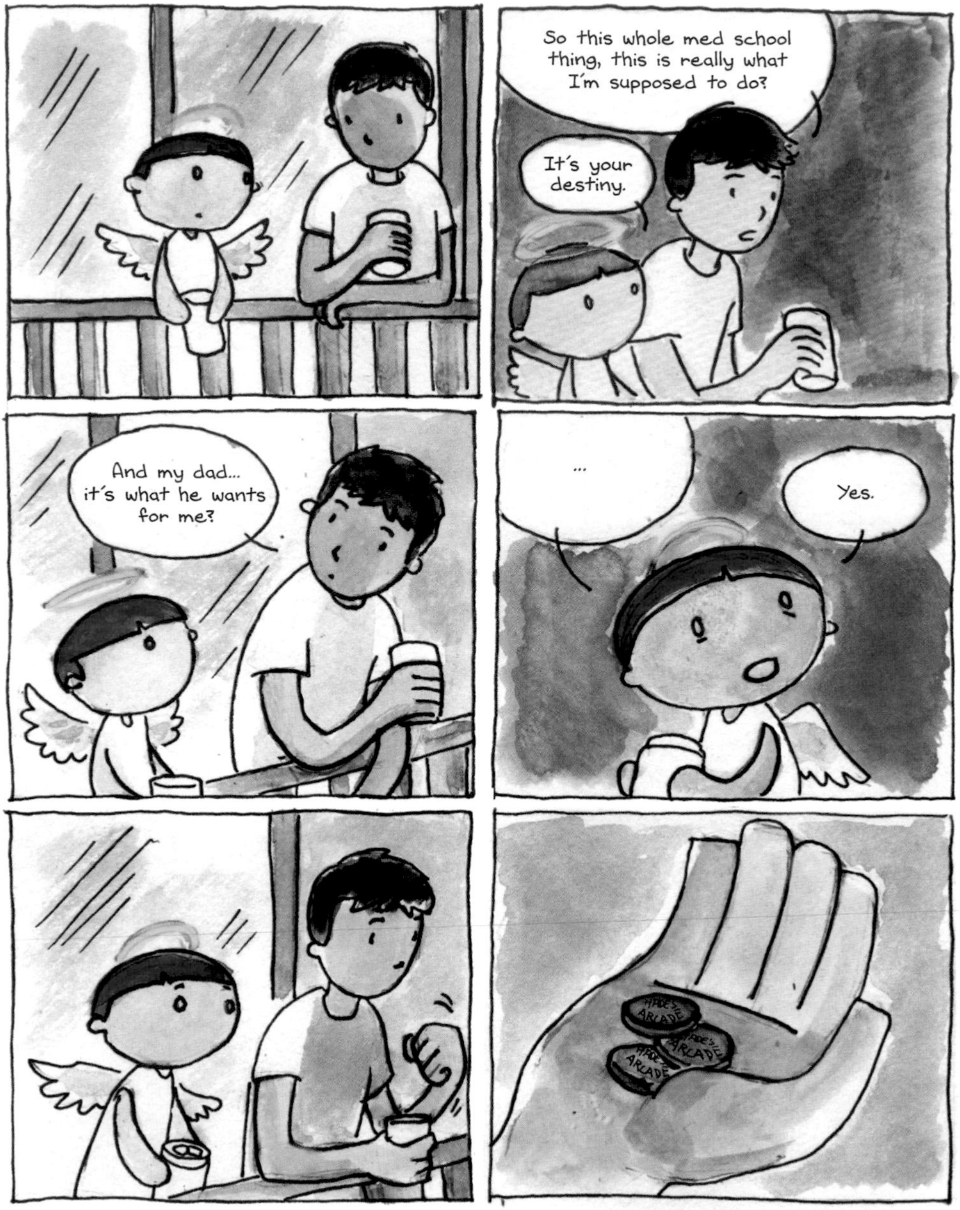
So this whole med school thing, this is really what I'm supposed to do?
It's your destiny.
And my dad... it's what he wants for me?
...
Yes.

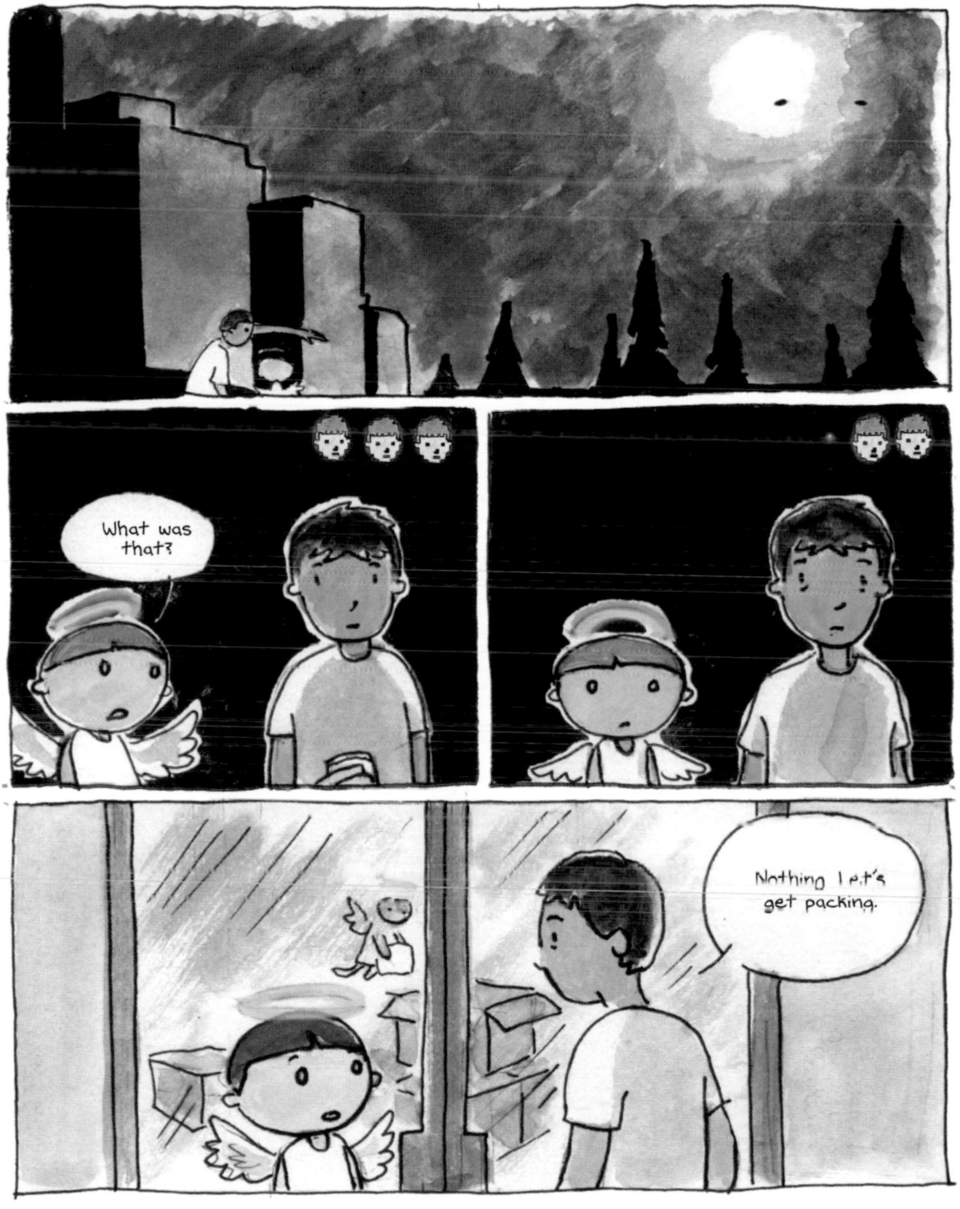
What was that?
Nothing Let's get packing.

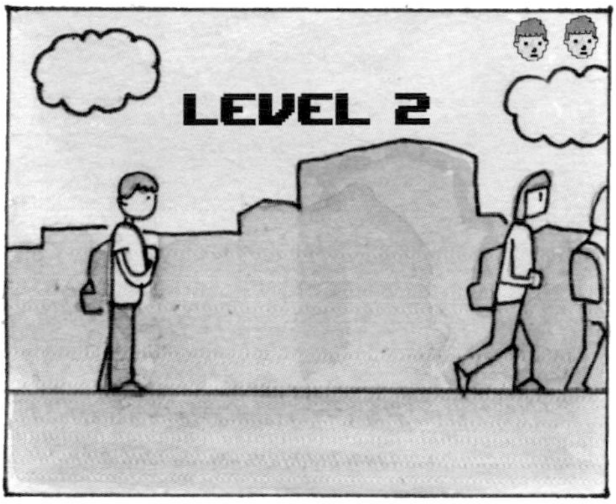
LEVEL 2

On the morning of my first day of med school, everything was *BEAUTIFUL*.

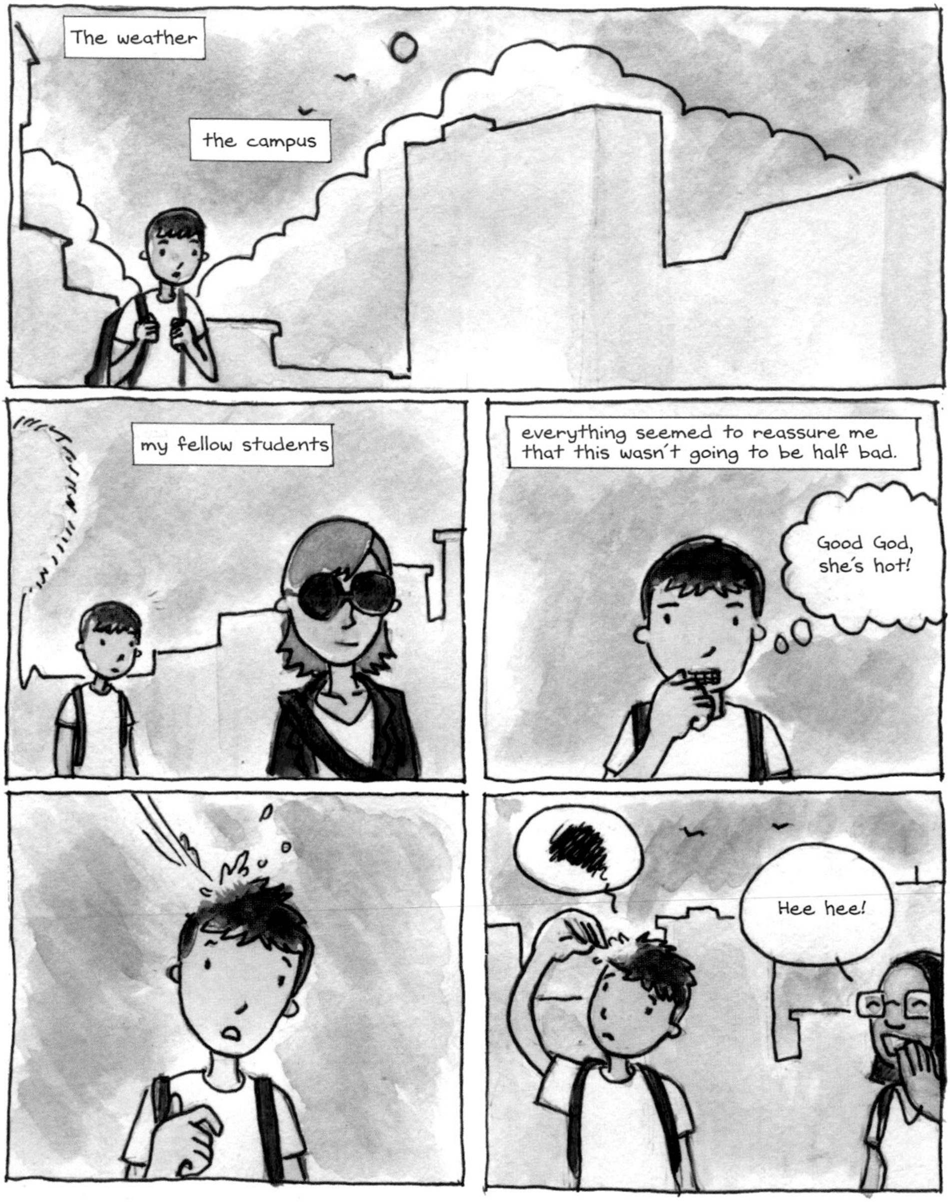
The weather
the campus
my fellow students
everything seemed to reassure me that this wasn´t going to be half bad.
Good God, she´s hot!
Hee hee!

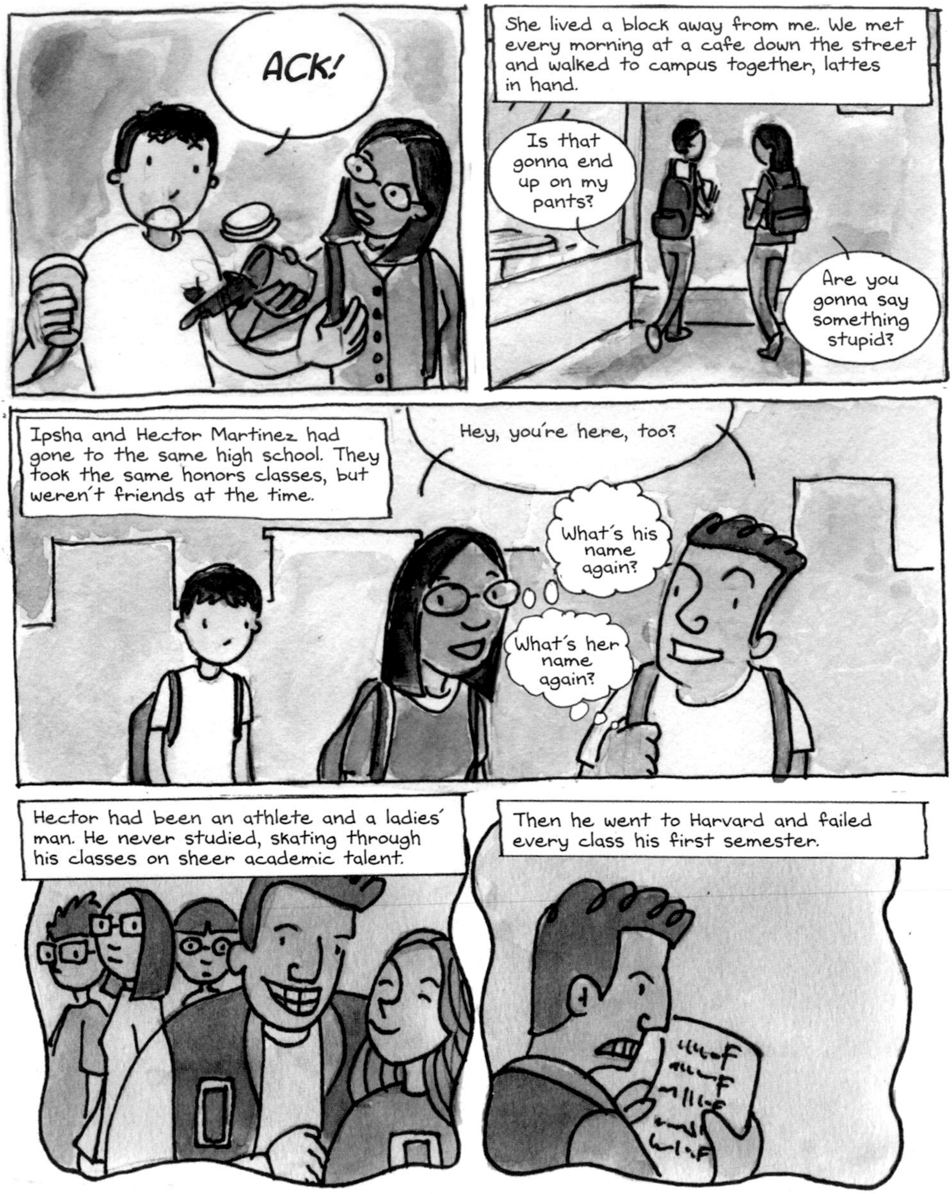
ACK!
She lived a block away from me. We met every morning at a cafe down the street and walked to campus together, lattes in hand.
Is that gonna end up on my pants?
Are you gonna say something stupid?
Ipsha and Hector Martinez had gone to the same high school. They took the same honors classes, but weren't friends at the time.
Hey, you're here, too?
What's his name again?
What's her name again?
Hector had been an athlete and a ladies' man. He never studied, skating through his classes on sheer academic talent.
Then he went to Harvard and failed every class his first semester.

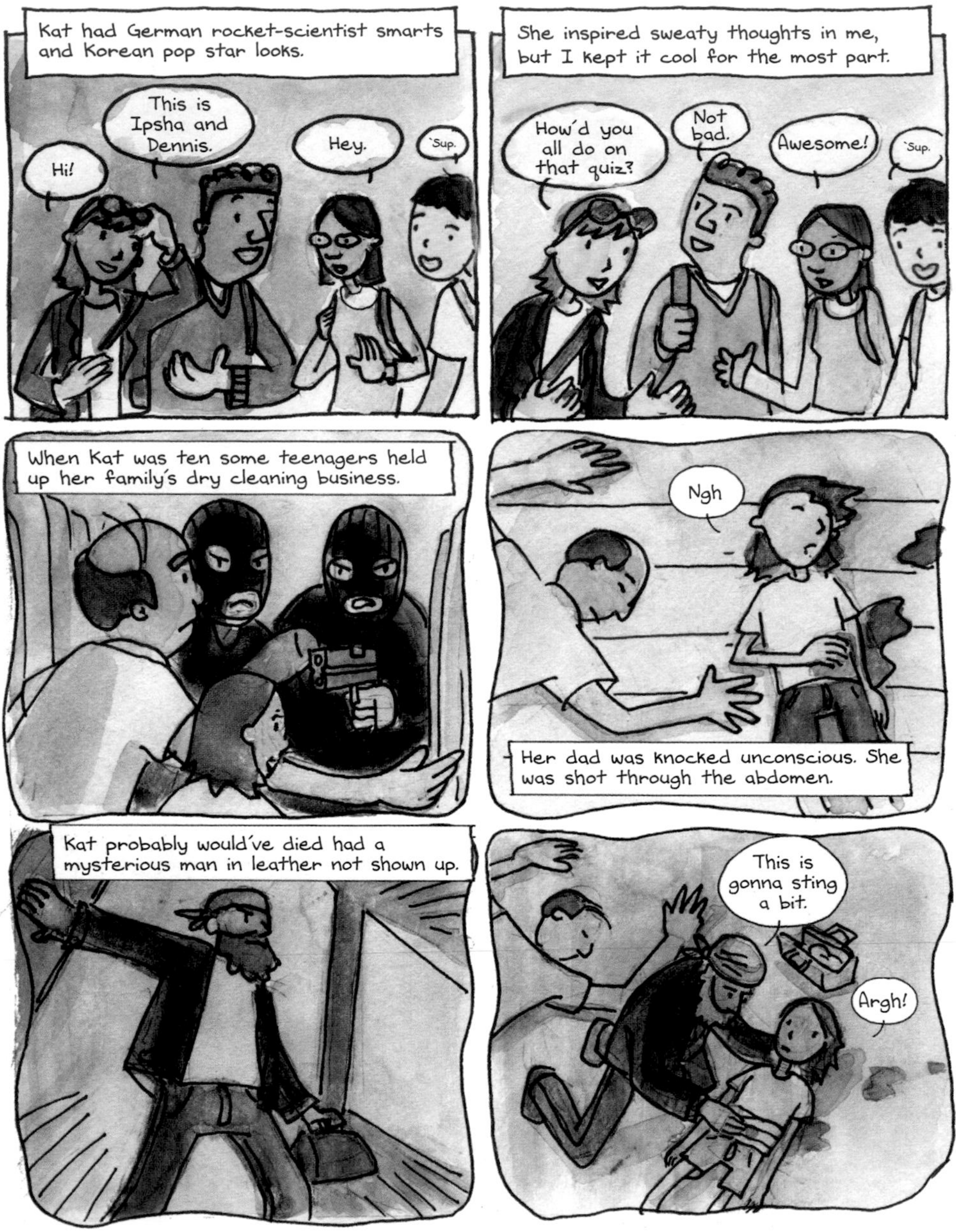
Kat had German rocket-scientist smarts and Korean pop star looks.
Hi!
This is Ipsha and Dennis.
Hey.
`Sup.
She inspired sweaty thoughts in me, but I kept it cool for the most part.
How'd you all do on that quiz?
Not bad.
Awesome!
`Sup.
When Kat was ten some teenagers held up her family's dry cleaning business.
Ngh
Her dad was knocked unconscious. She was shot through the abdomen.
Kat probably would've died had a mysterious man in leather not shown up.
This is gonna sting a bit.
Argh!

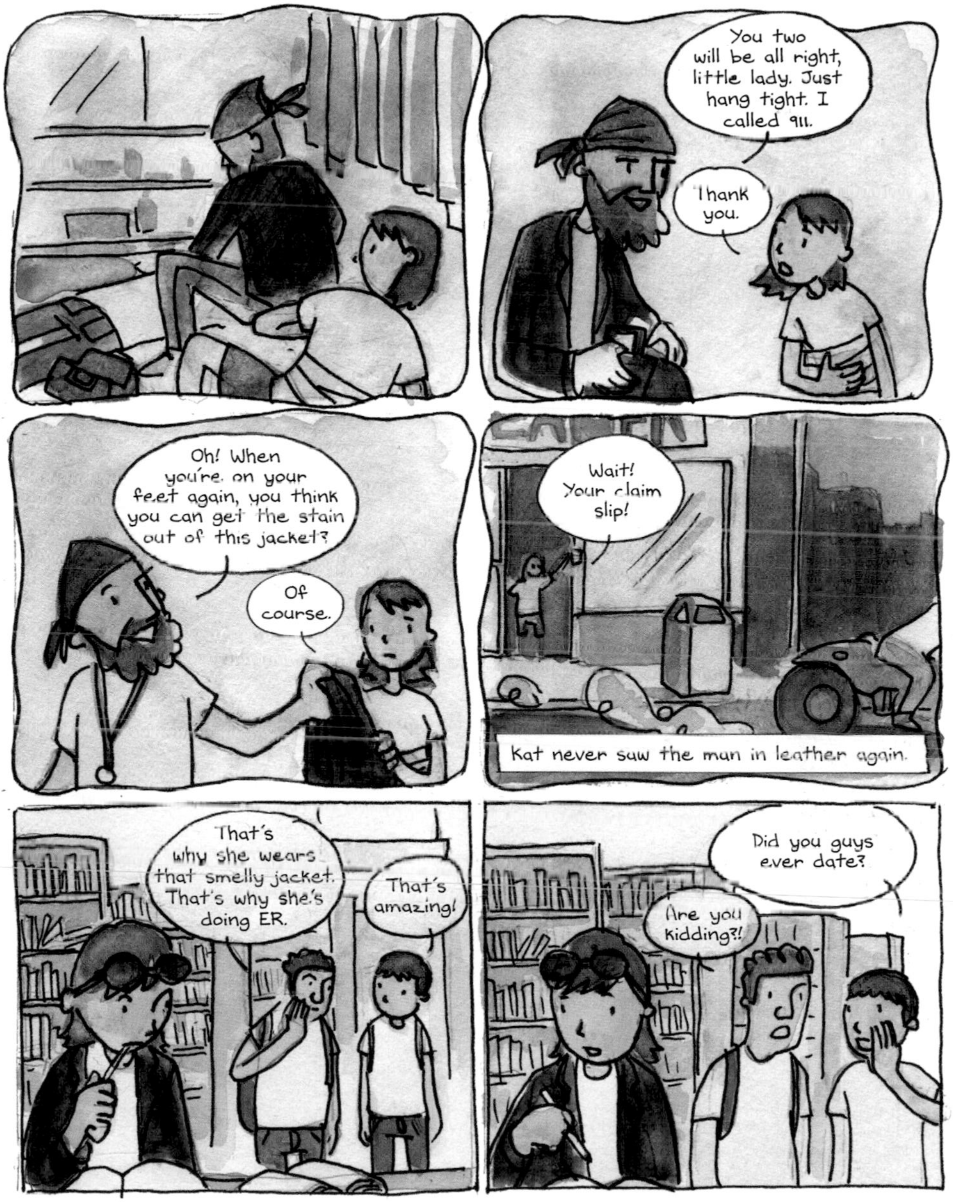
You two will be all right, little lady. Just hang tight. I called 911.
Thank you.
Oh! When you're on your feet again, you think you can get the stain out of this jacket?
Of course.
Wait! Your claim slip!
Kat never saw the man in leather again.
That's why she wears that smelly jacket. That's why she's doing ER.
That's amazing!
Did you guys ever date?
Are you kidding?!

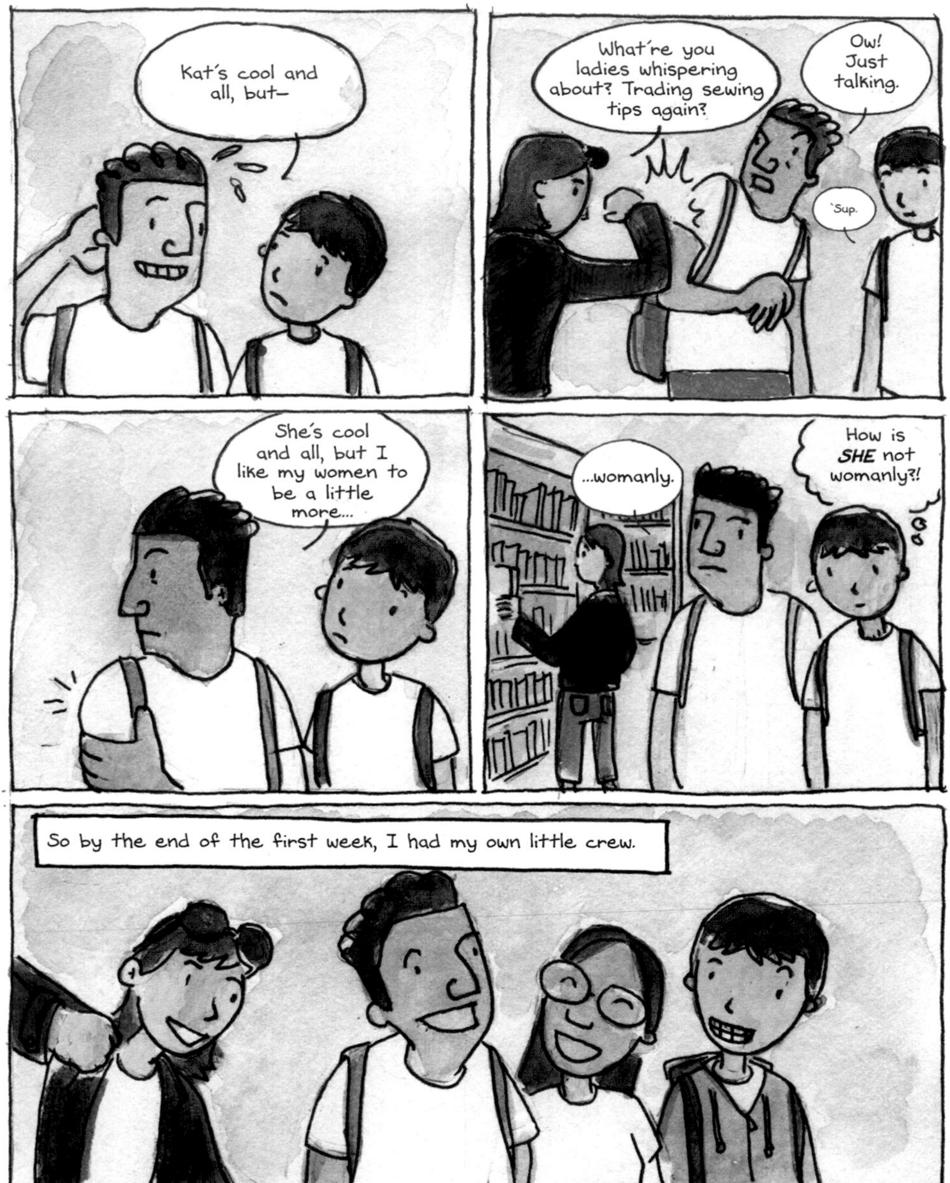
Kat's cool and all, but–
What're you ladies whispering about? Trading sewing tips again?
Ow! Just talking.
'Sup.
She's cool and all, but I like my women to be a little more...
...womanly.
How is SHE not womanly?!
So by the end of the first week, I had my own little crew.

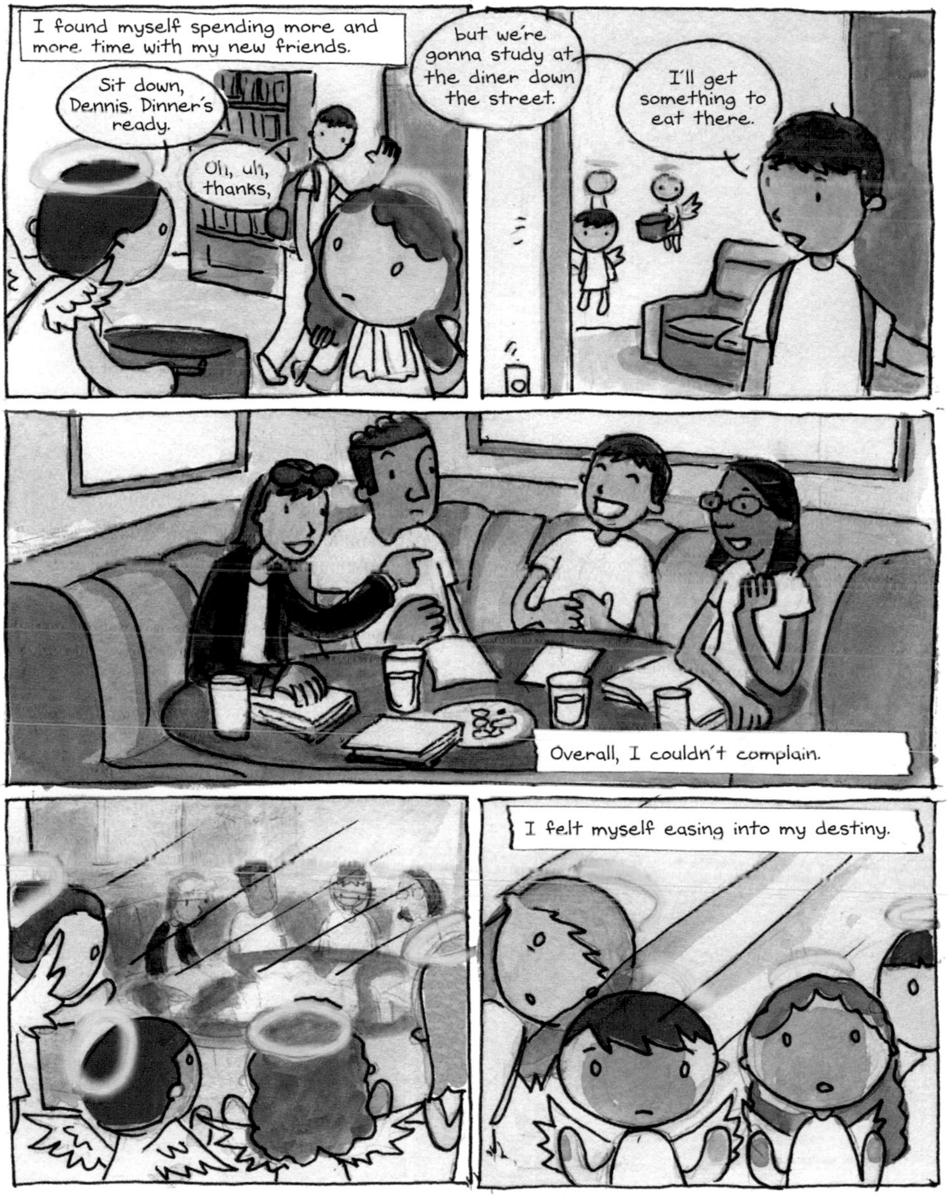
I found myself spending more and more time with my new friends.
Sit down, Dennis. Dinner's ready.
Oh, uh, thanks,
but we're gonna study at the diner down the street.
I'll get something to eat there.
Overall, I couldn't complain.
I felt myself easing into my destiny.

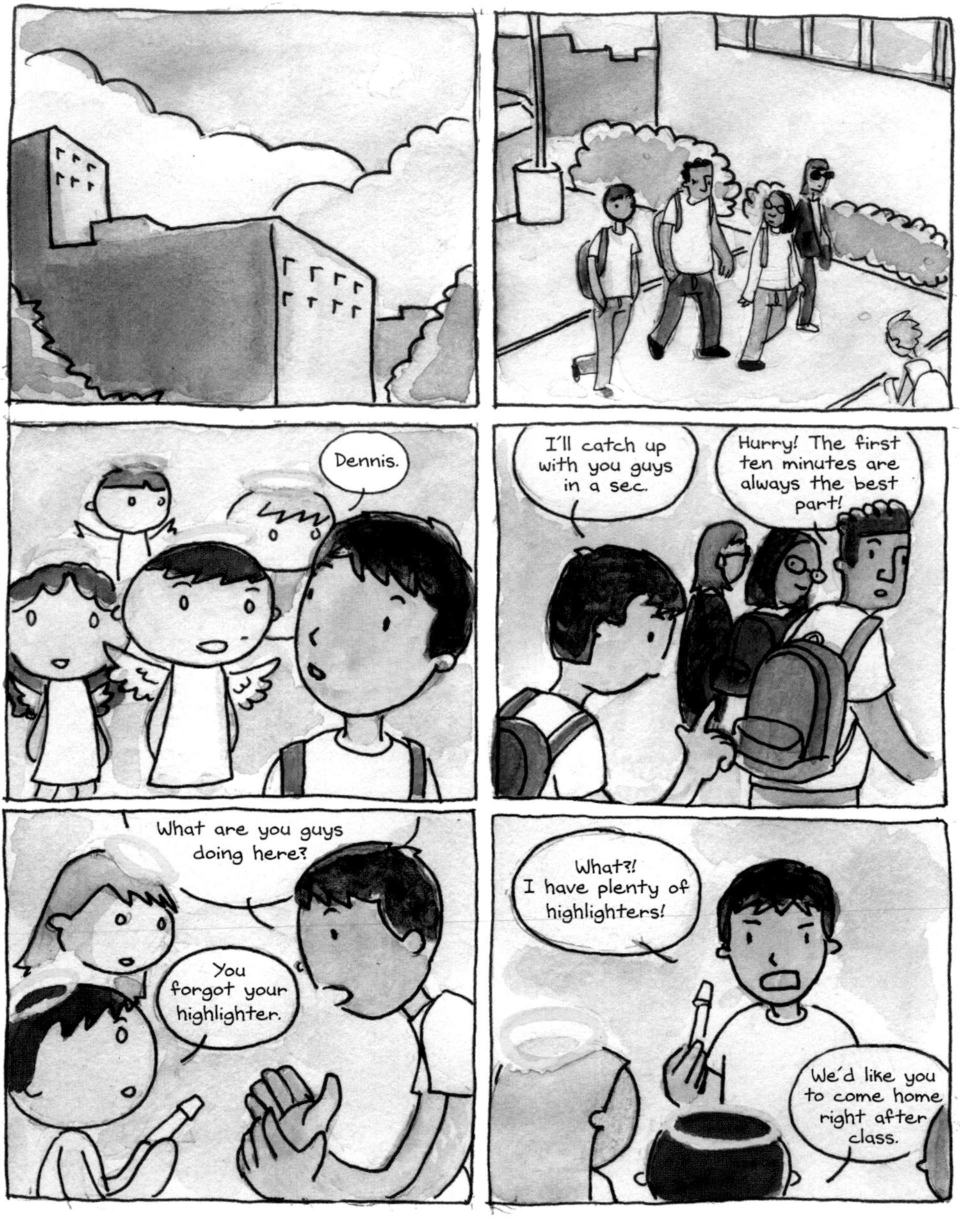
Dennis.
I'll catch up with you guys in a sec.
Hurry! The first ten minutes are always the best part!
What are you guys doing here?
You forgot your highlighter.
What?! I have plenty of highlighters!
We'd like you to come home right after class.

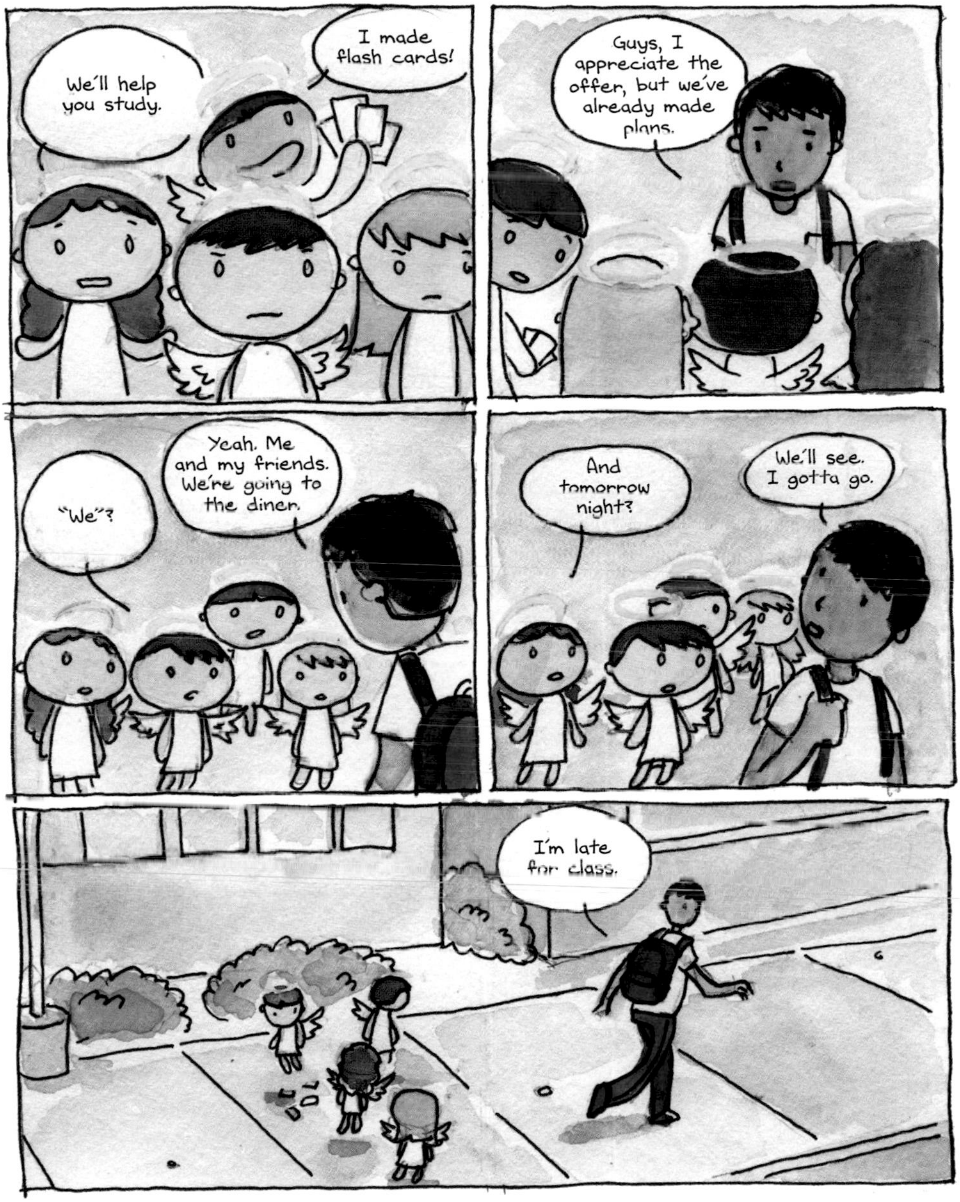
We'll help you study.
I made flash cards!
Guys, I appreciate the offer, but we've already made plans.
"We"?
Yeah. Me and my friends. We're going to the diner.
And tomorrow night?
We'll see. I gotta go.
I'm late for class.

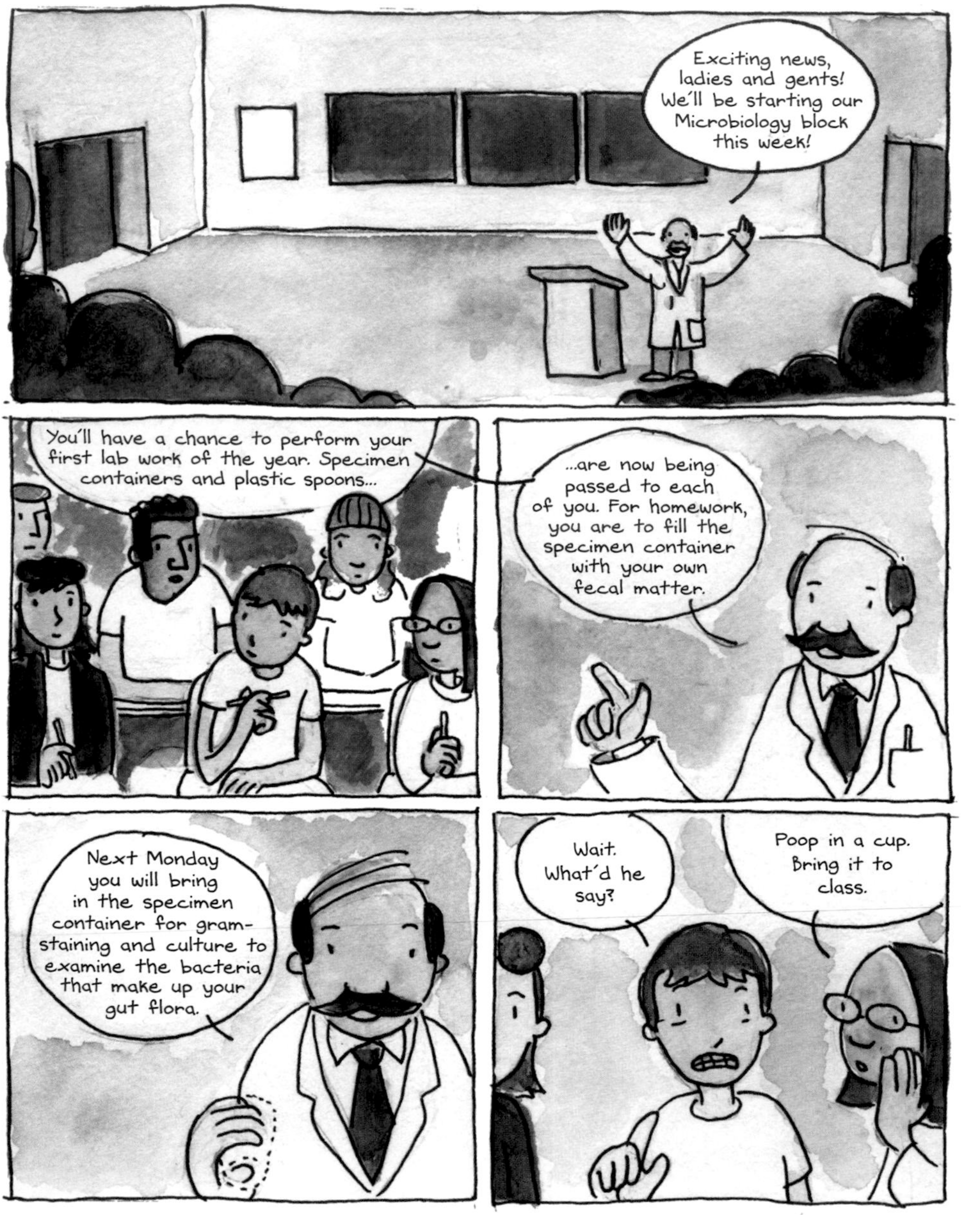
Exciting news, ladies and gents! We'll be starting our Microbiology block this week!
You'll have a chance to perform your first lab work of the year. Specimen containers and plastic spoons...
...are now being passed to each of you. For homework, you are to fill the specimen container with your own fecal matter.
Next Monday you will bring in the specimen container for gram-staining and culture to examine the bacteria that make up your gut flora.
Wait. What'd he say?
Poop in a cup. Bring it to class.

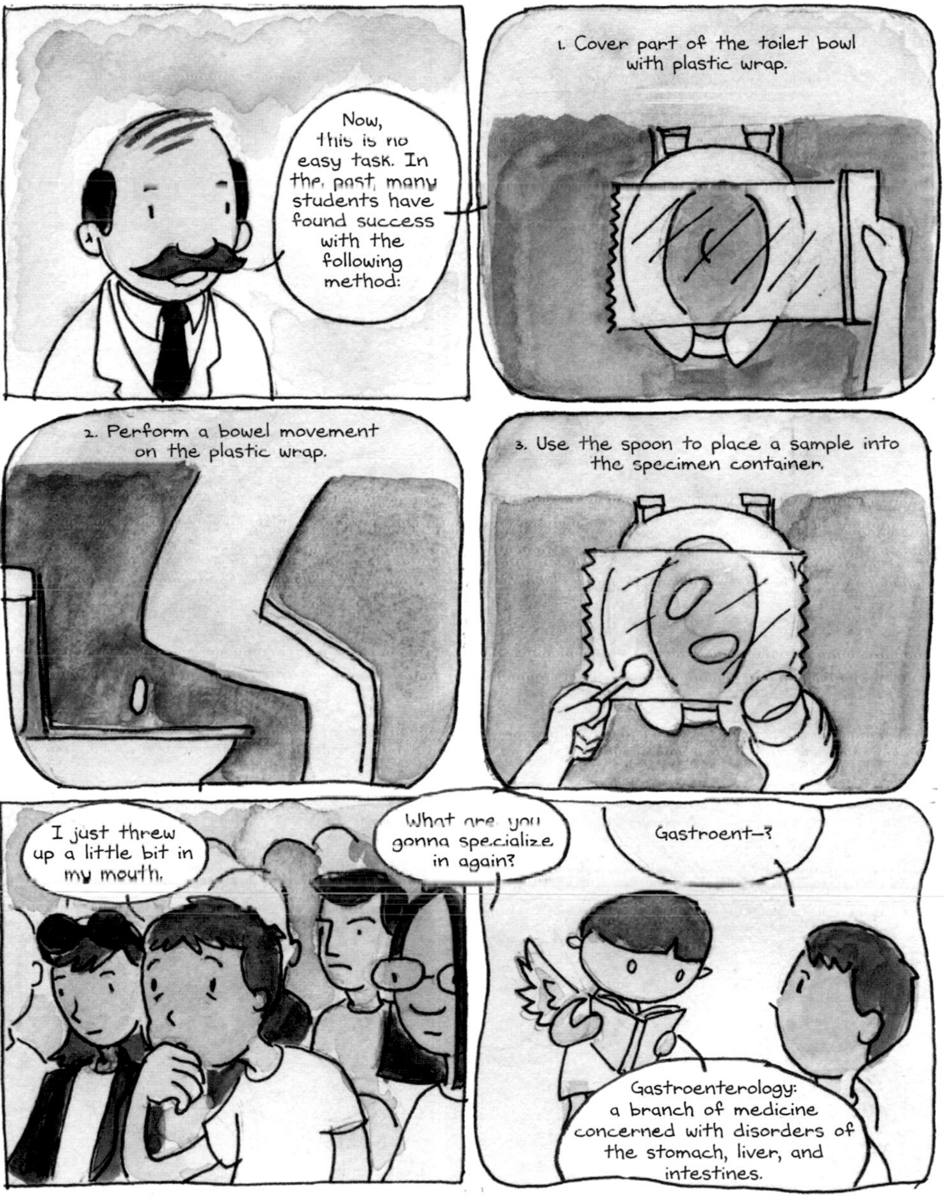
Now, this is no easy task. In the past, many students have found success with the following method:
1. Cover part of the toilet bowl with plastic wrap.
2. Perform a bowel movement on the plastic wrap.
3. Use the spoon to place a sample into the specimen container.
I just threw up a little bit in my mouth.
What are you gonna specialize in again?
Gastroent–?
Gastroenterology: a branch of medicine concerned with disorders of the stomach, liver, and intestines.

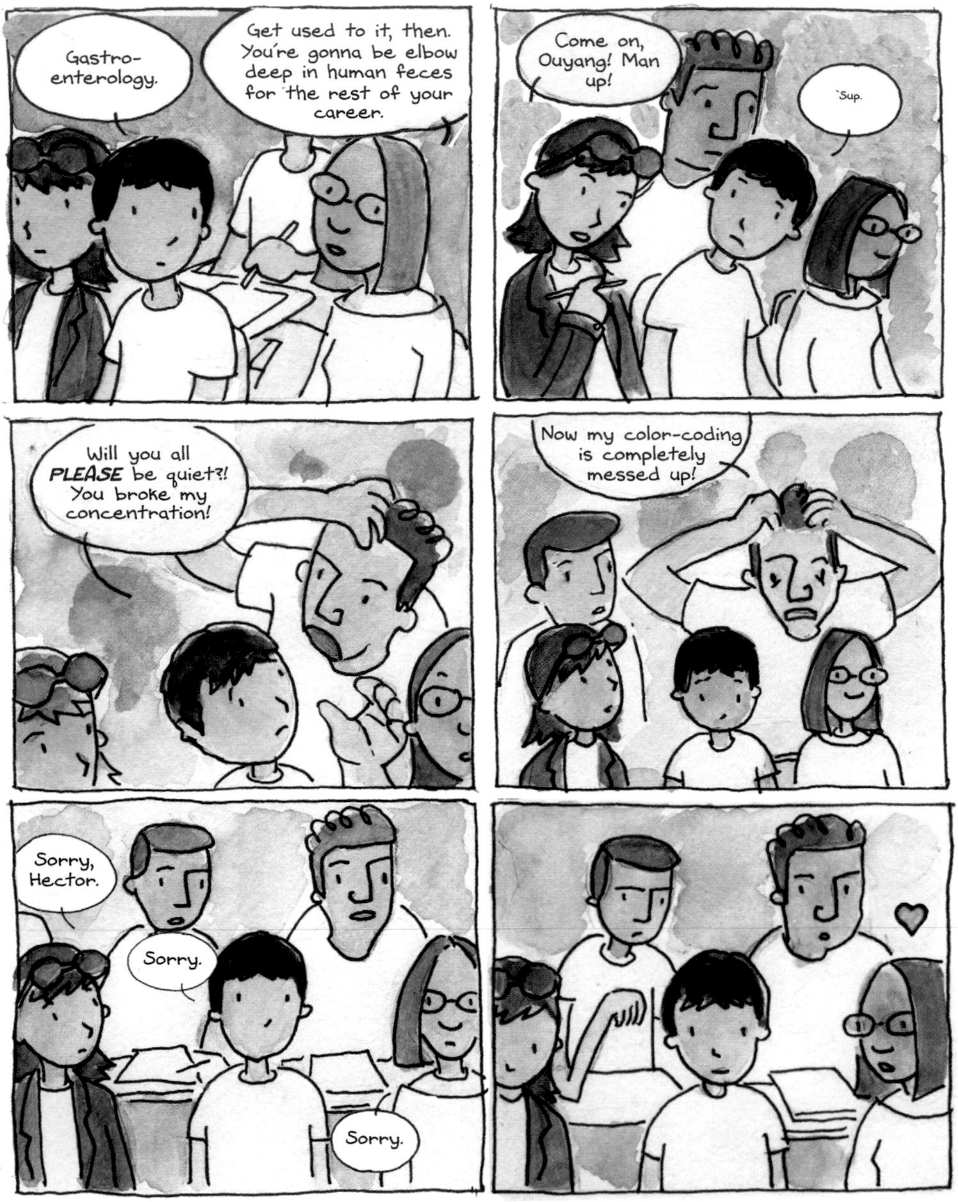
Gastro-enterology.
Get used to it, then. You're gonna be elbow deep in human feces for the rest of your career.
Come on, Ouyang! Man up!
'Sup.
Will you all PLEASE be quiet?! You broke my concentration!
Now my color-coding is completely messed up!
Sorry, Hector.
Sorry.
Sorry.

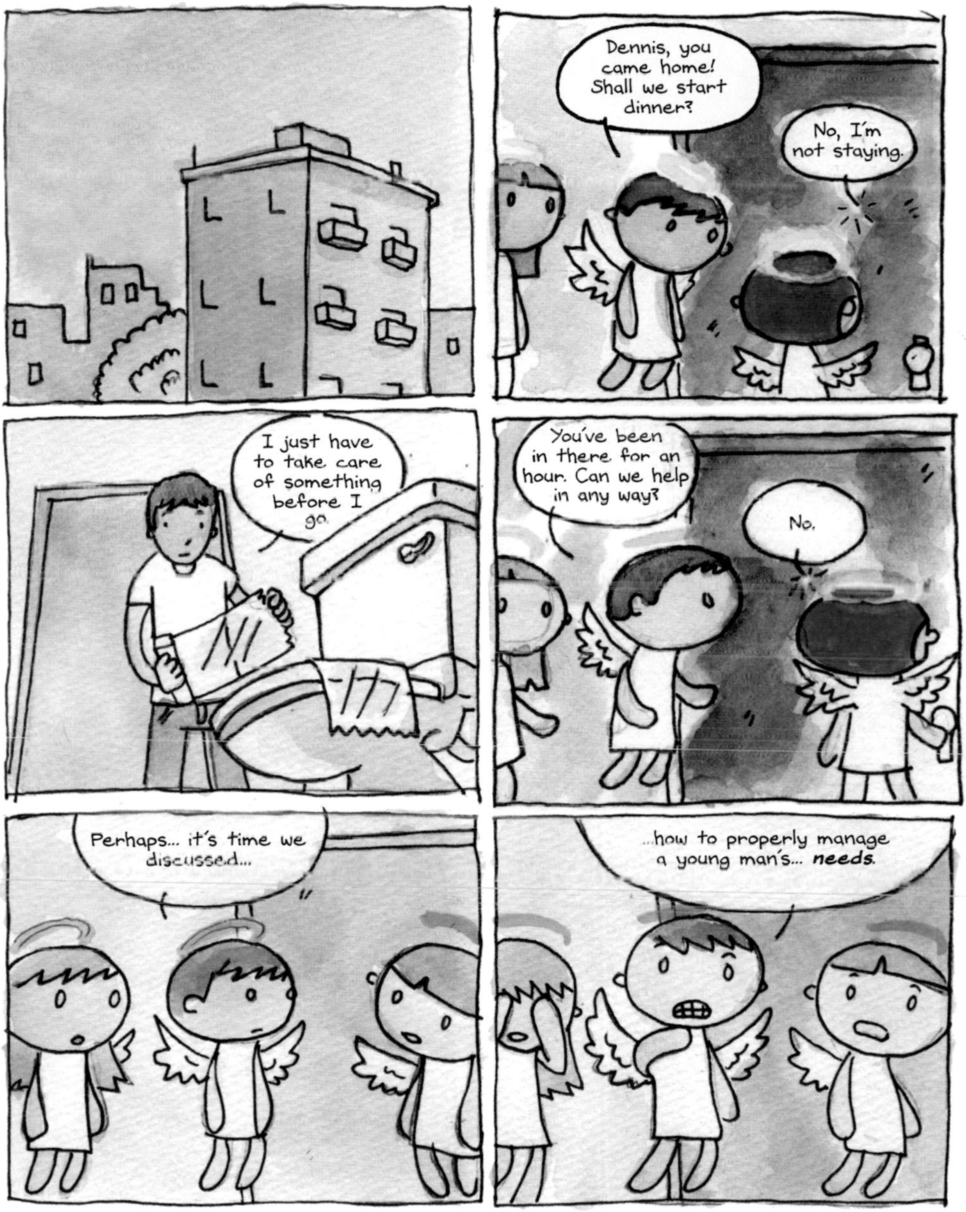
Dennis, you came home! Shall we start dinner?
No, I'm not staying.
I just have to take care of something before I go.
You've been in there for an hour. Can we help in any way?
No.
Perhaps... it's time we discussed...
...how to properly manage a young man's... **needs**.

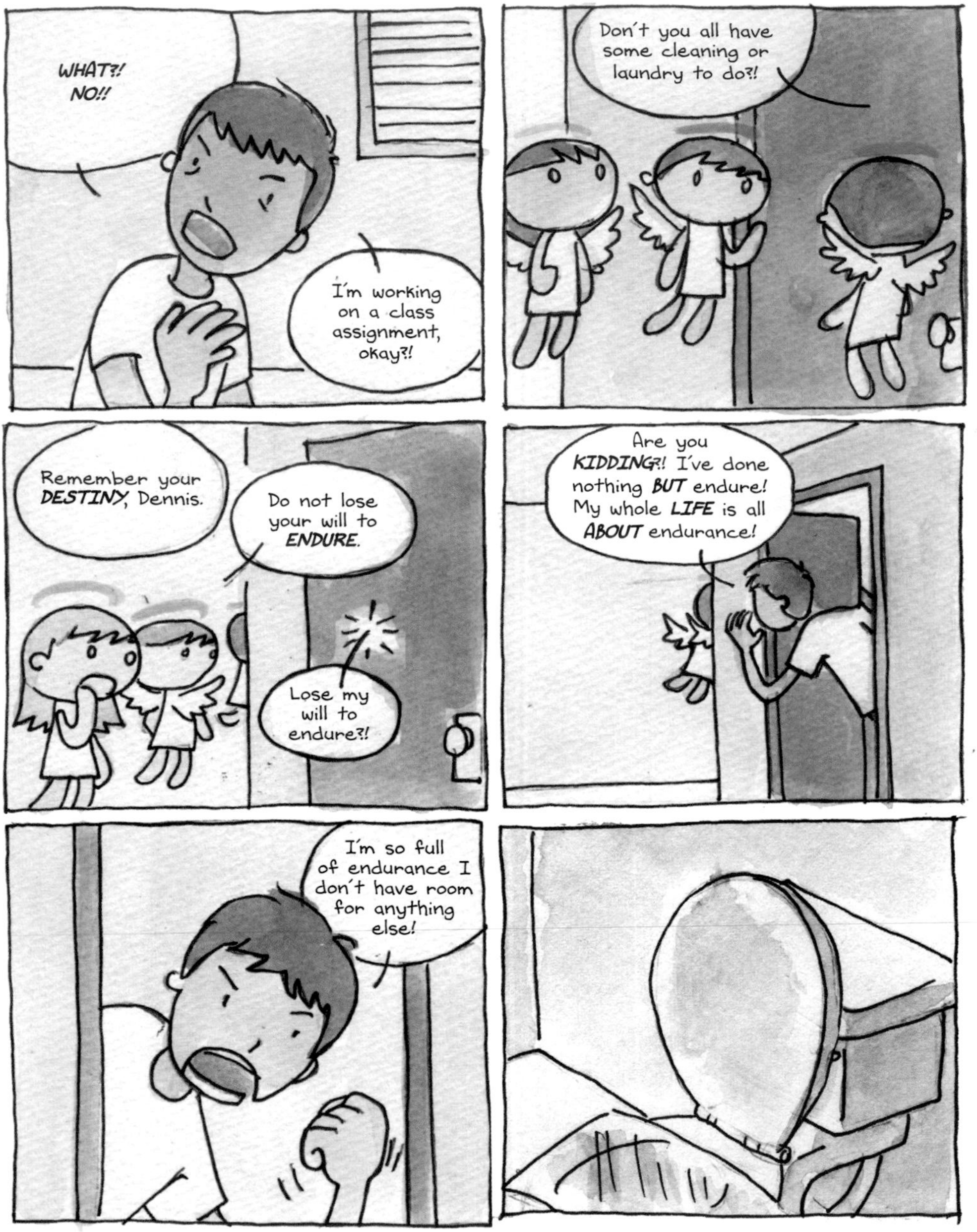
WHAT?! NO!!
I'm working on a class assignment, okay?!
Don't you all have some cleaning or laundry to do?!
Remember your DESTINY, Dennis.
Do not lose your will to ENDURE.
Lose my will to endure?!
Are you KIDDING?! I've done nothing BUT endure! My whole LIFE is all ABOUT endurance!
I'm so full of endurance I don't have room for anything else!

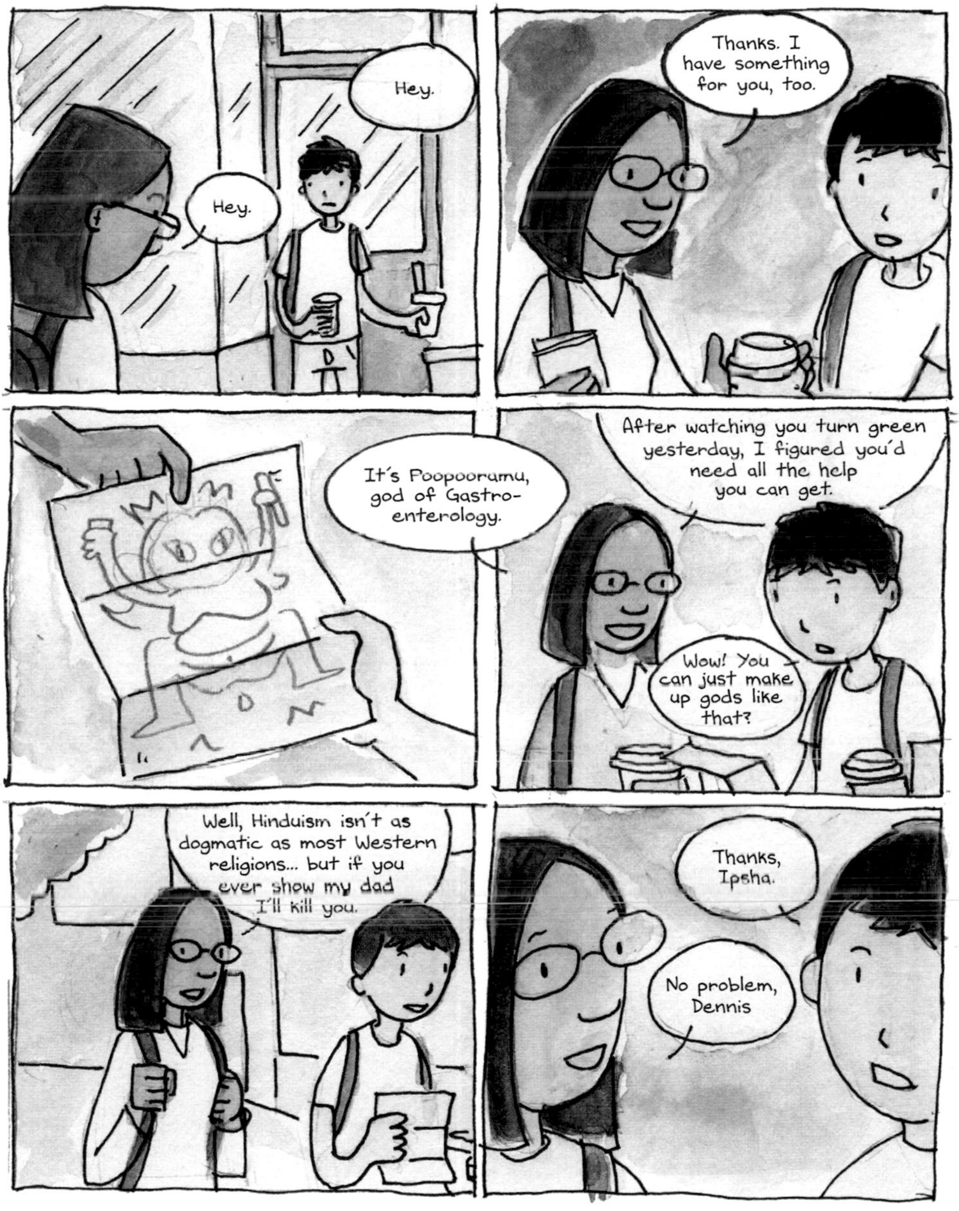
Hey.
Hey.
Thanks. I have something for you, too.
It's Poopooramu, god of Gastro-enterology.
After watching you turn green yesterday, I figured you'd need all the help you can get.
Wow! You can just make up gods like that?
Well, Hinduism isn't as dogmatic as most Western religions... but if you ever show my dad I'll kill you.
Thanks, Ipsha.
No problem, Dennis

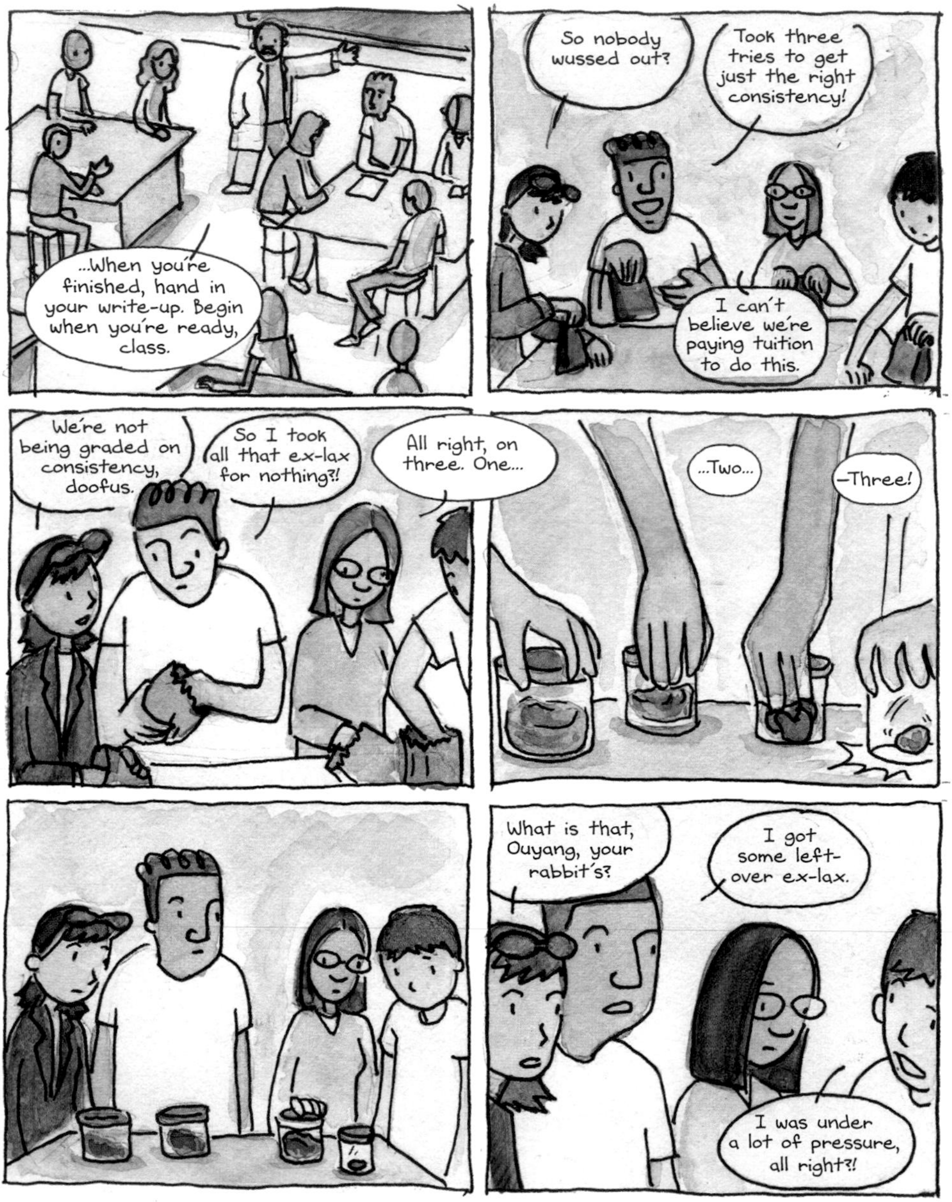
...When you're finished, hand in your write-up. Begin when you're ready, class.
So nobody wussed out?
Took three tries to get just the right consistency!
I can't believe we're paying tuition to do this.
We're not being graded on consistency, doofus.
So I took all that ex-lax for nothing?!
All right, on three. One...
...Two...
–Three!
What is that, Ouyang, your rabbit's?
I got some left-over ex-lax.
I was under a lot of pressure, all right?!

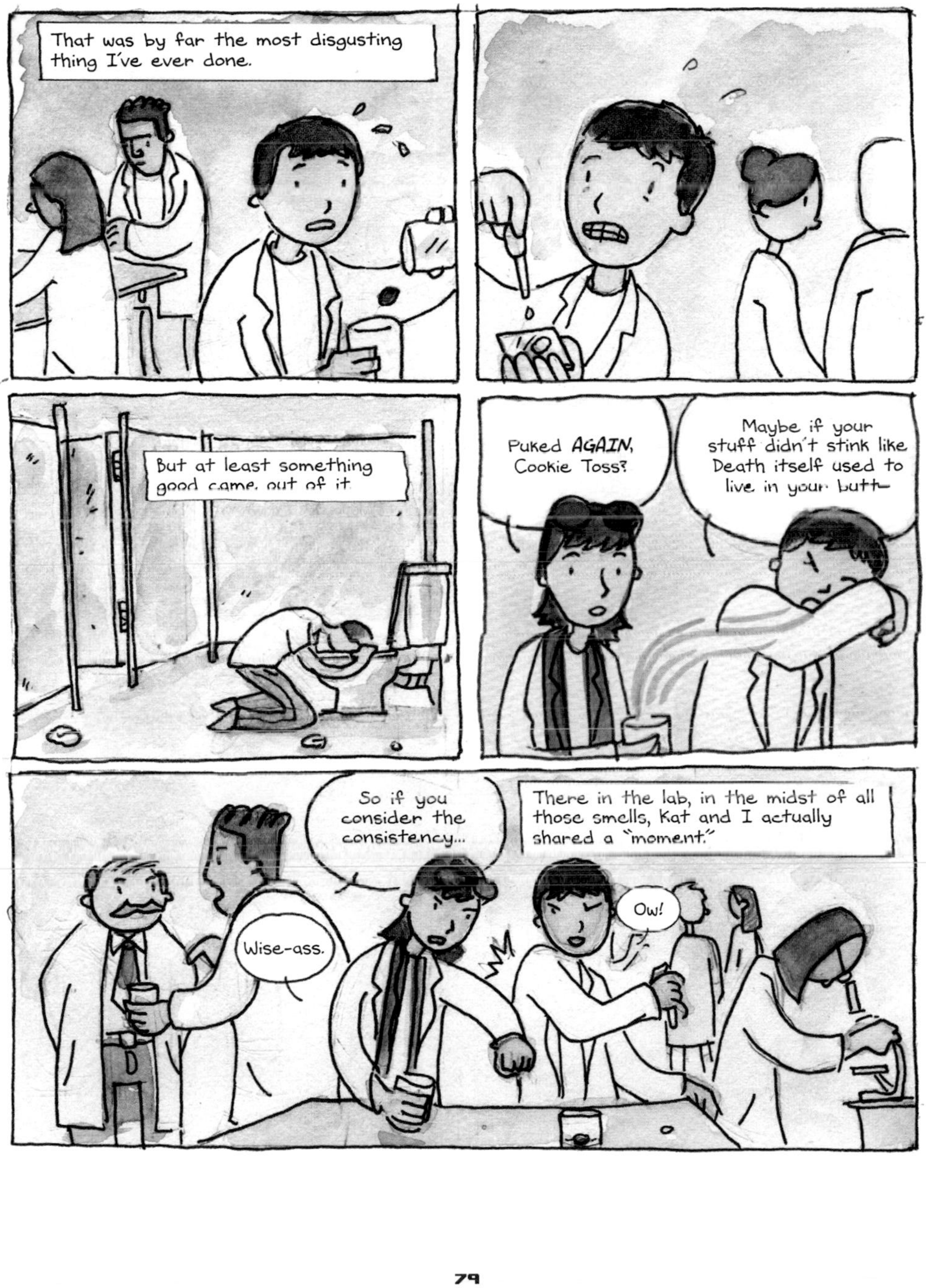
That was by far the most disgusting thing I've ever done.
But at least something good came out of it.
Puked AGAIN, Cookie Toss?
Maybe if your stuff didn't stink like Death itself used to live in your butt—
So if you consider the consistency...
There in the lab, in the midst of all those smells, Kat and I actually shared a "moment."
Wise-ass.
Ow!

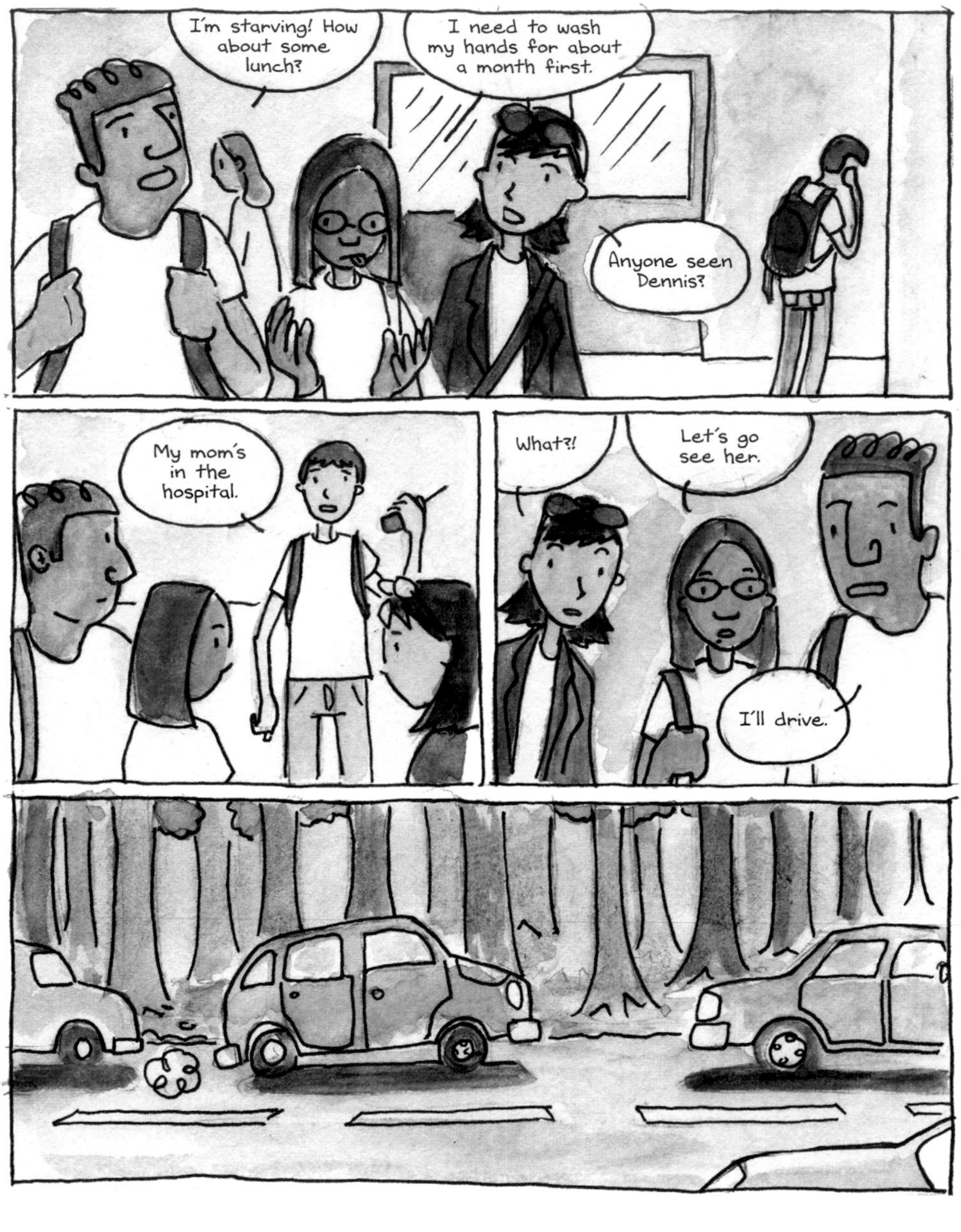
I'm starving! How about some lunch?
I need to wash my hands for about a month first.
Anyone seen Dennis?
My mom's in the hospital.
What?!
Let's go see her.
I'll drive.

85

We've been at it for five hours straight! Time to loosen up a little with some music.
Wait—Hector wants to "loosen up"?
The night before a big test?
Shh. If you listen carefully, you can hear the monkeys flying out of my butt.
I read this study linking music to increased brain activity.

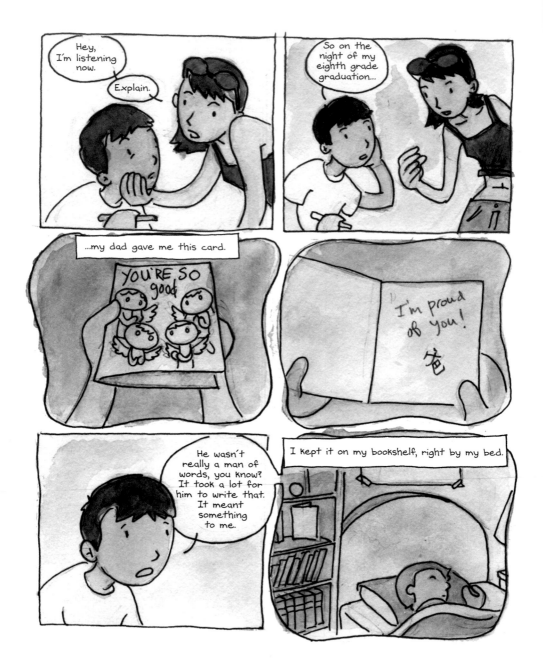

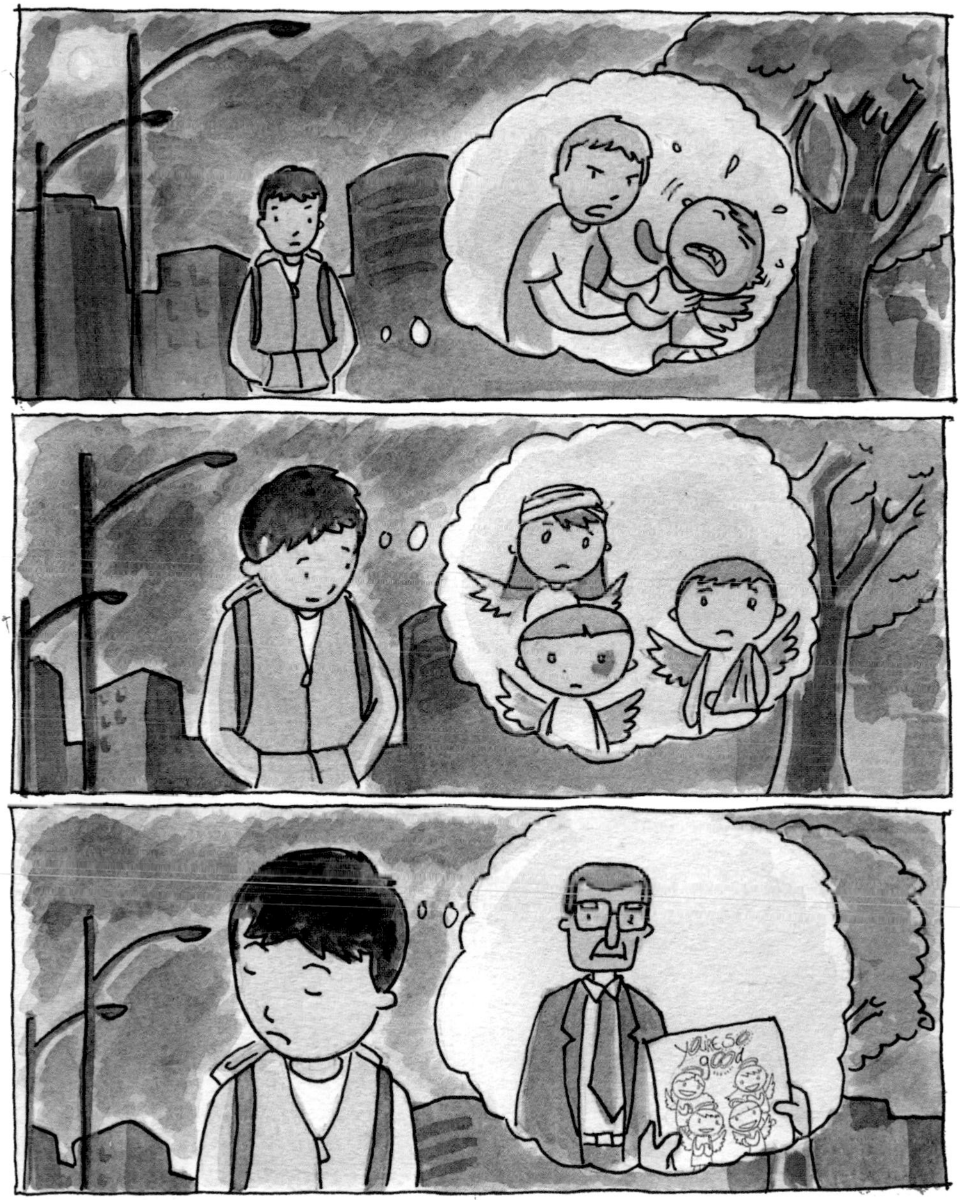
YOURE SO good

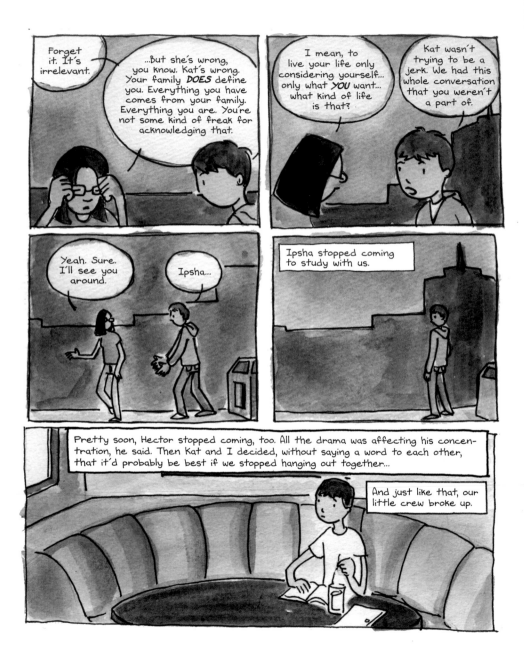

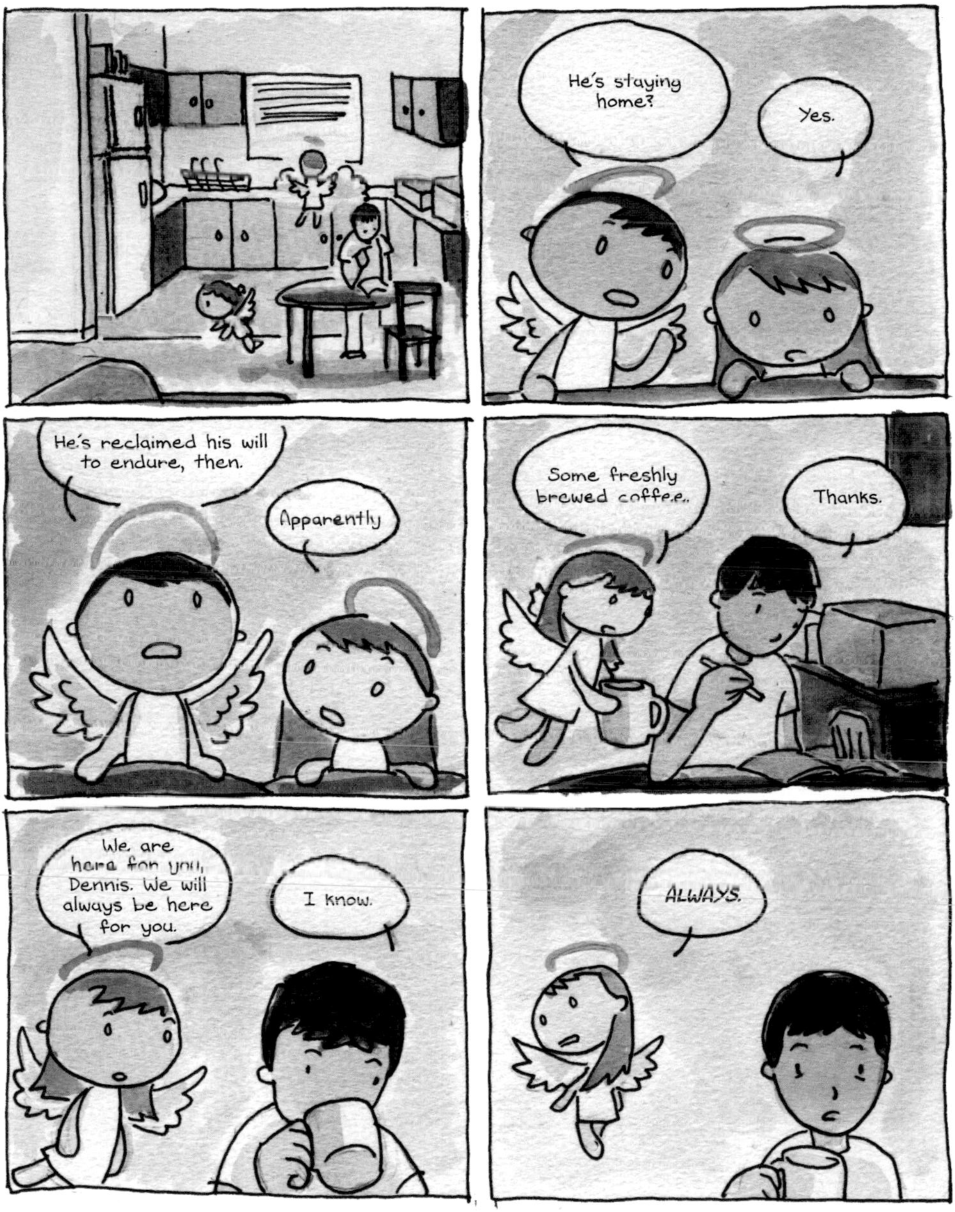
He's staying home?
Yes.
He's reclaimed his will to endure, then.
Apparently
Some freshly brewed coffee..
Thanks.
We are here for you, Dennis. We will always be here for you.
I know.
ALWAYS.

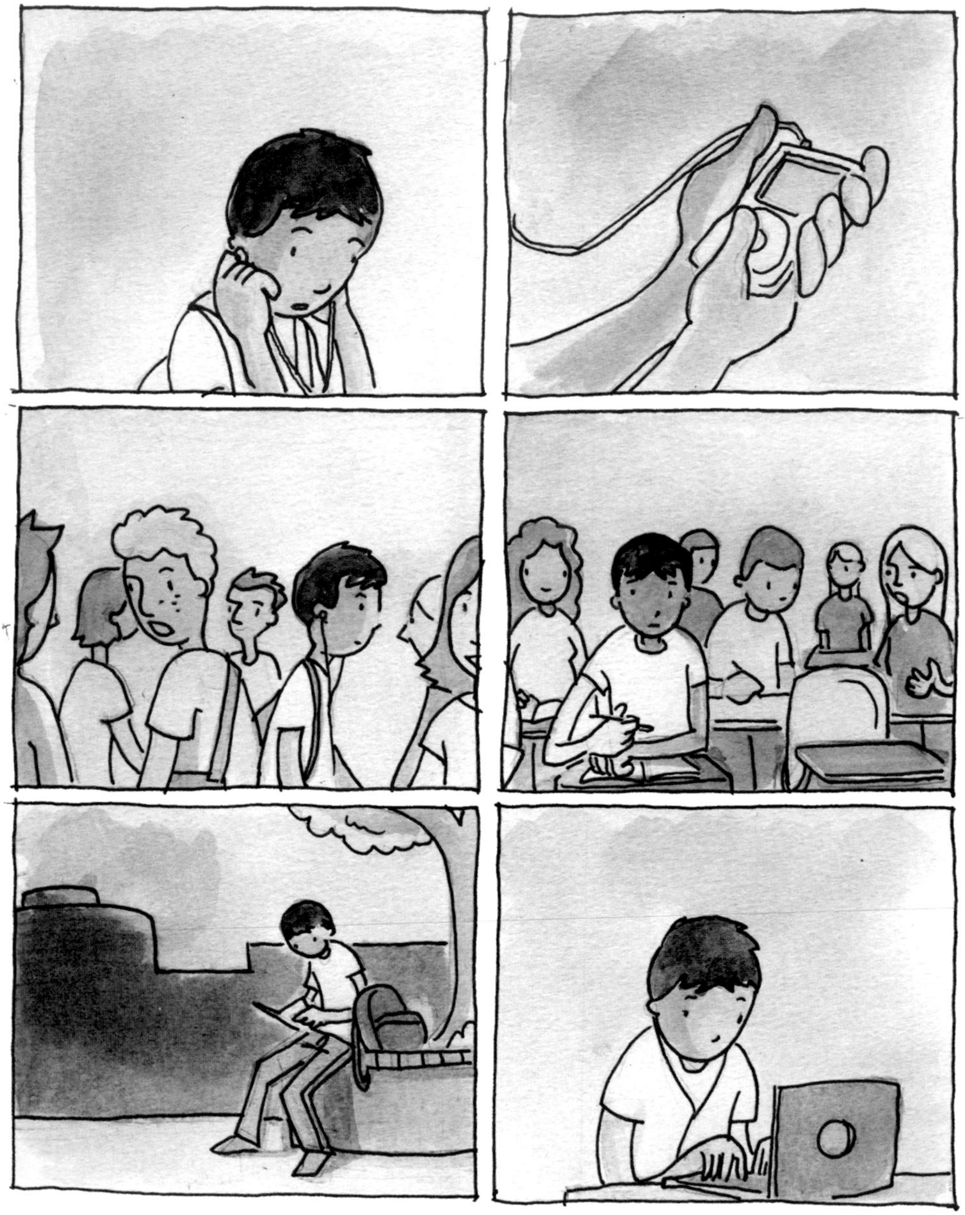

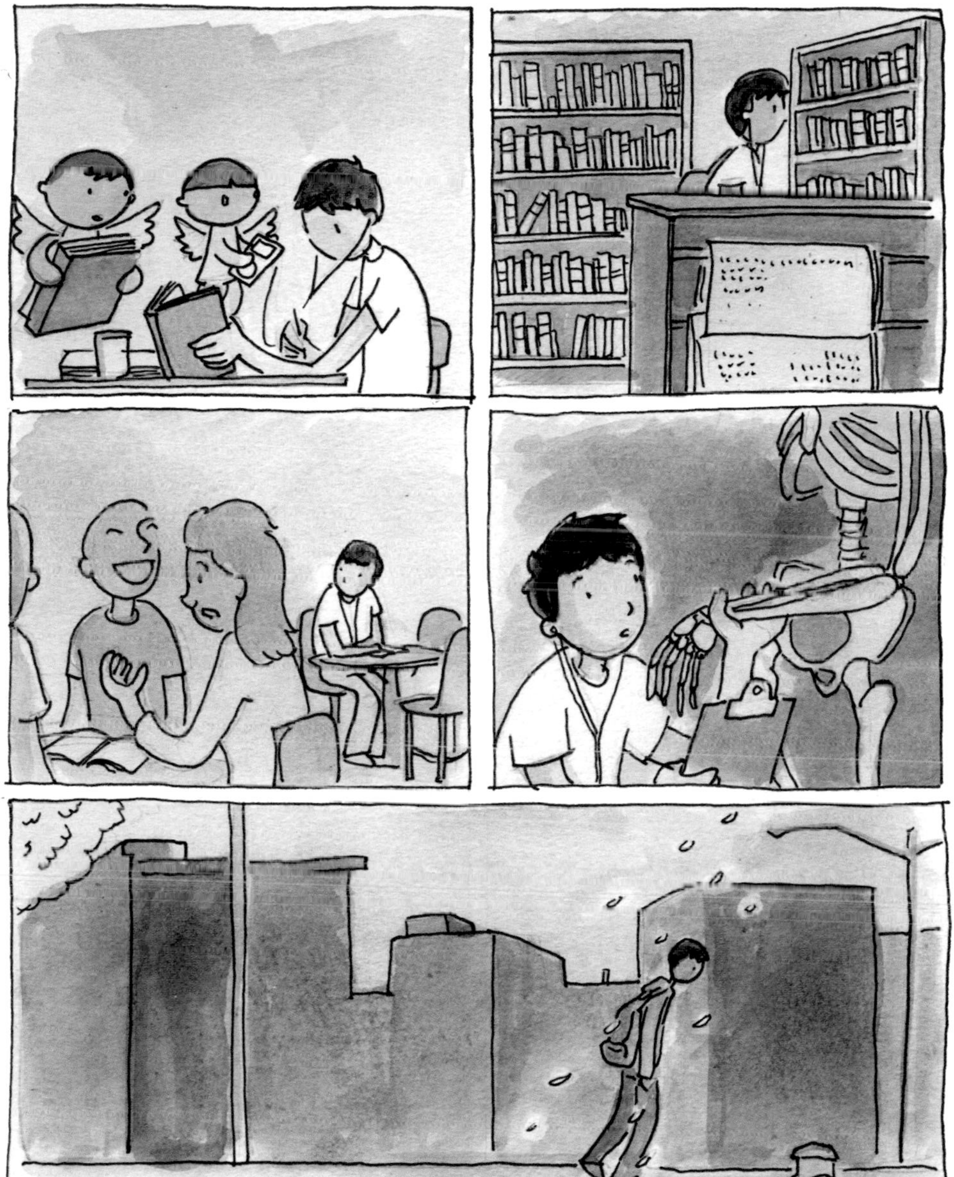

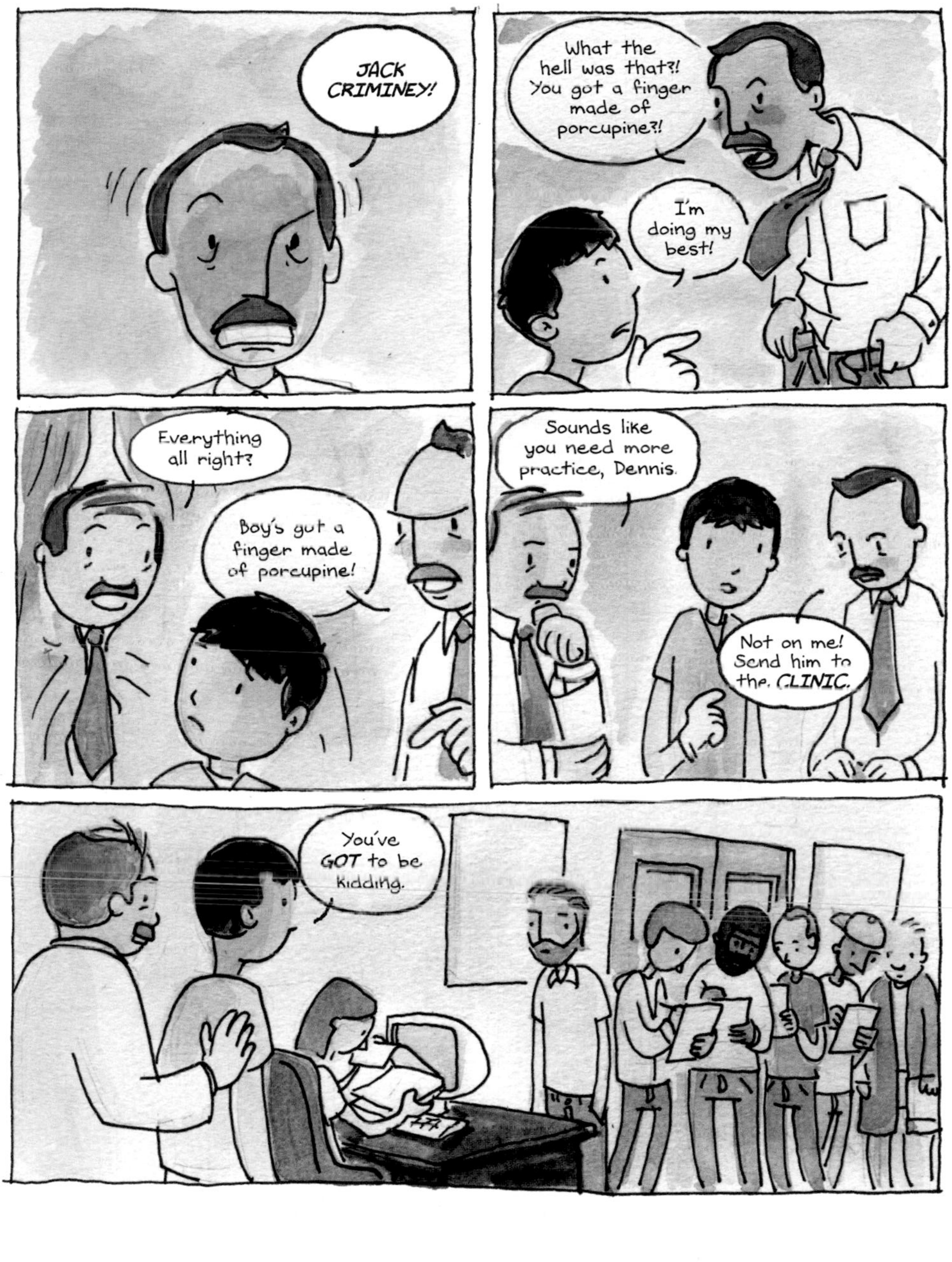
JACK CRIMINEY!
What the hell was that?! You got a finger made of porcupine?!
I'm doing my best!
Everything all right?
Boy's got a finger made of porcupine!
Sounds like you need more practice, Dennis.
Not on me! Send him to the CLINIC.
You've GOT to be kidding.

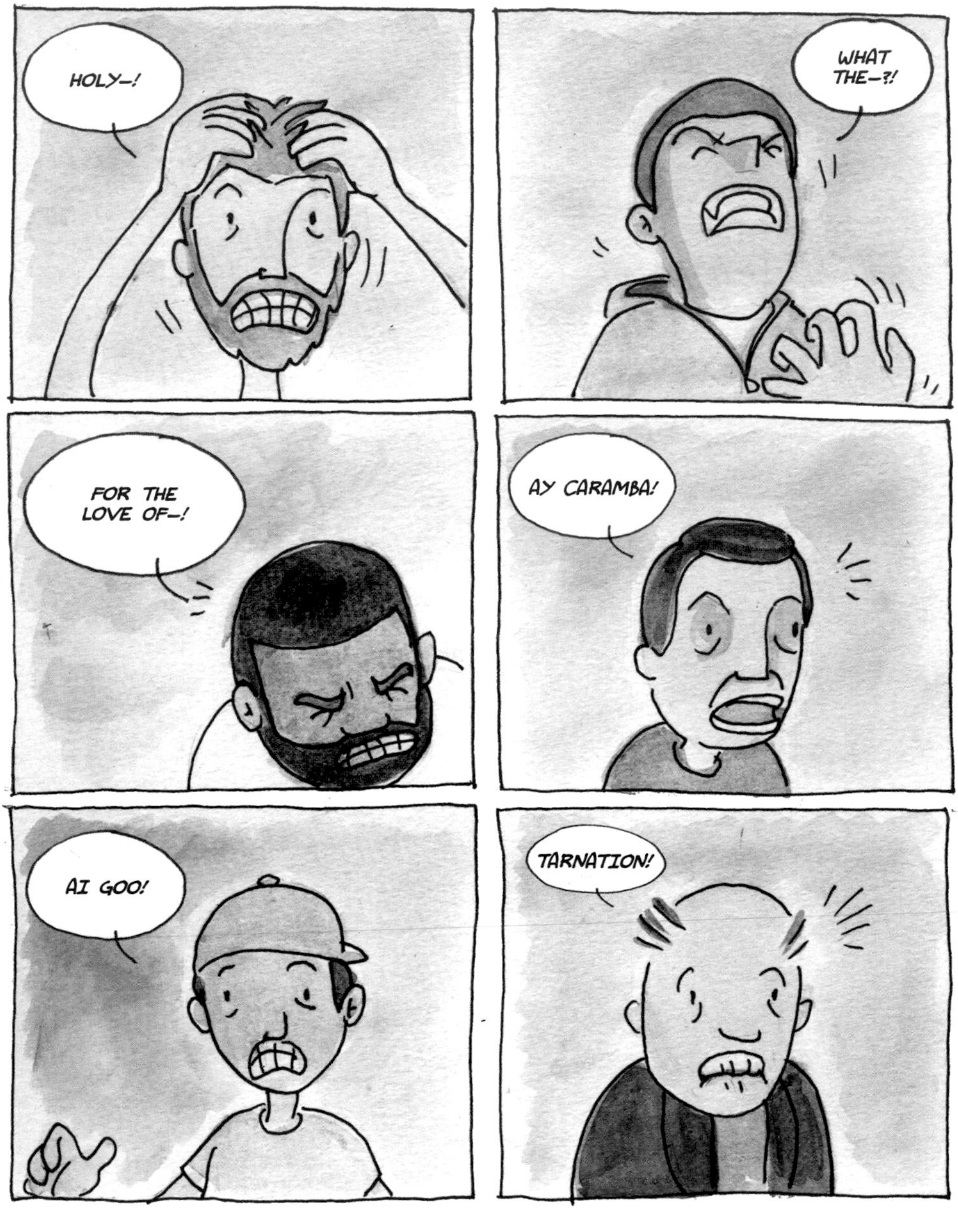
HOLY–!
WHAT THE–?!
FOR THE LOVE OF–!
AY CARAMBA!
AI GOO!
TARNATION!

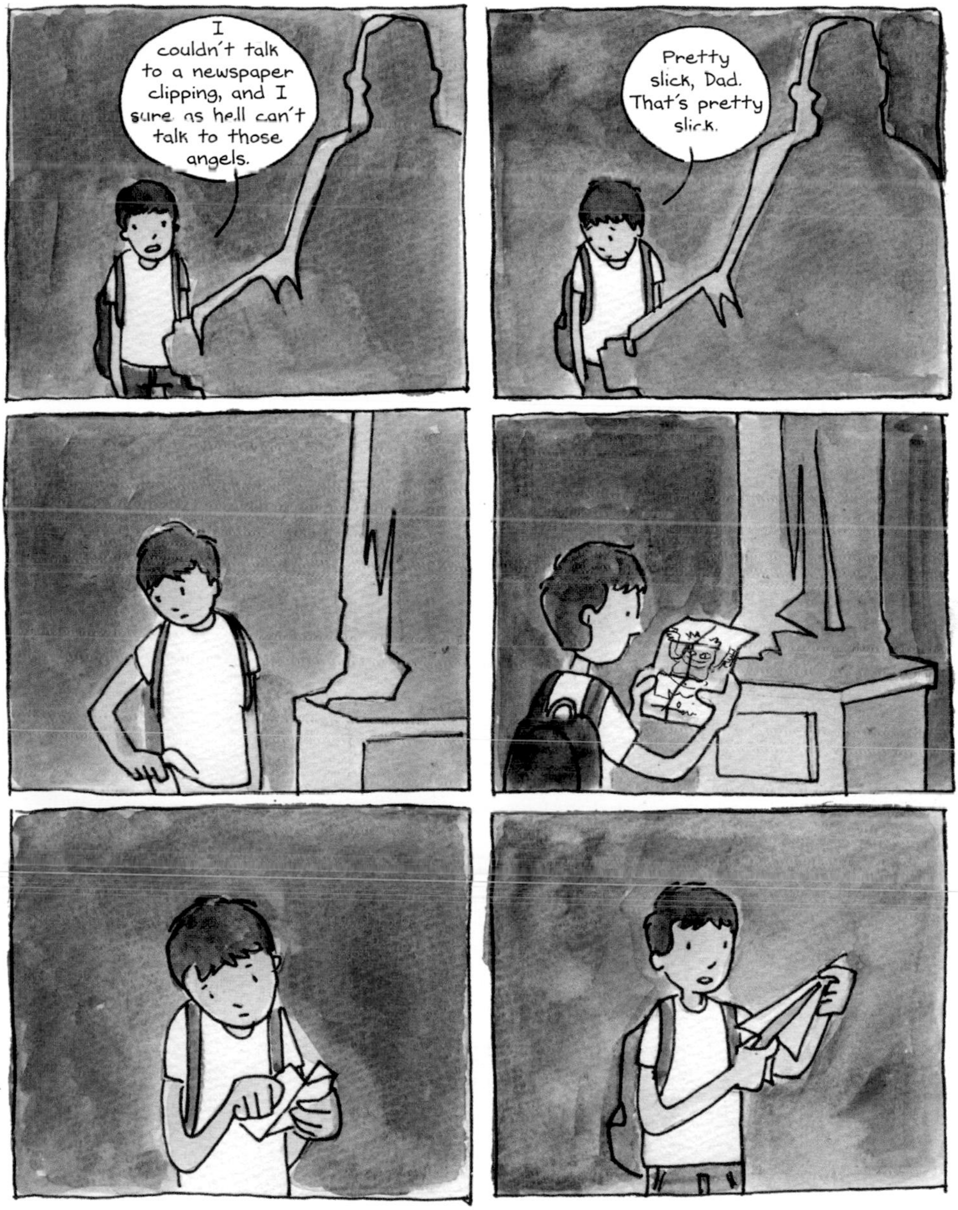
I couldn't talk to a newspaper clipping, and I sure as hell can't talk to those angels.
Pretty slick, Dad. That's pretty slick.

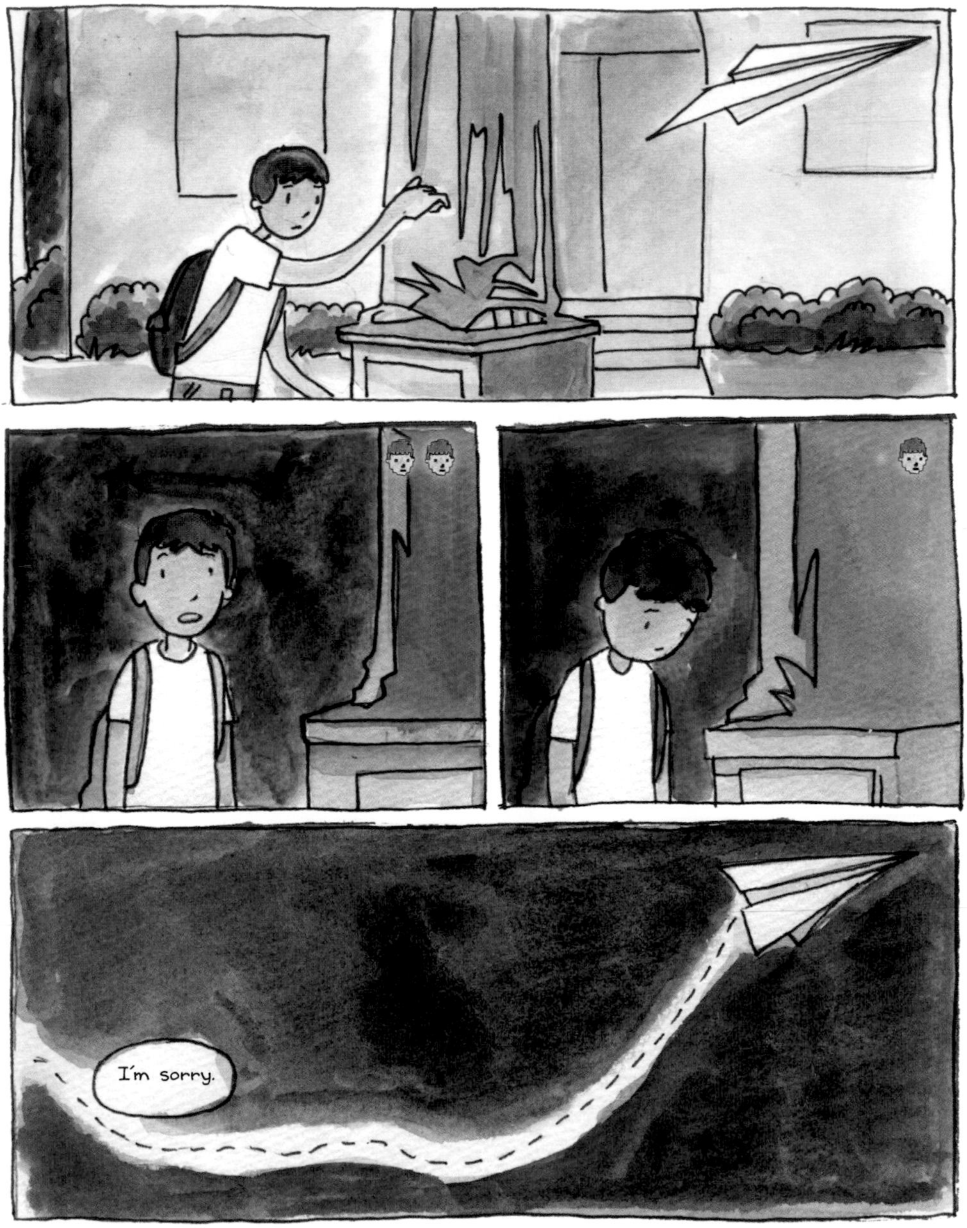
I'm sorry.

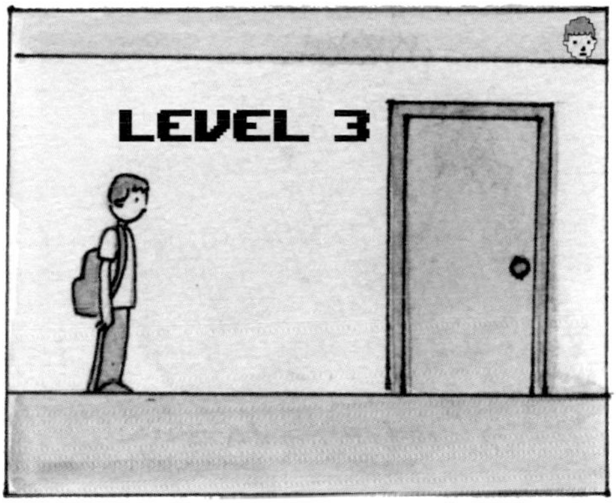
LEVEL 3

I knew exactly what I was going to say and
how I was going to say it. It was my life.
I wanted it back.

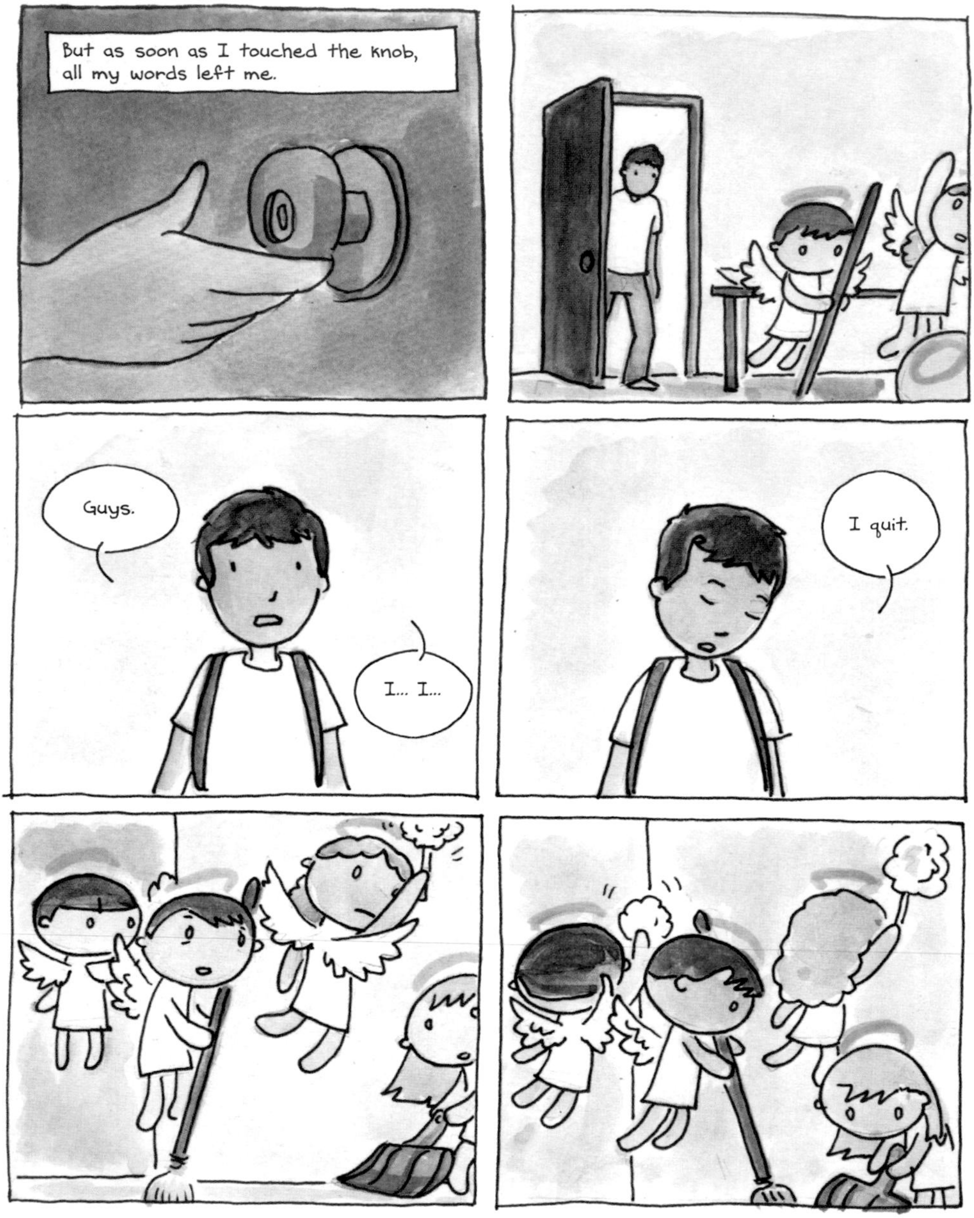
But as soon as I touched the knob, all my words left me.
Guys.
I... I...
I quit.

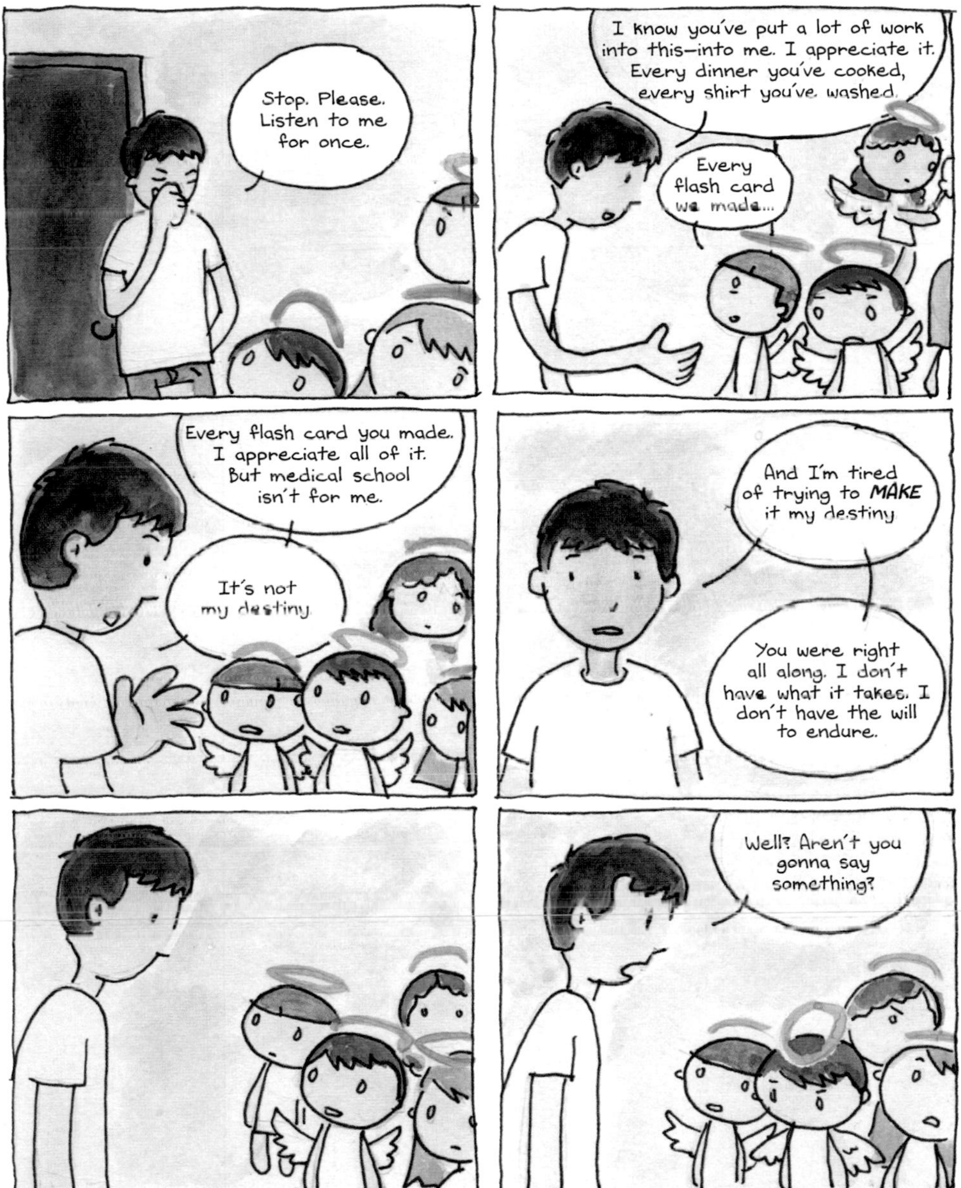

Stop. Please. Listen to me for once.
I know you've put a lot of work into this—into me. I appreciate it. Every dinner you've cooked, every shirt you've washed.
Every flash card we made...
Every flash card you made. I appreciate all of it. But medical school isn't for me.
It's not my destiny.
And I'm tired of trying to *MAKE* it my destiny.
You were right all along. I don't have what it takes. I don't have the will to endure.
Well? Aren't you gonna say something?

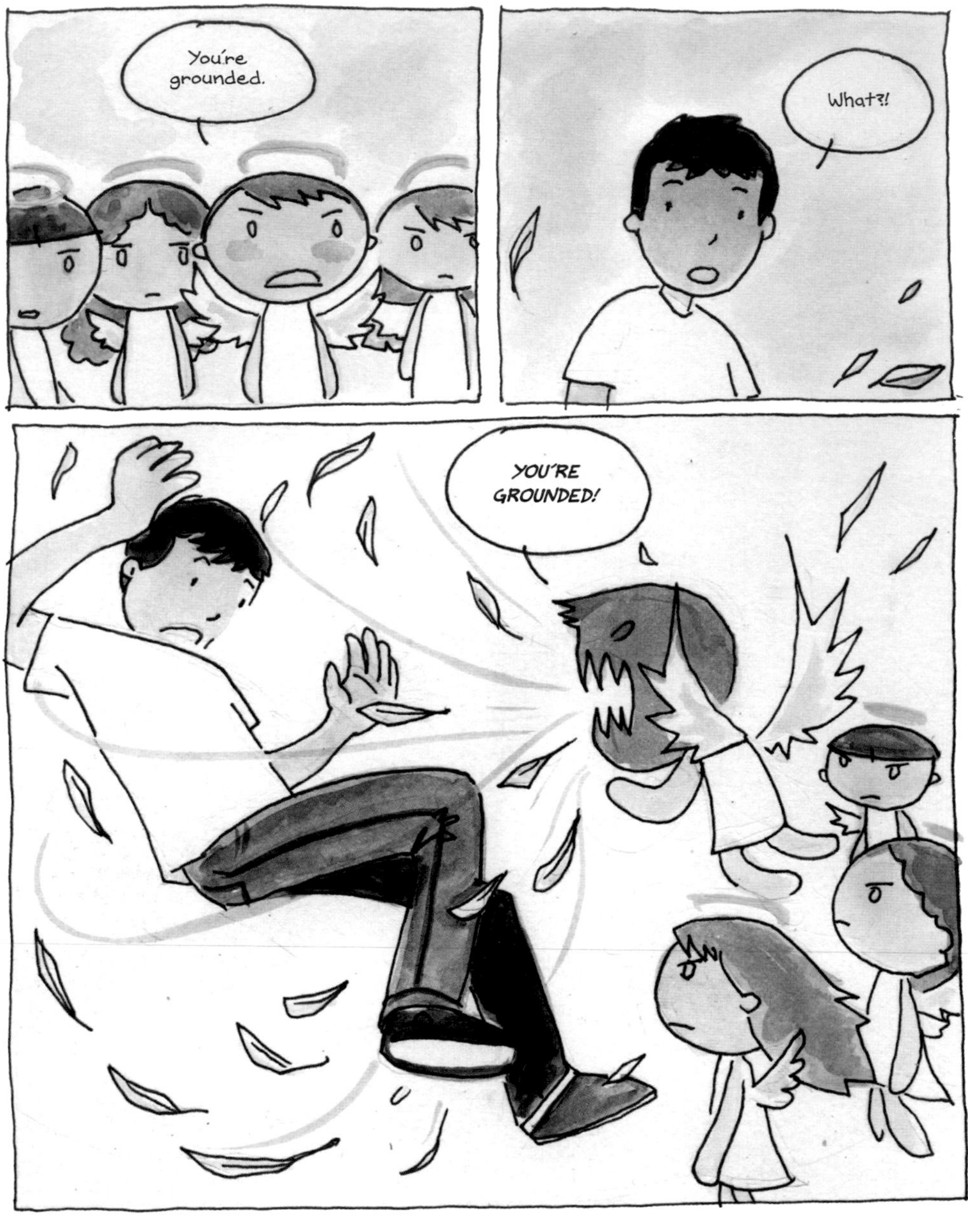
You're grounded.
What?!
YOU'RE GROUNDED!

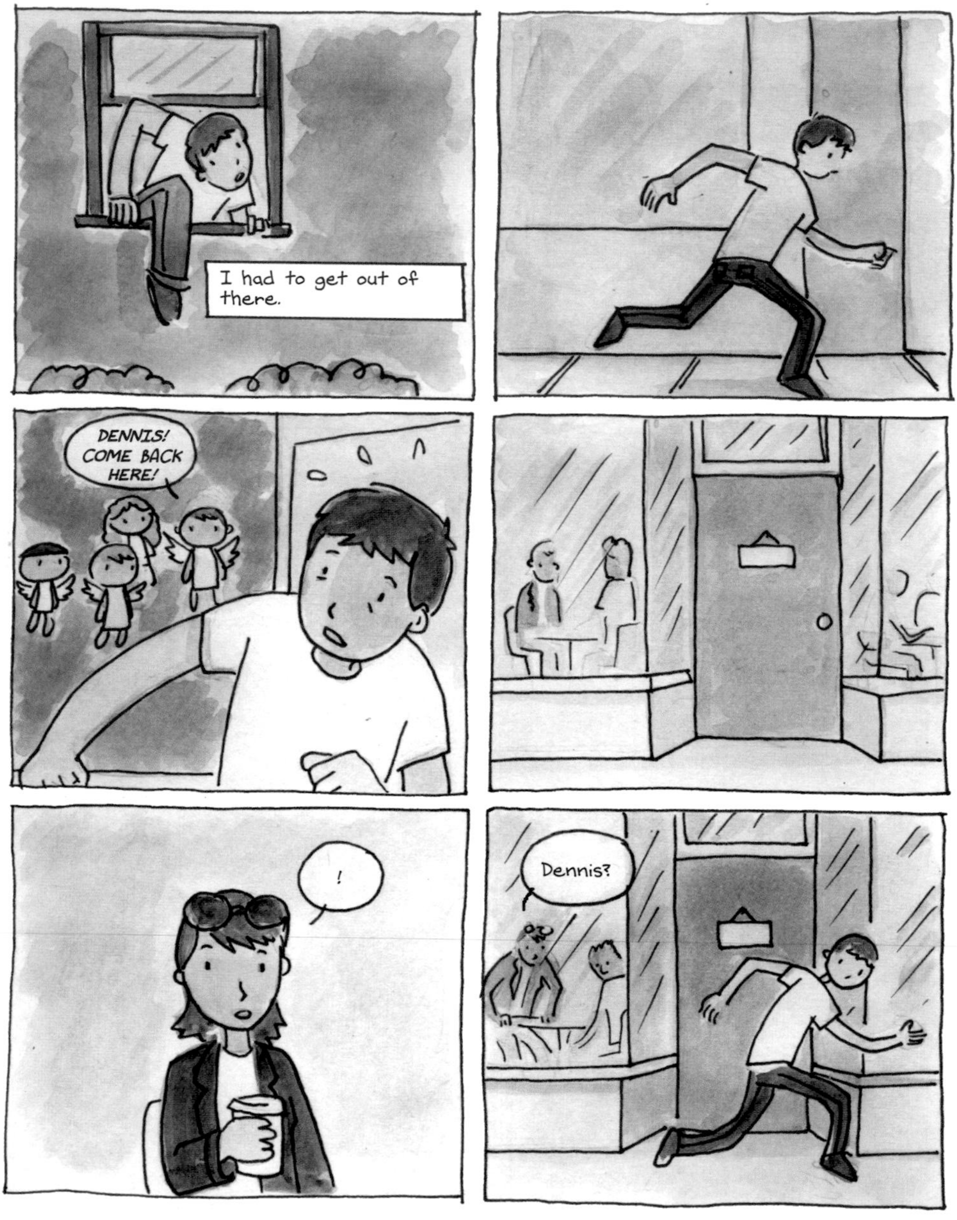
I had to get out of there.
DENNIS! COME BACK HERE!
!
Dennis?

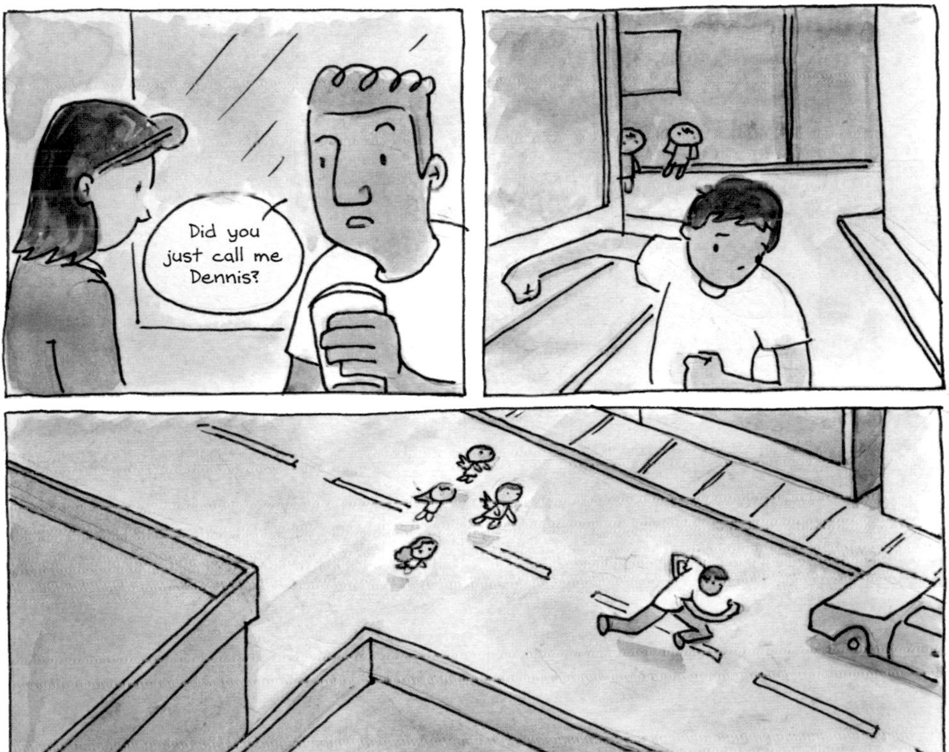
Did you just call me Dennis?
These streets are like a maze...
Wait a minute... I'm running through a maze...

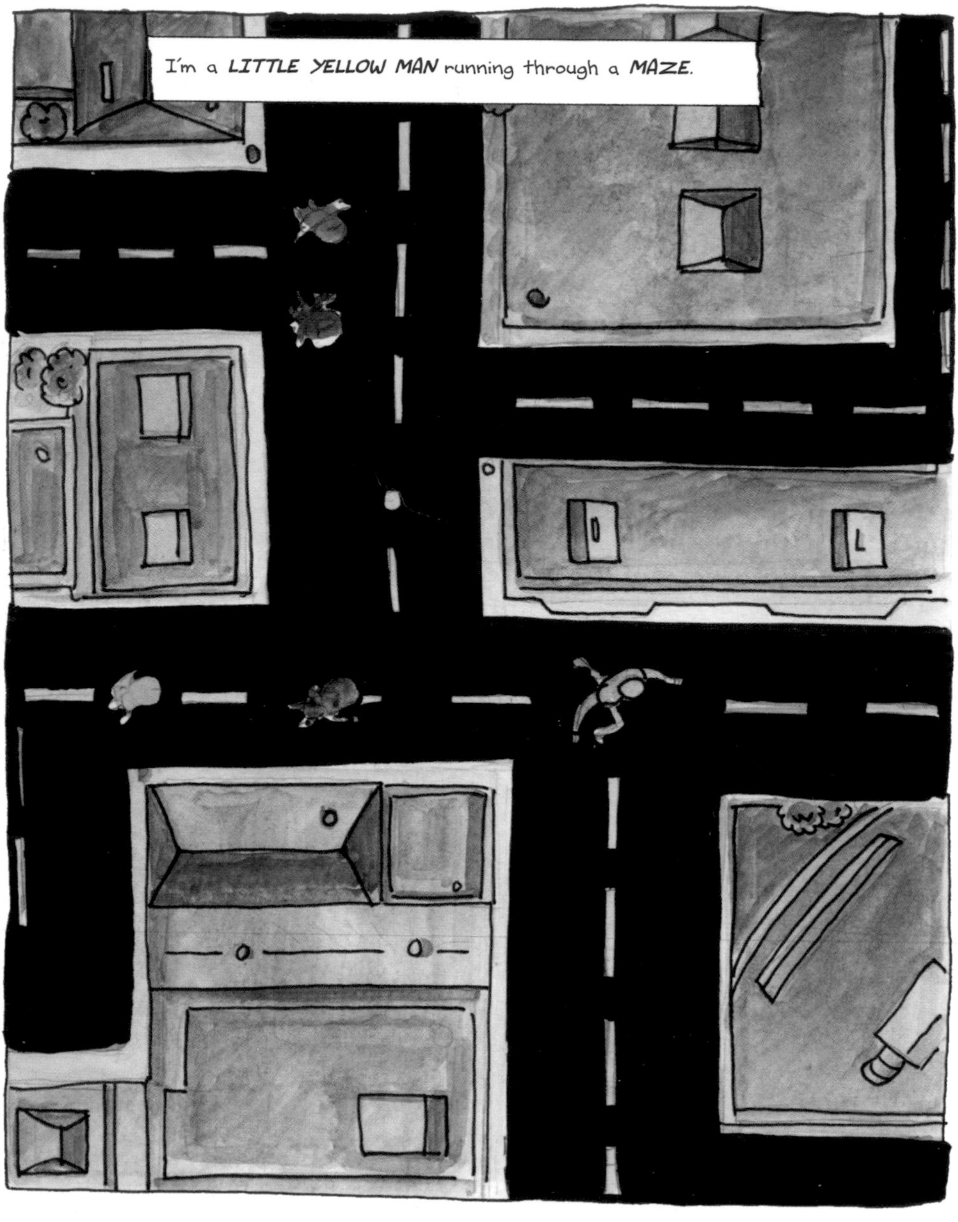
I'm a LITTLE YELLOW MAN running through a MAZE.

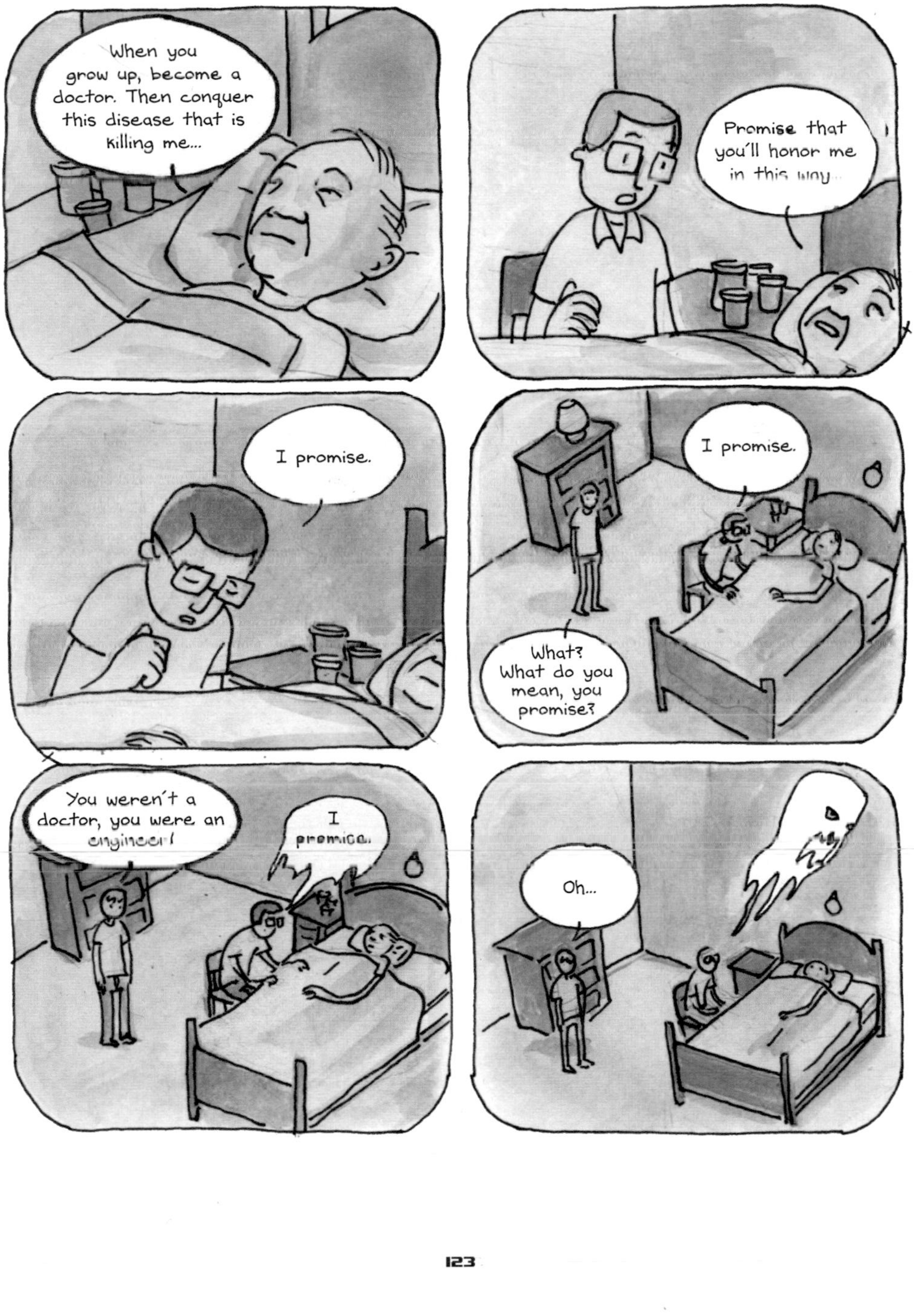
When you grow up, become a doctor. Then conquer this disease that is killing me...
Promise that you'll honor me in this way...
I promise.
I promise.
What? What do you mean, you promise?
You weren't a doctor, you were an engineer!
I promise.
Oh...

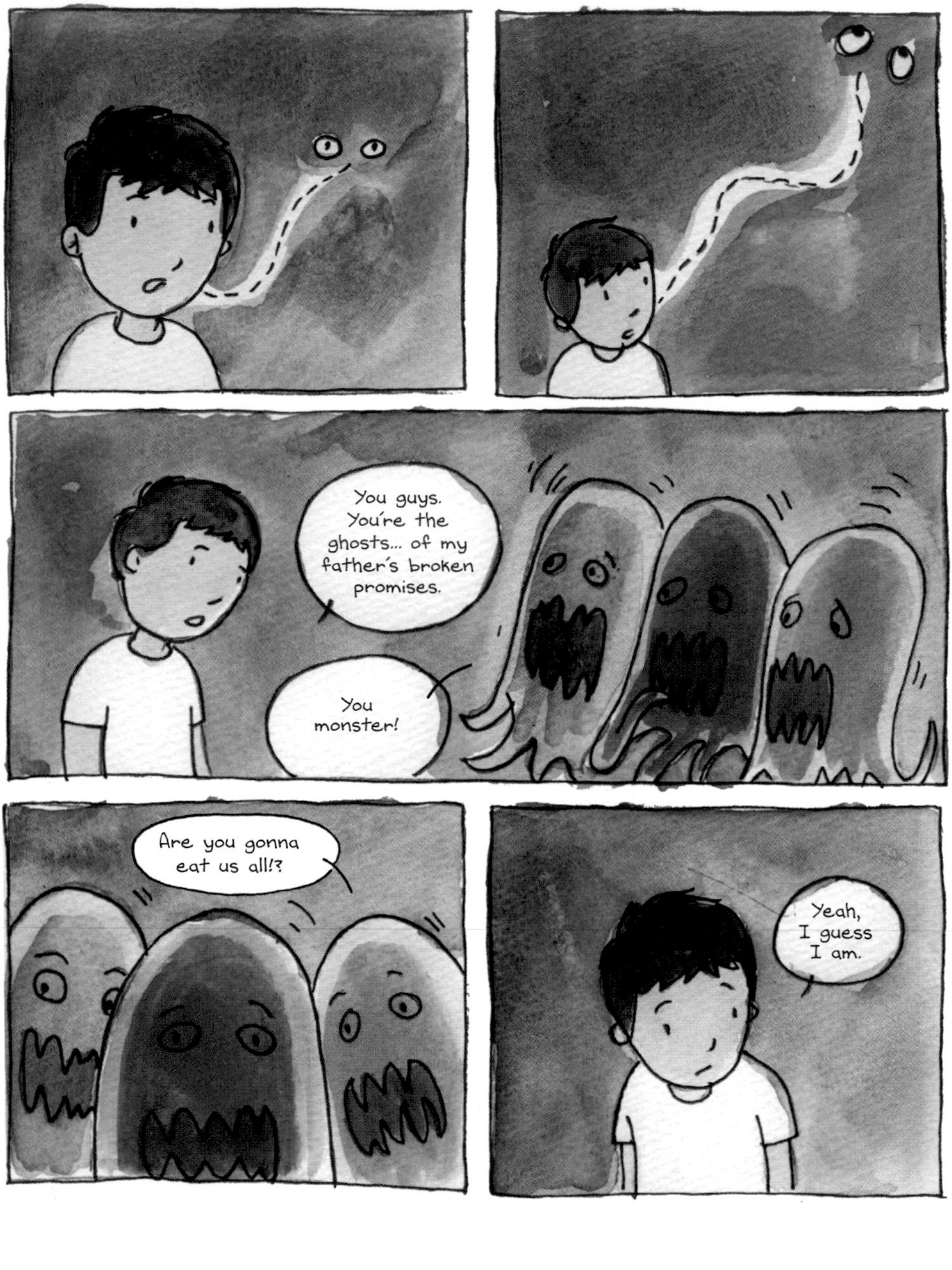
You guys. You're the ghosts... of my father's broken promises.
You monster!
Are you gonna eat us all!?
Yeah, I guess I am.

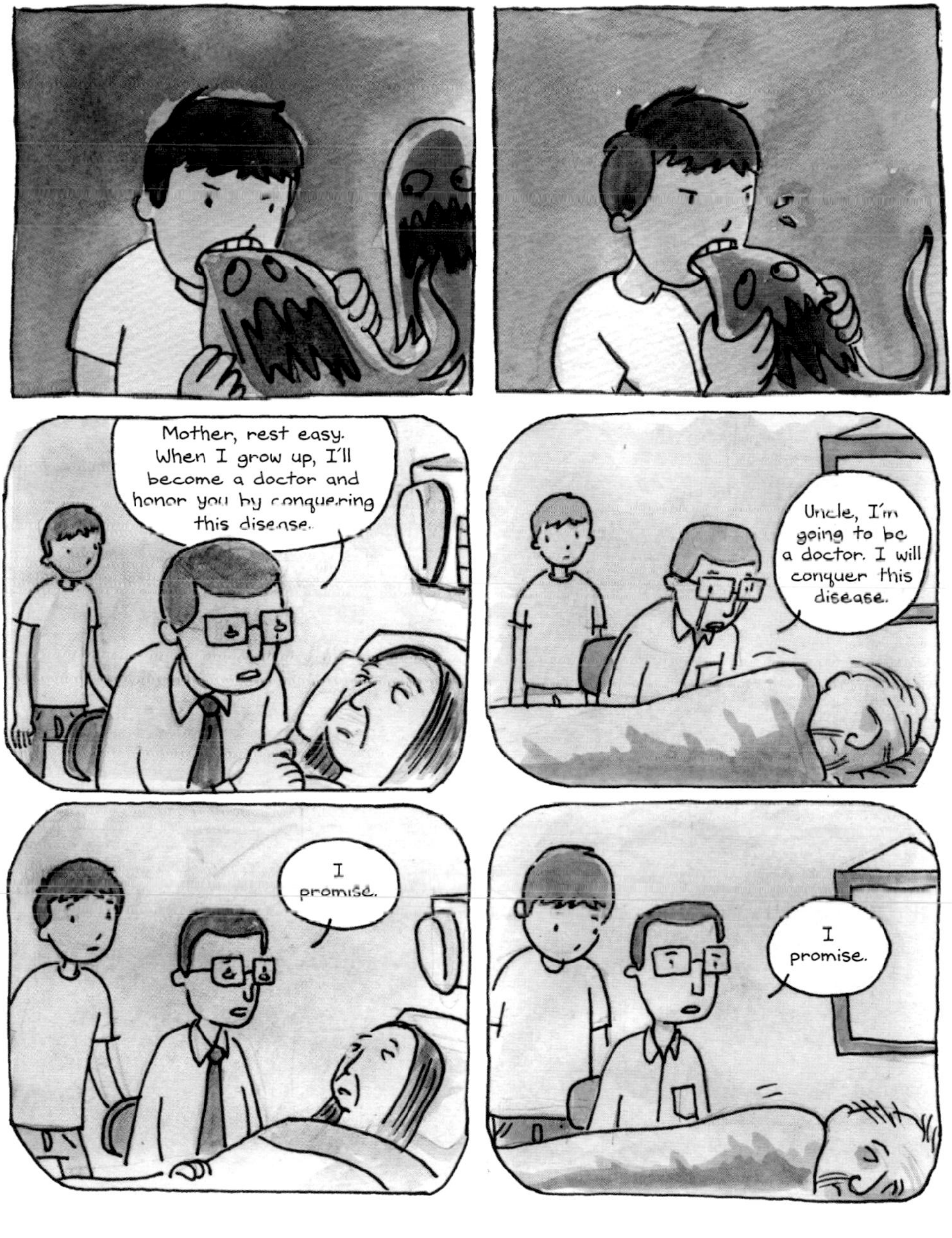
Mother, rest easy. When I grow up, I'll become a doctor and honor you by conquering this disease.
Uncle, I'm going to be a doctor. I will conquer this disease.
I promise.
I promise.

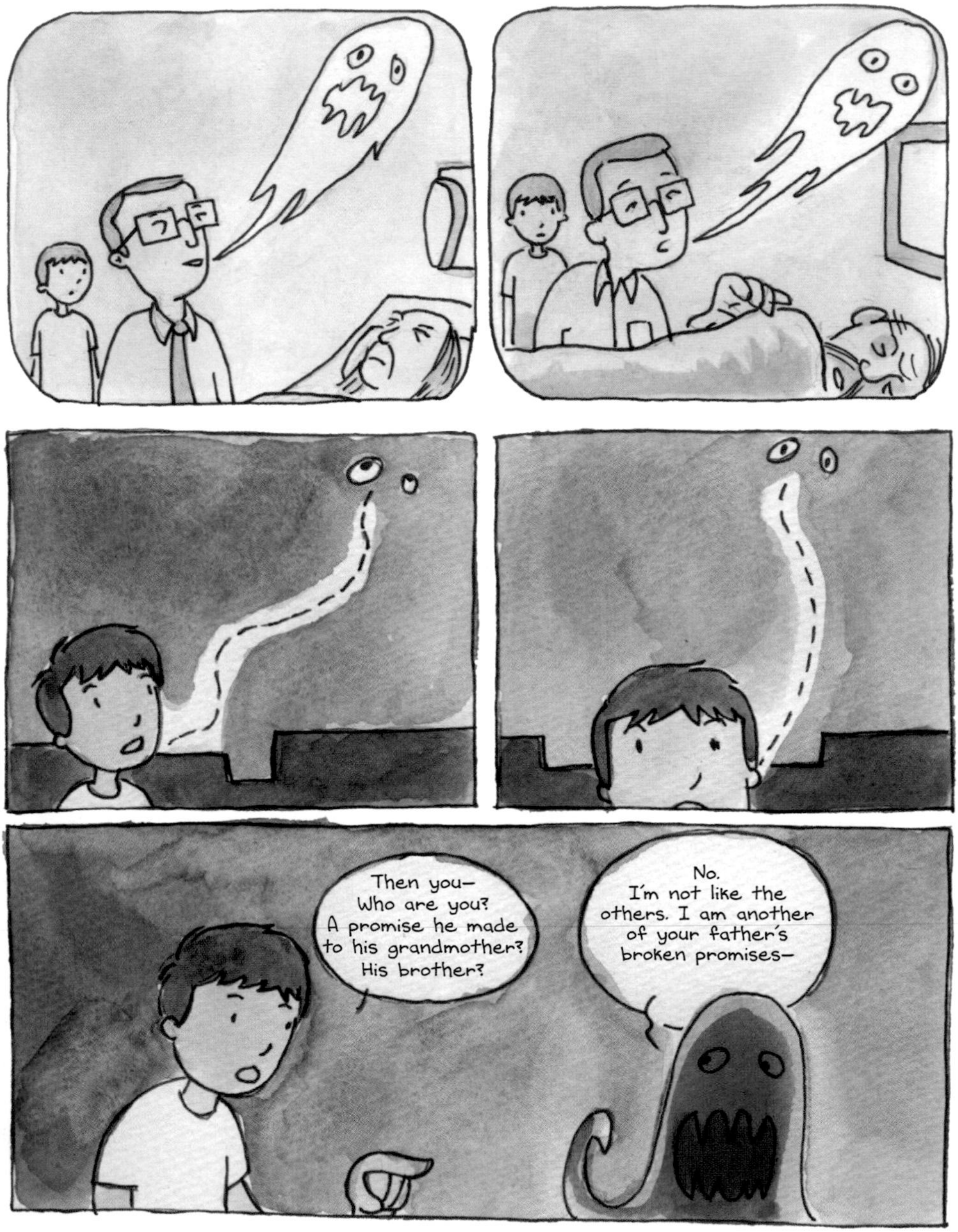
Then you— Who are you? A promise he made to his grandmother? His brother?
No. I'm not like the others. I am another of your father's broken promises—

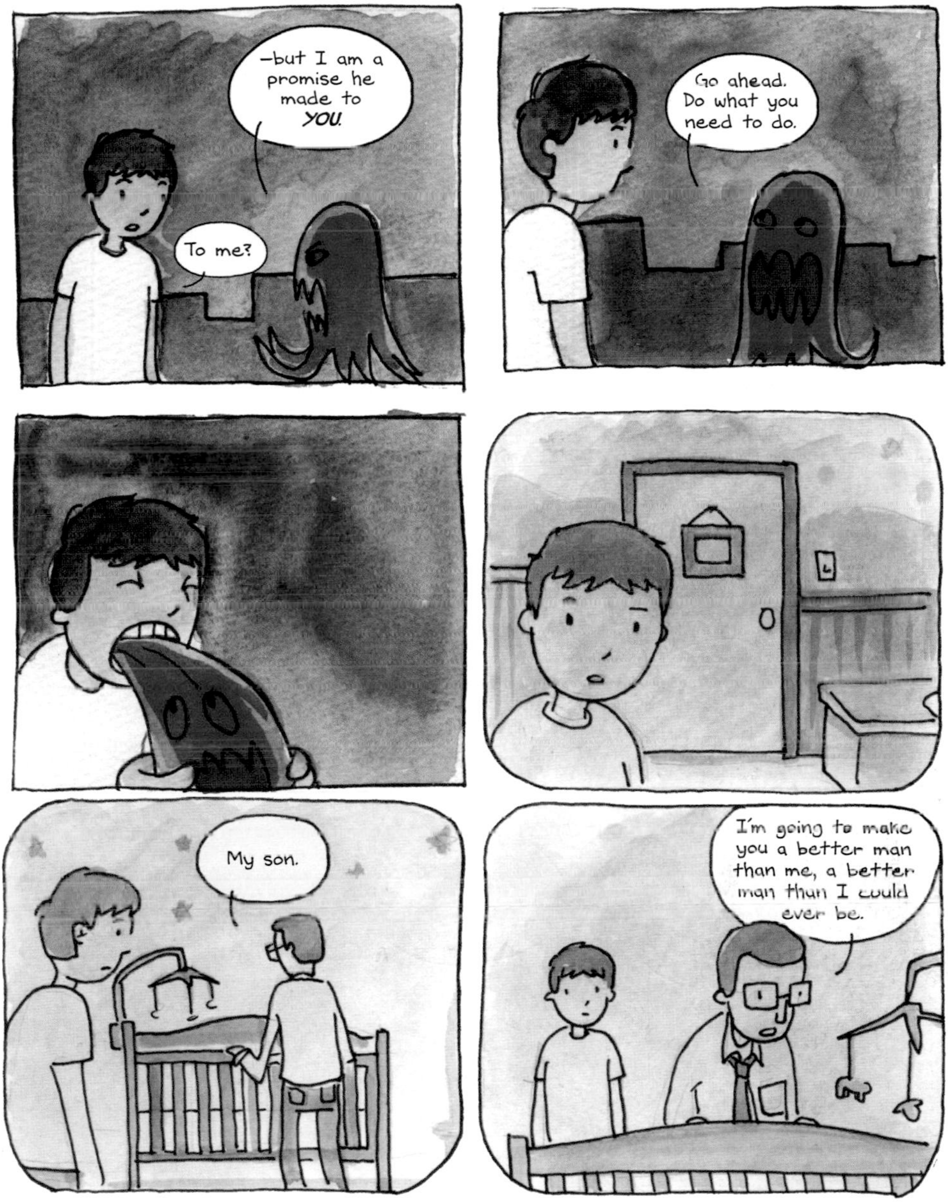

—but I am a promise he made to *YOU.*
To me?
Go ahead. Do what you need to do.
My son.
I'm going to make you a better man than me, a better man than I could ever be.

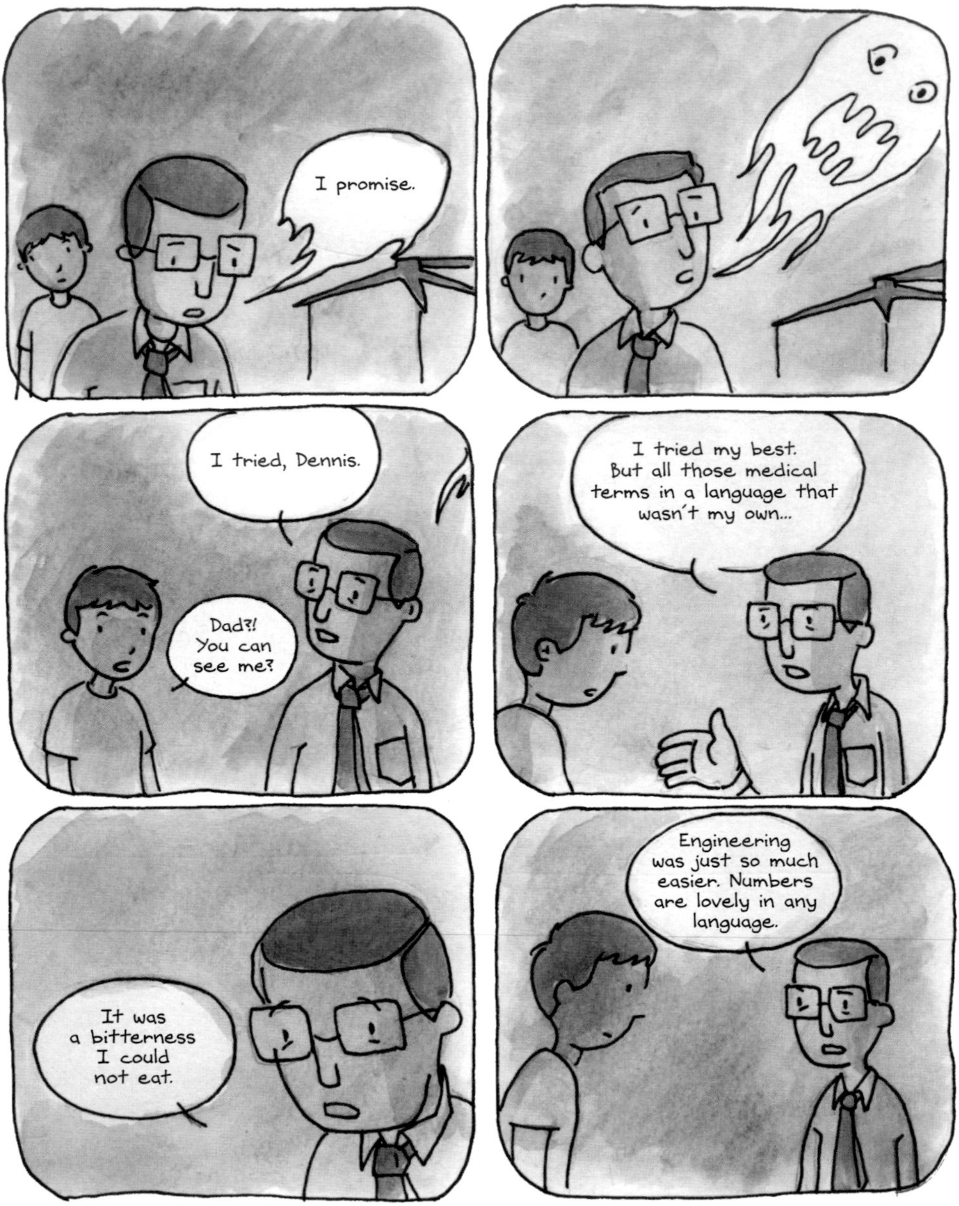
I promise.
I tried, Dennis.
Dad?! You can see me?
I tried my best. But all those medical terms in a language that wasn't my own...
It was a bitterness I could not eat.
Engineering was just so much easier. Numbers are lovely in any language.

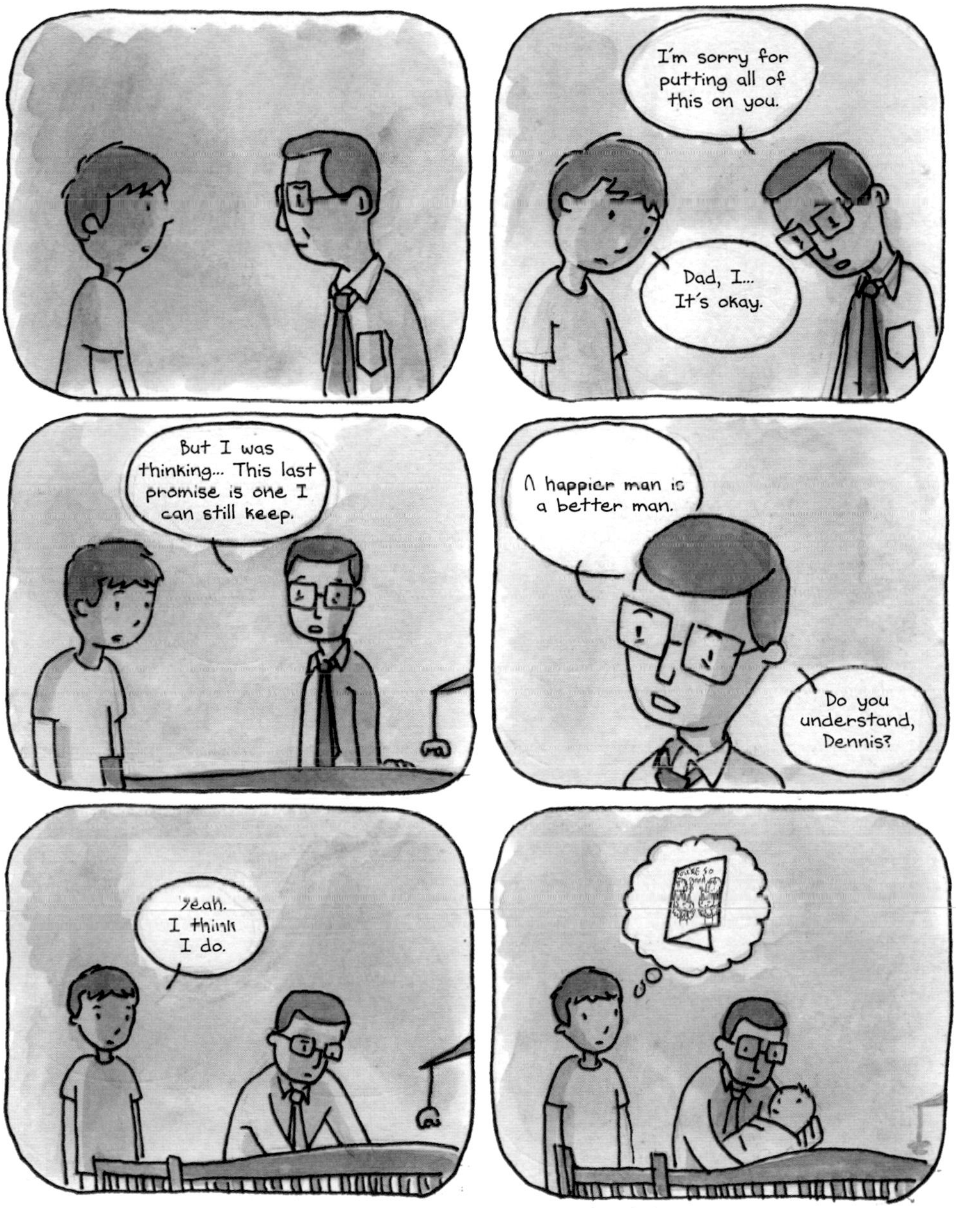
I'm sorry for putting all of this on you.
Dad, I... It's okay.
But I was thinking... This last promise is one I can still keep.
A happier man is a better man.
Do you understand, Dennis?
Yeah. I think I do.

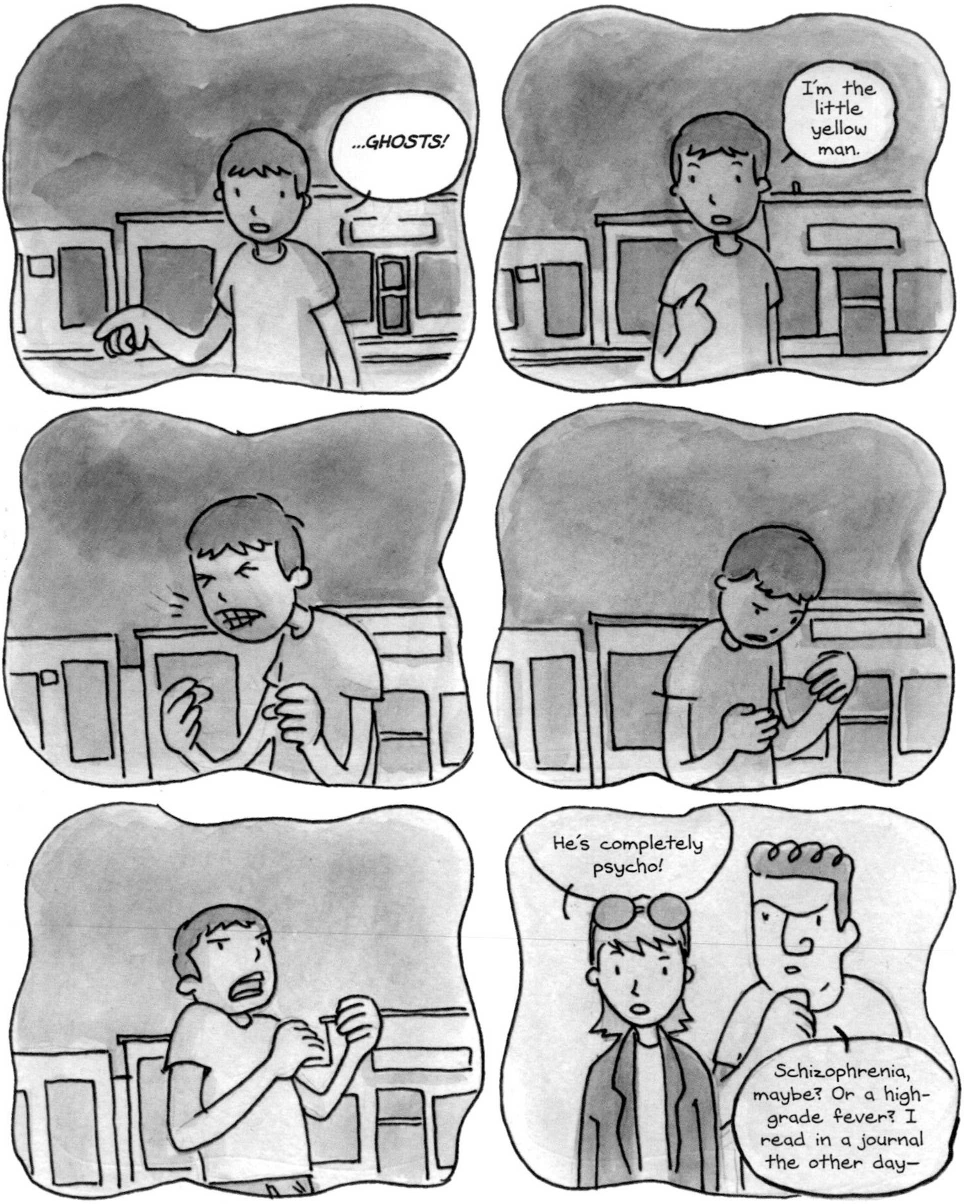
...GHOSTS!
I'm the little yellow man.
He's completely psycho!
Schizophrenia, maybe? Or a high-grade fever? I read in a journal the other day—

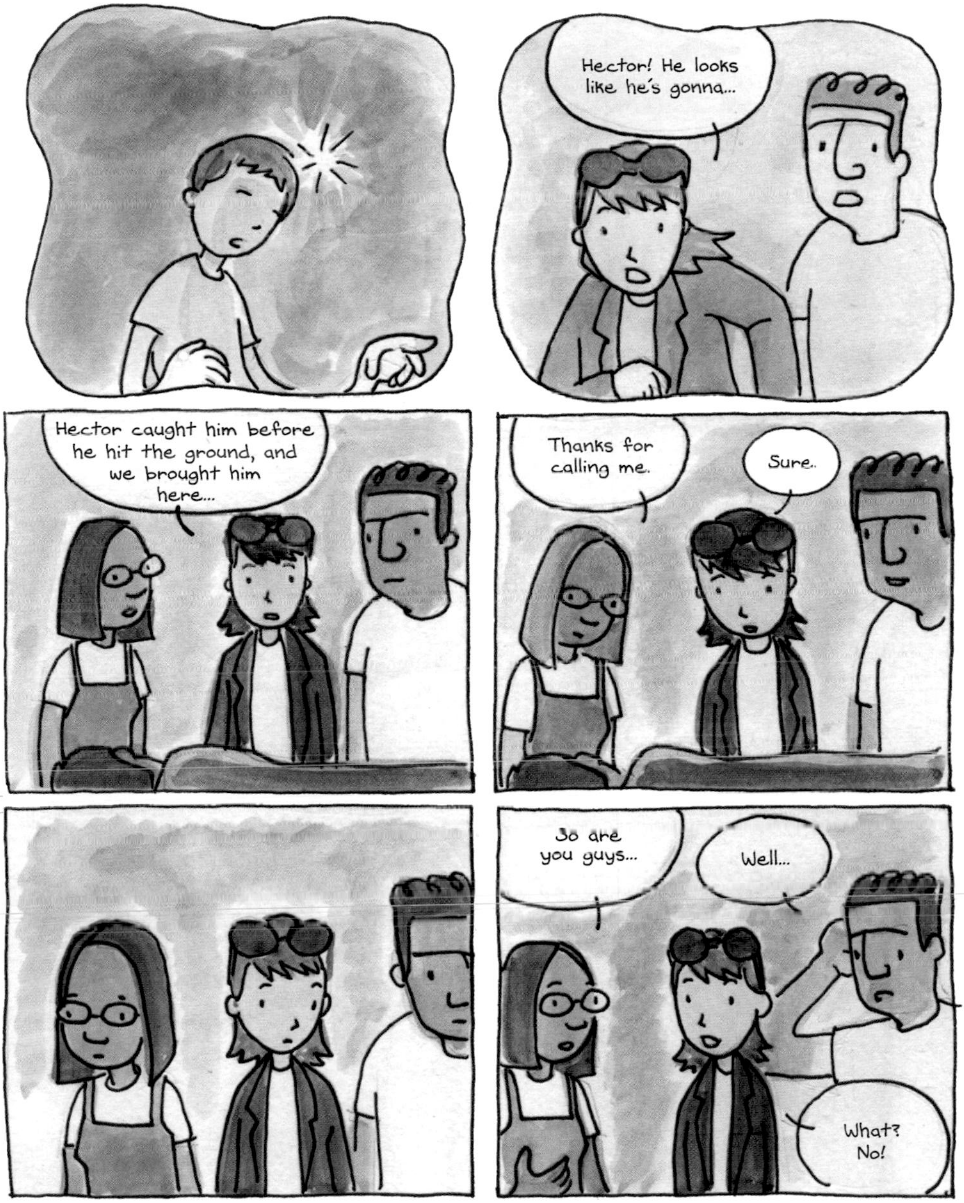
Hector! He looks like he's gonna...
Hector caught him before he hit the ground, and we brought him here...
Thanks for calling me.
Sure..
So are you guys...
Well...
What? No!

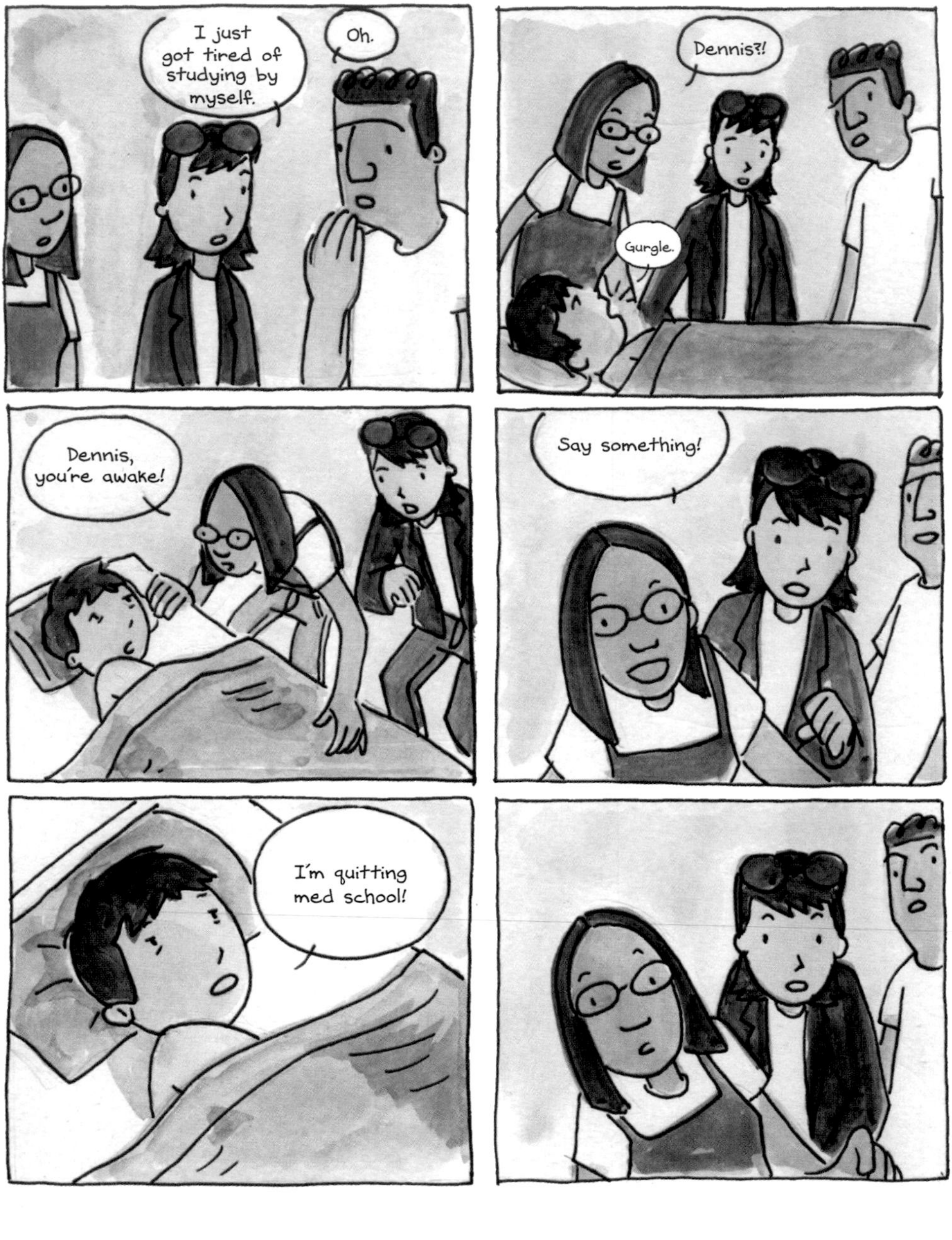
I just got tired of studying by myself.
Oh.
Dennis?!
Gurgle.
Dennis, you're awake!
Say something!
I'm quitting med school!

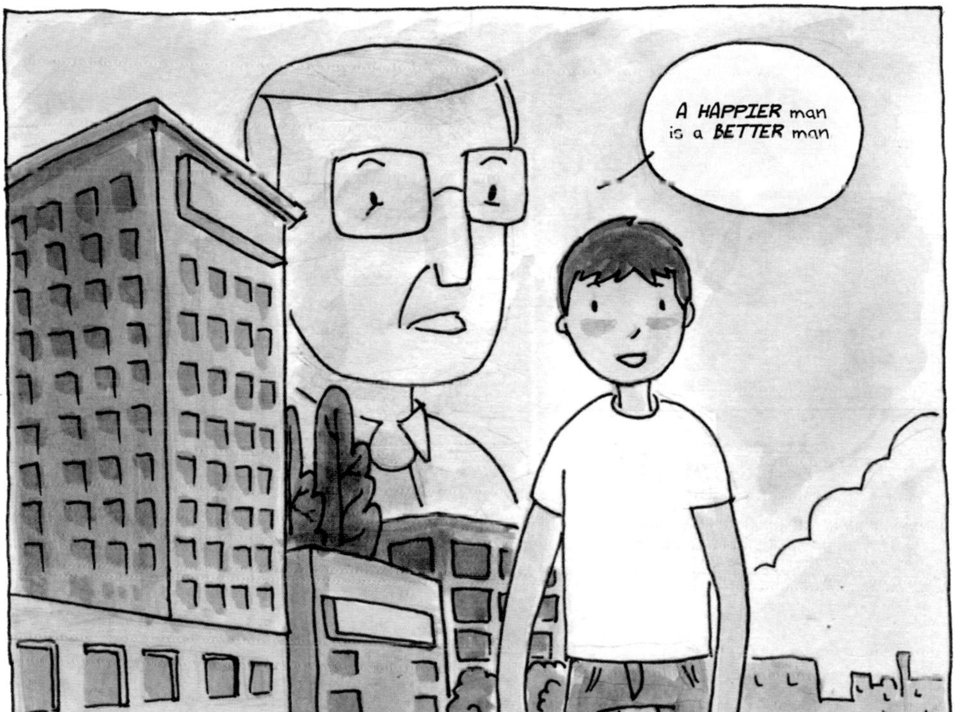
A **HAPPIER** man is a **BETTER** man
The next morning I walked out of med school—

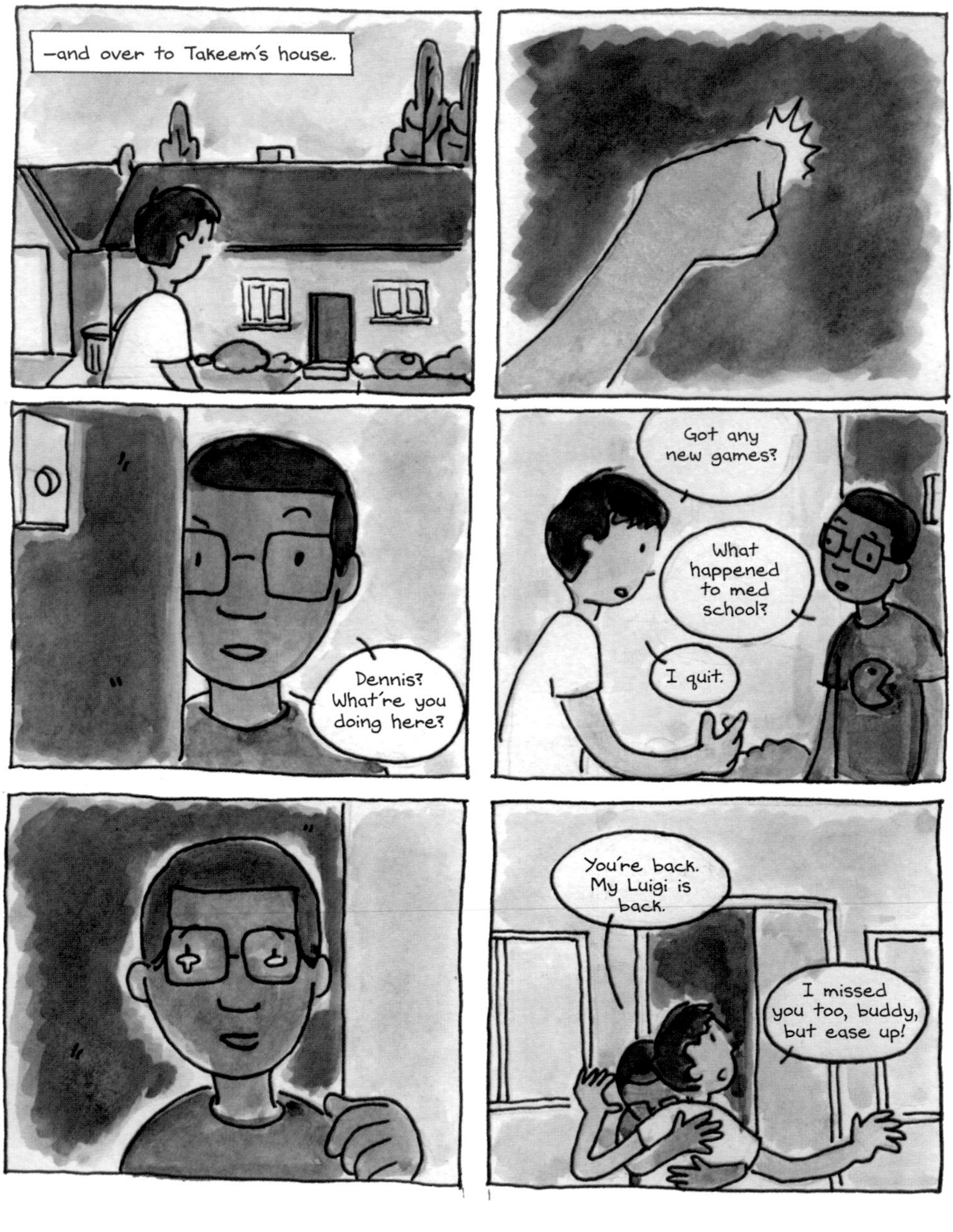
—and over to Takeem's house.
Dennis? What're you doing here?
Got any new games?
What happened to med school?
I quit.
You're back. My Luigi is back.
I missed you too, buddy, but ease up!

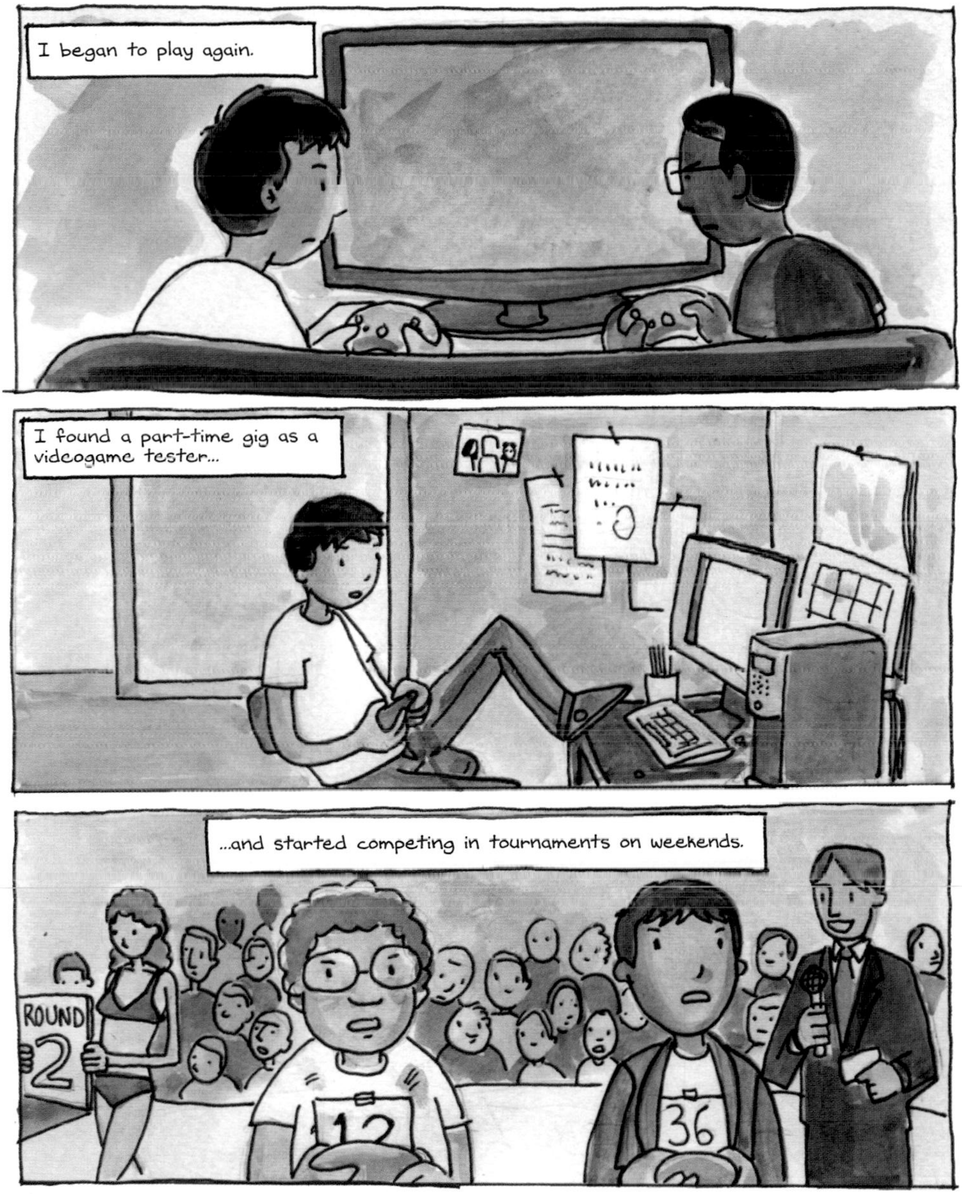
I began to play again.
I found a part-time gig as a videogame tester...
...and started competing in tournaments on weekends.
ROUND 2
12
36

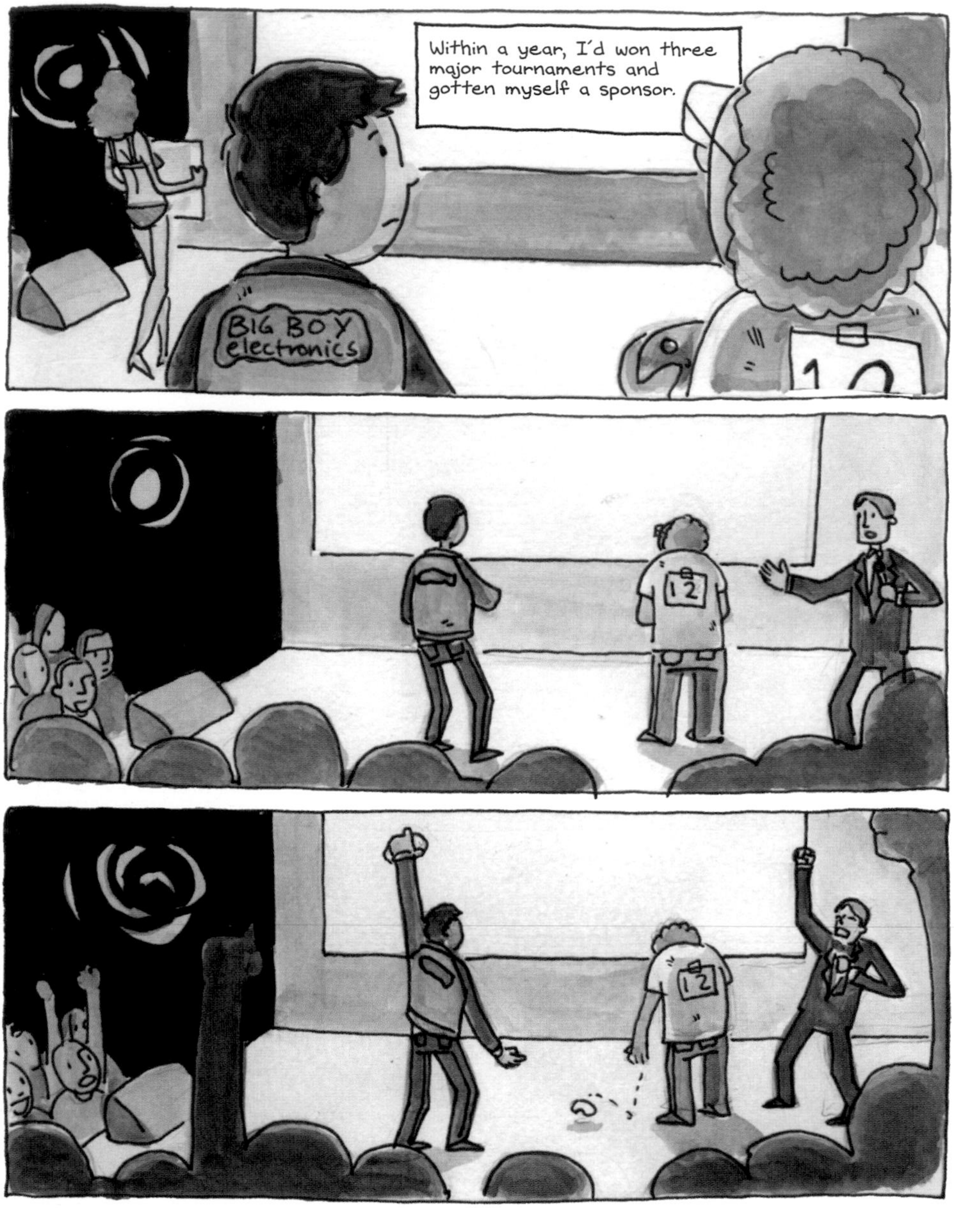
Within a year, I'd won three
major tournaments and
gotten myself a sponsor.
BIG BOY
electronics
12
12

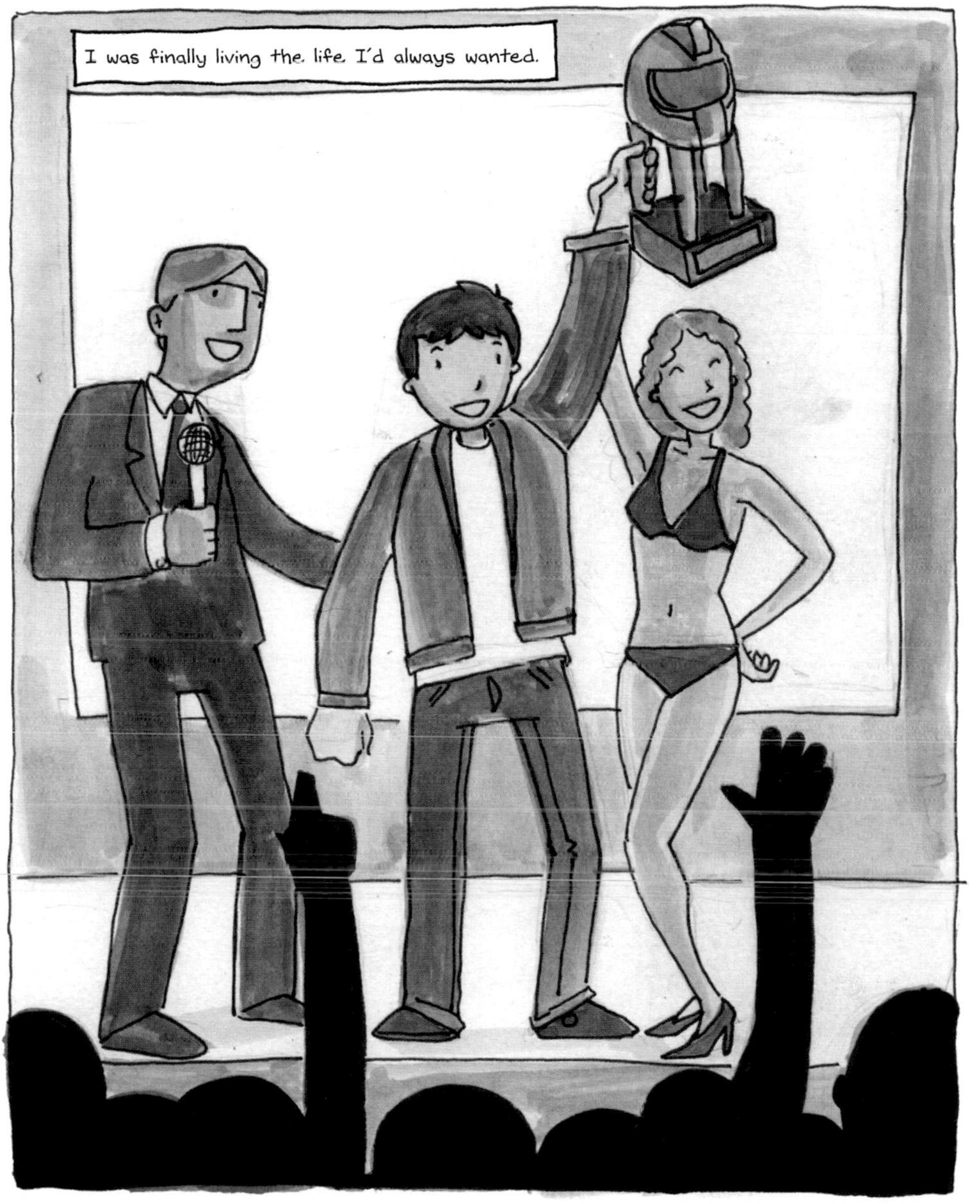
I was finally living the life I'd always wanted.

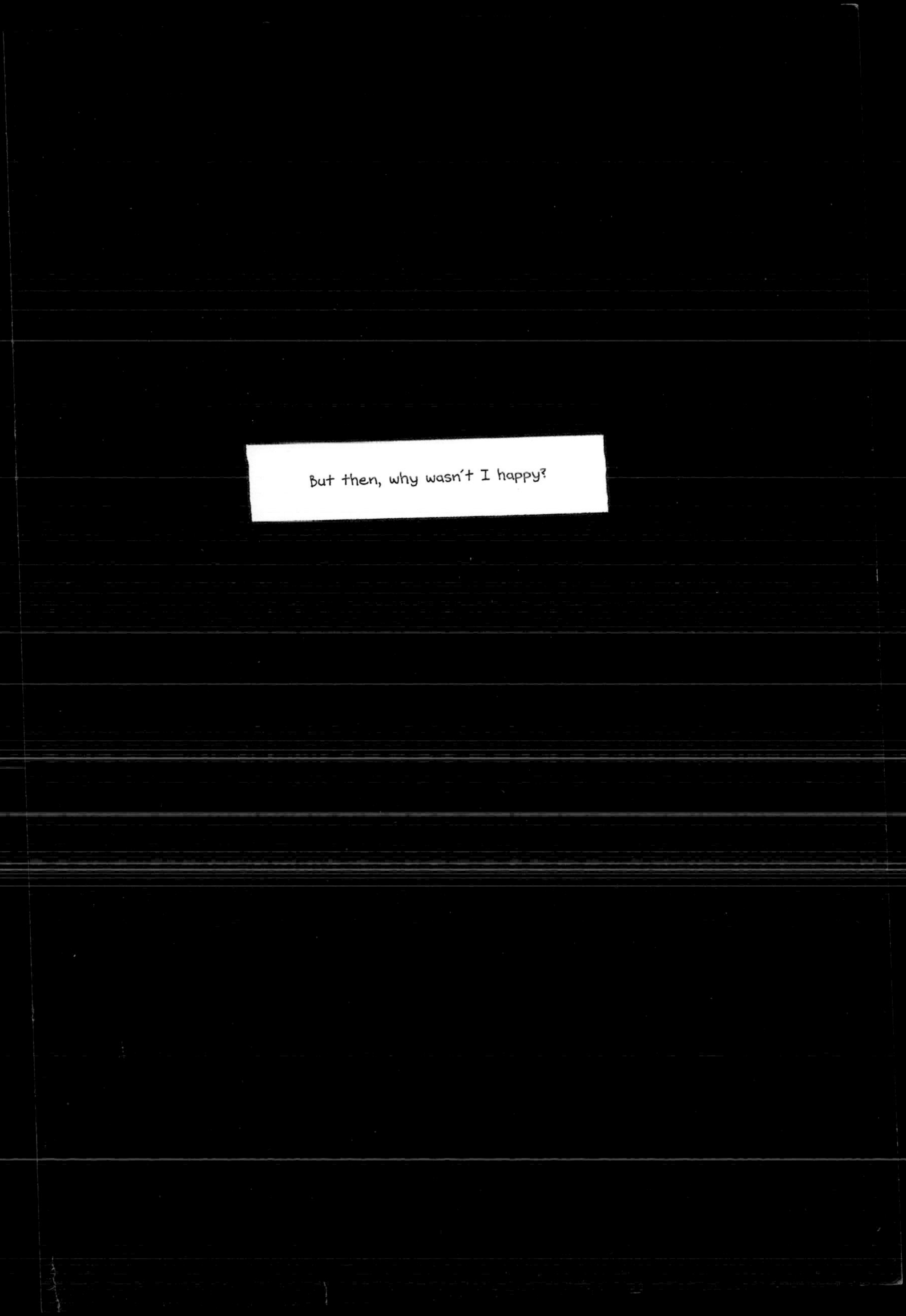
But then, why wasn't I happy?

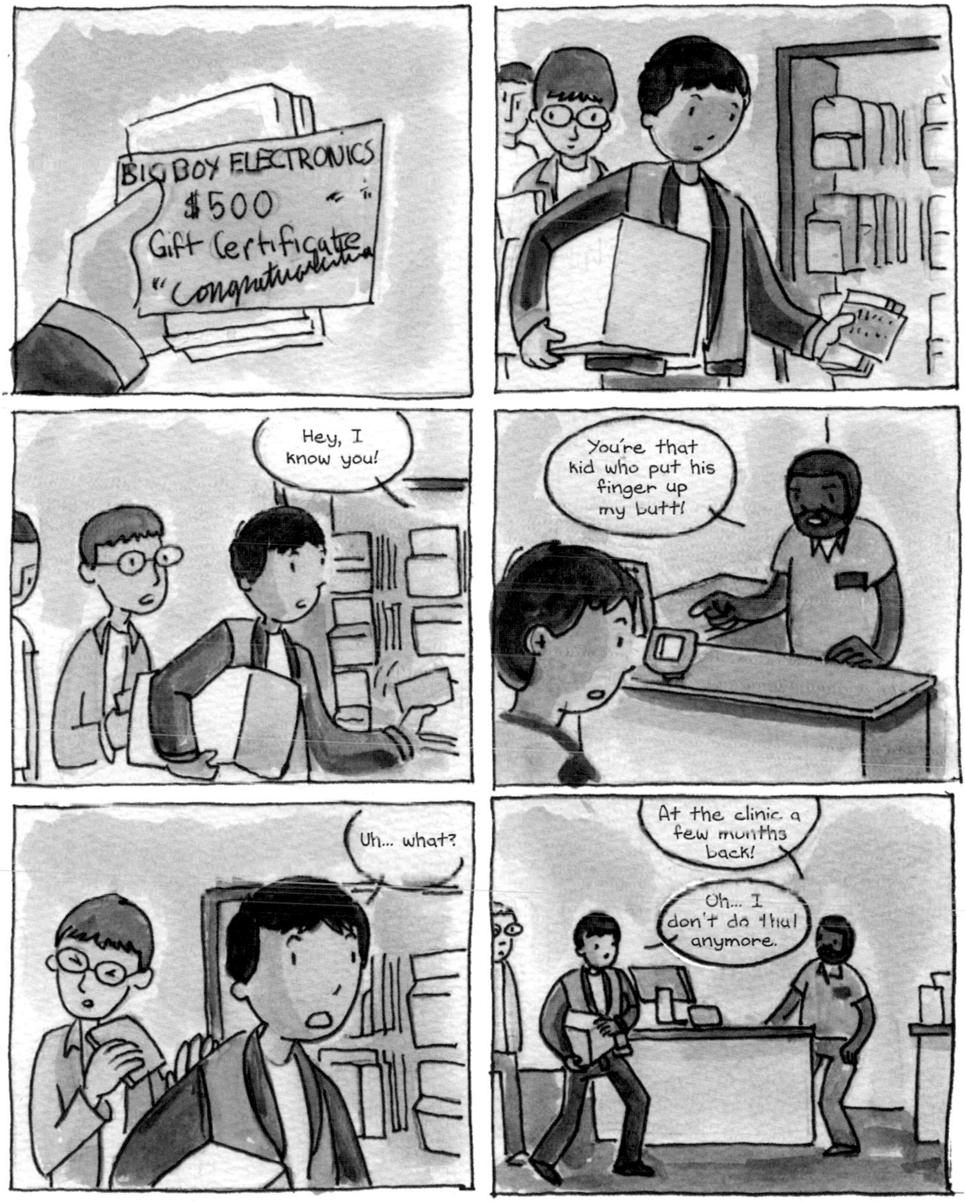
BIG BOY ELECTRONICS
$500
Gift Certificate
Hey, I know you!
You're that kid who put his finger up my butt!
Uh... what?
At the clinic a few months back!
Oh... I don't do that anymore.

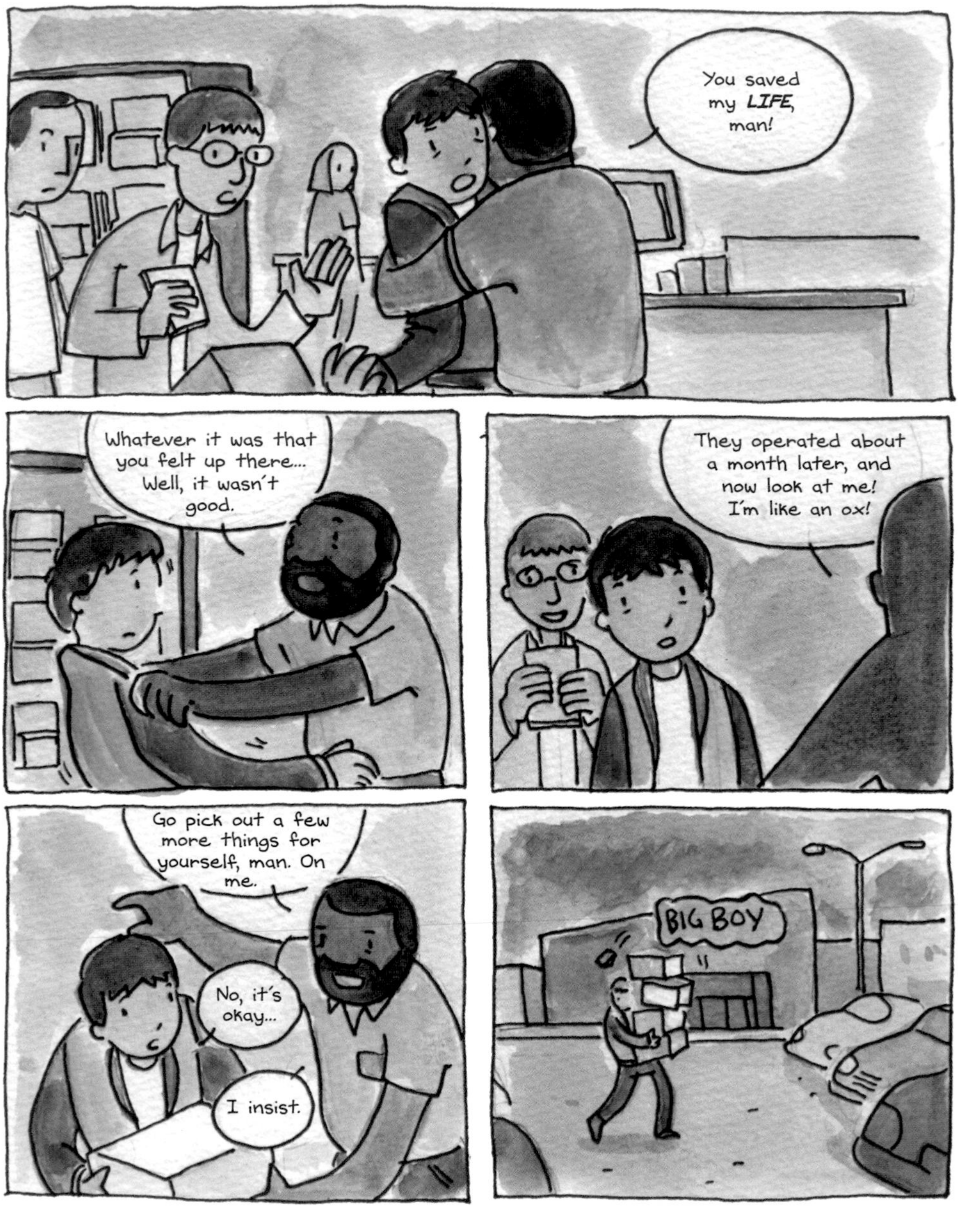
You saved my **LIFE**, man!
Whatever it was that you felt up there... Well, it wasn't good.
They operated about a month later, and now look at me! I'm like an ox!
Go pick out a few more things for yourself, man. On me.
No, it's okay...
I insist.
BIG BOY

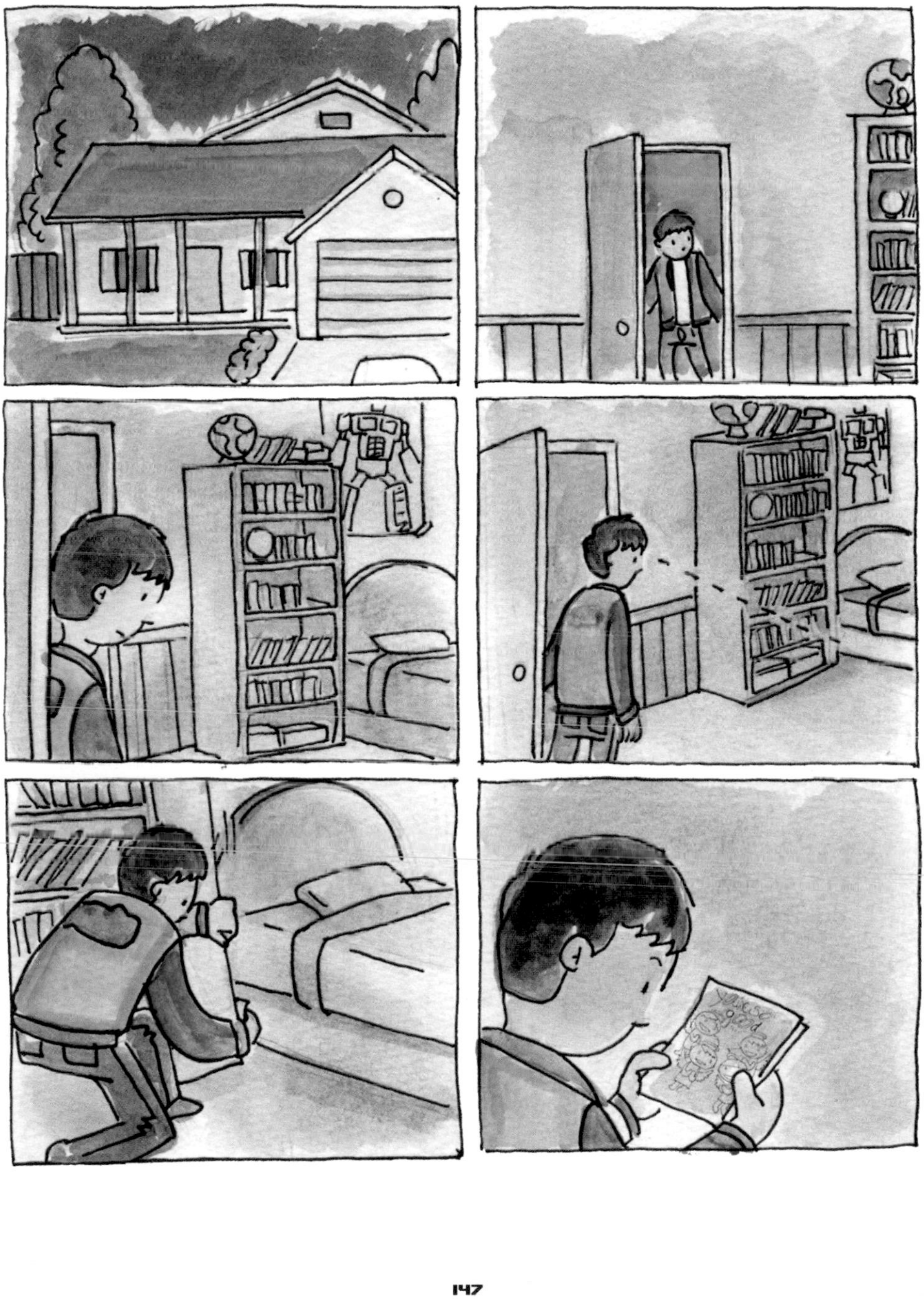

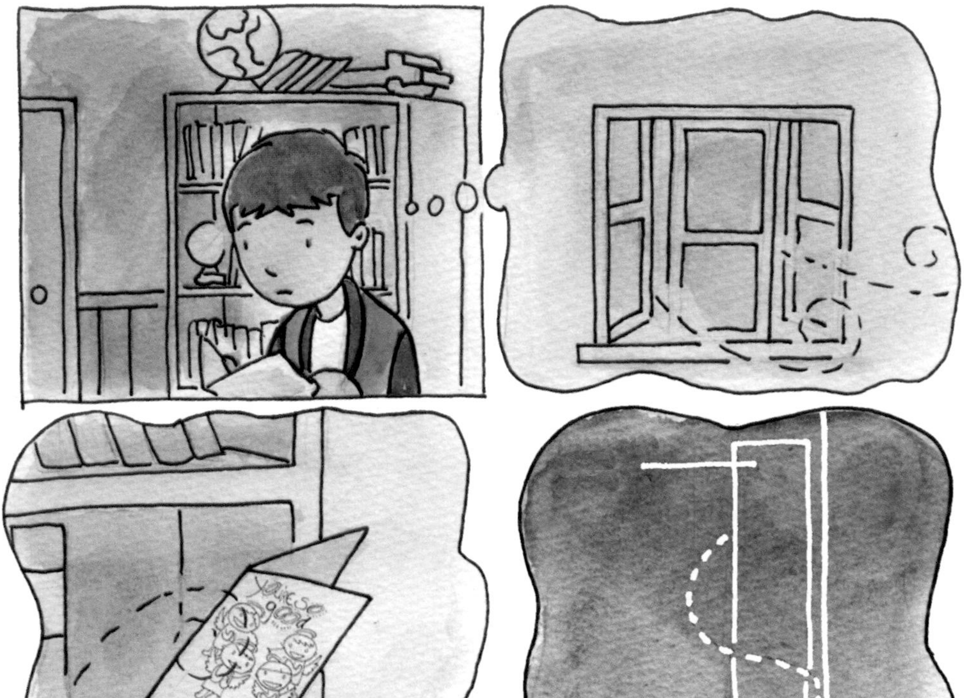
You're so good

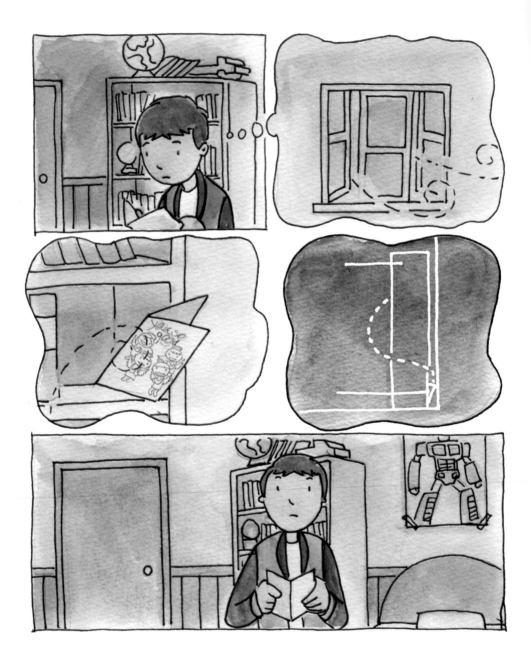

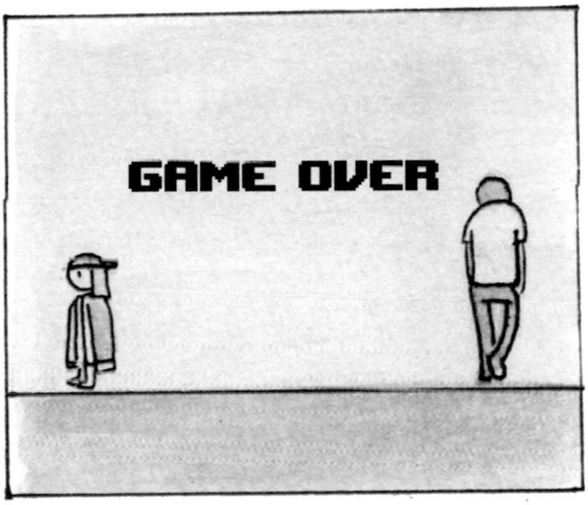
GAME OVER

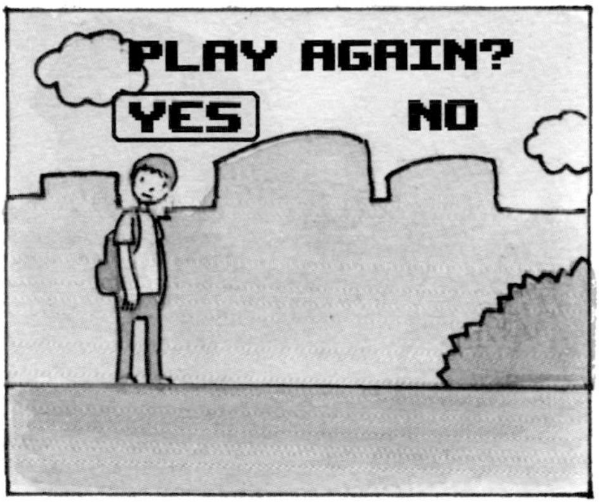
PLAY AGAIN?
YES
NO

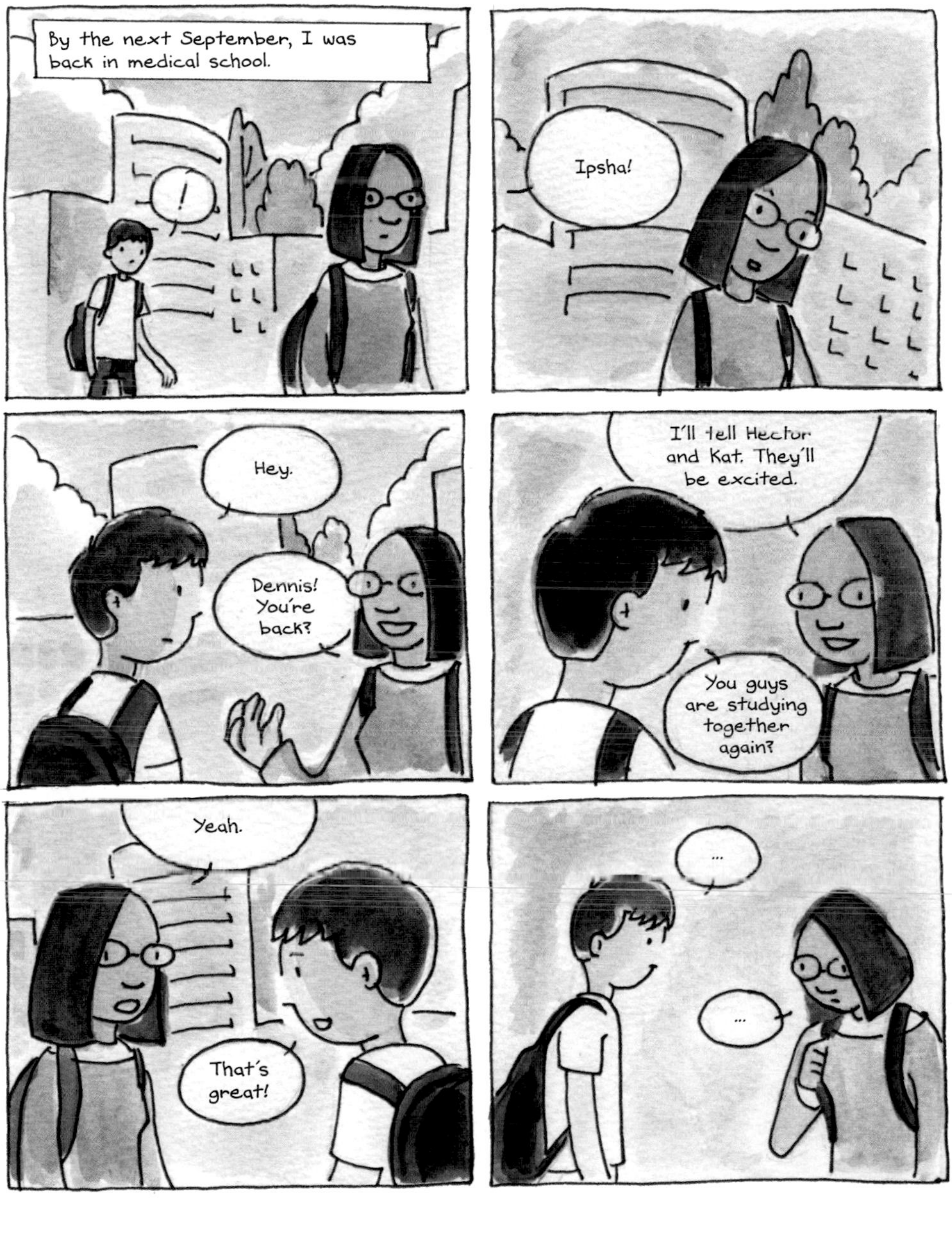
By the next September, I was back in medical school.
!
Ipsha!
Hey.
Dennis! You're back?
I'll tell Hector and Kat. They'll be excited.
You guys are studying together again?
Yeah.
That's great!
...
...

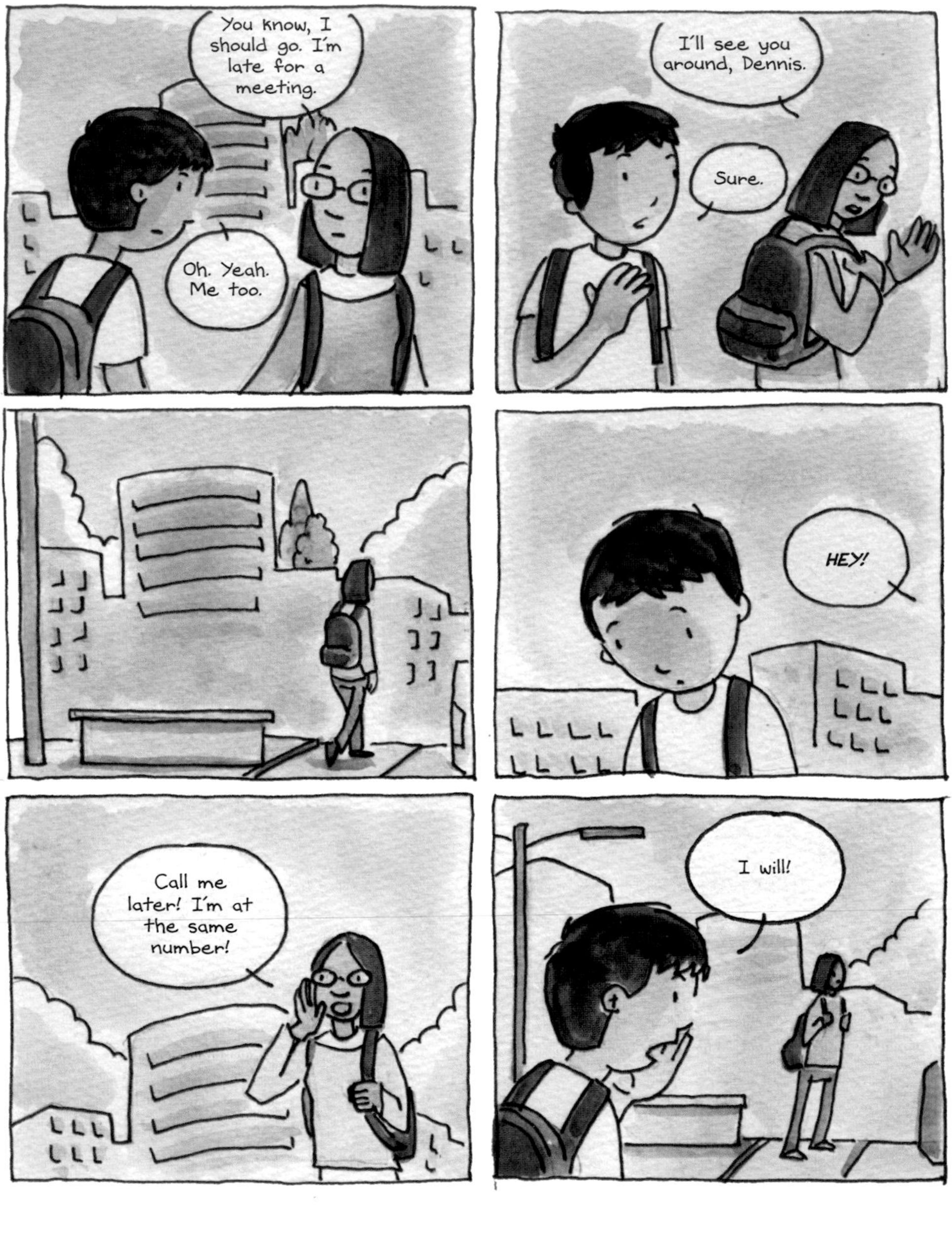
You know, I should go. I'm late for a meeting.
Oh. Yeah. Me too.
I'll see you around, Dennis.
Sure.
HEY!
Call me later! I'm at the same number!
I will!

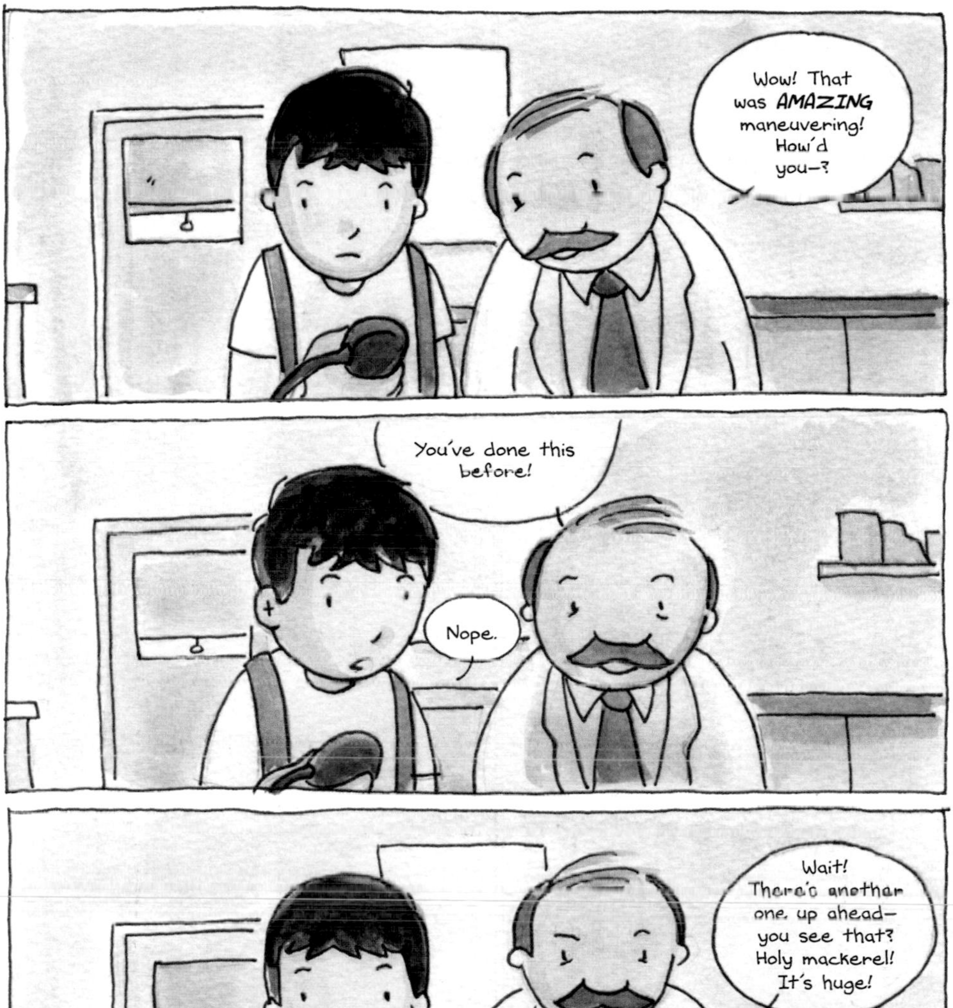
Wow! That was AMAZING maneuvering! How'd you–?
You've done this before!
Nope.
Wait! There's another one up ahead– you see that? Holy mackerel! It's huge!

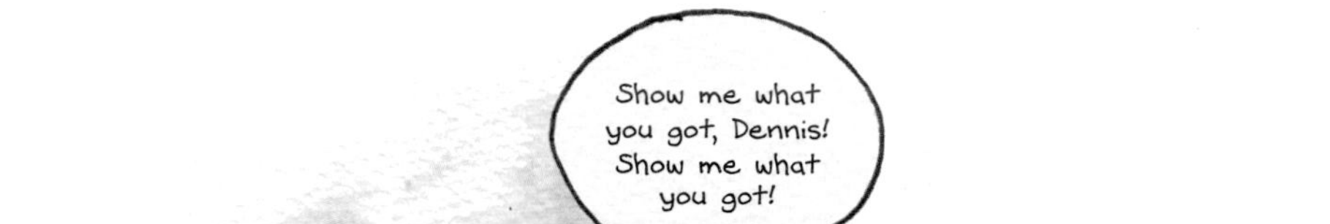
Show me what you got, Dennis! Show me what you got!

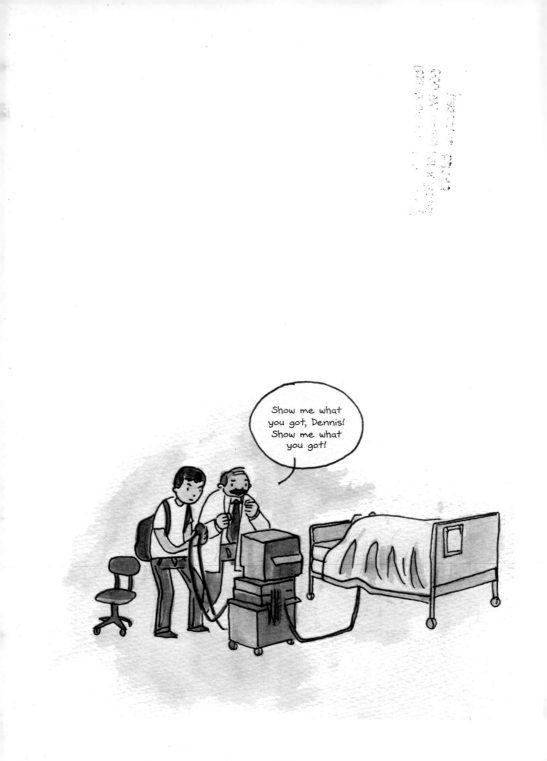